Praise for *A Dog's Purpose*

"I loved this book."   —Temple Grandin,
New York Times bestselling author

"*Marley & Me* combined with *Tuesdays with Morrie*."
—*Kirkus Reviews*

"An amazing book. I laughed and smiled and cried. Wise . . . and sure to open the hearts of all who read it."   —Alice Walker,
Pulitzer Prize–winning author
of *The Color Purple*

"Anyone who has ever loved a dog needs to read this wise, touching, often hilarious book."
—Dr. Marty Becker, resident veterinarian
on *Good Morning America*

"This book gives you a glimpse into the heart and mind of a dog—and will change your view of our furry friends forever."   —*Guideposts*

Praise for *A Dog's Journey*

"Once again endearing himself to animal lovers, Cameron explores the concept of canine karma with acute sensitivity and exhibits cunning insight into life from a dog's perspective."   —*Booklist*

"Full of humor, heartbreak, and insights that sneak up on you . . . a whopping good yarn."
—*The Denver Post*

"Transfixing and heartwarming . . . Will have you hooked until the last page is turned—just be sure to have plenty of Kleenex on hand."   —*Modern Dog*

A DOG'S JOURNEY

W. BRUCE CAMERON

A TOM DOHERTY ASSOCIATES BOOK • NEW YORK

This is a work of fiction. All of the characters, organizations, and events portrayed in this novel are either products of the author's imagination or are used fictitiously.

A DOG'S JOURNEY

Copyright © 2012 by W. Bruce Cameron

All rights reserved.

A Forge Book
Published by Tom Doherty Associates
175 Fifth Avenue
New York, NY 10010

www.tor-forge.com

Forge® is a registered trademark of Macmillan Publishing Group, LLC.

ISBN 978-0-7653-6829-4

Our books may be purchased in bulk for promotional, educational, or business use. Please contact your local bookseller or the Macmillan Corporate and Premium Sales Department at 1-800-221-7945, macmillan.com.

First Edition: May 2012
First Mass Market Edition: May 2017

Printed in the United States of America

0 9 8 7 6 5 4 3 2 1

*To all the people who work so hard
to rescue, foster, and save animals who
find themselves lost in the world*

[ONE]

As I sat in the sun on the wooden dock that jutted out into the pond, I knew this to be true: my name was Buddy, and I was a good dog.

The fur on my legs was as black as the rest of me, but down at my paws it had, over time, become tinged with white. I had lived a long and full life with a boy named Ethan, spending many lazy afternoons on this very dock, here on the Farm, enjoying a swim or barking at the ducks.

This was the second summer without Ethan. When he died I felt a pain inside me much sharper than any other I'd ever felt. Now the pain was less, more like a stomachache, but I still felt it all the time. Only sleep soothed it away—in my sleep, Ethan ran with me through my dreams.

I was an old dog and knew that someday soon a much deeper sleep would come, as it had always come for me before. It came for me when I was named Toby, in my silly first life, when I had no real purpose but to play with other dogs. It came for me when I was named Bailey, when I first met my boy and loving him became my whole focus. It came for me when I was Ellie, when my job was to Work, to Find people, and to Save them. So when the deeper sleep came for me next, at the end of this life, as Buddy, I felt sure that I would not live again, that I had fulfilled my purpose and there was no reason for me to be a dog anymore. So whether it happened this summer or the next didn't matter. Ethan, loving Ethan, was my ultimate purpose, and I had done it as well as I could. I was a good dog.

And yet . . .

And yet as I sat there I was watching one of the many children from Ethan's family striding unsteadily toward the end of the dock. She hadn't been walking very long in her life, so every step was a wobble. She wore white puffy pants and a thin shirt. I pictured jumping in the water and pulling her to the surface by that shirt, and I let out a soft whimper.

The child's mother's name was Gloria. She was on the dock, too, lying motionless on a reclined chair with bits of vegetables placed on both of her eyes. Her hand had been holding a leash that went to the little girl's waist, but the leash had gone slack in Gloria's hand and was now trailing behind the child as she headed for the end of the dock and the pond beyond.

As a puppy my reaction to a limp leash was always

to explore, and this little girl's response was just the same.

This was Gloria's second visit to the Farm. The previous time was in the wintertime. Ethan had still been alive, and Gloria had handed the baby to him and called him Grandpa. After Gloria left, Ethan and his mate, Hannah, said the name Gloria out loud many times over many nights, with sad emotions underlying their conversations.

They also said the name Clarity. The baby's name was Clarity, though often Gloria called her Clarity June.

I felt certain that Ethan would want me to watch over Clarity, who always seemed to be getting into trouble. Just the other day I had sat by miserably while the baby crawled under the bird feeder and stuffed handfuls of fallen seeds into her mouth. It was one of my main jobs to terrorize the squirrels when they did this, but I wasn't sure what to do when I caught Clarity at it, even though I knew that for a child to eat birdseed was probably against a rule. And I was right about that—when I finally barked a few times, Gloria sat up from where she had been lying facedown on a towel and she was very angry.

I glanced at Gloria now. Should I bark? Children often jumped into the pond but never when they were as young as this little girl, though the way she was going it seemed inevitable she was going to get wet. Babies were only allowed in the water with adults holding them. I looked back toward the house. Hannah was outside, kneeling and playing with flowers up by the driveway, too far away to do anything if Clarity fell in the pond. I was pretty sure Hannah would want me to watch over Clarity, too. It was my new purpose.

Clarity was getting closer to the edge. I let out another whimper, a louder one.

"Hush," Gloria said without opening her eyes. I didn't understand the word, but the sharp tone was unmistakable.

Clarity didn't even look back. When she got to the edge of the dock, she teetered briefly and then fell straight off the front.

My nails dug into the wood as I lunged off the side of the dock and into the warm water. Clarity bobbed up a little, her little limbs working frantically, but her head was mostly below the pond's surface. I reached her in seconds, my teeth gently snagging the shirt. I pulled her head out of the water and turned for the shore.

Gloria started screaming, "Oh my God! Clarity!" She ran around and waded into the water just as my feet found purchase on the mucky bottom of the pond.

"Bad dog!" she shouted as she snatched Clarity from me. "You are a bad, bad dog!"

I hung my head in shame.

"Gloria! What happened?" Hannah shouted as she came running up.

"Your dog just knocked the baby into the water. Clarity could have drowned! I had to jump in to save her and now I'm all wet!"

The distress in everyone's voices was very plain.

"Buddy?" Hannah said.

I didn't dare look at her. I wagged my tail a little and it splashed the surface of the pond. I didn't know what I had done wrong, but clearly I had upset everyone.

Everyone, that is, except Clarity. I risked a glance at her because I could sense her straining in her mother's arms, her little hands reaching out toward me.

"Bubby," Clarity gurgled. Her pants were streaming water down her legs. I dropped my eyes again.

Gloria blew out some air. "Hannah, would you mind taking the baby? Her diaper's all wet and I want to lie on my stomach so I'll be the same color on both sides."

"Sure," Hannah said. "Come on, Buddy."

Thankful we had *that* over with, I leaped out of the water, wagging my tail.

"Don't shake!" Gloria said, dancing away from me on the dock. I heard the warning in her voice, though I wasn't sure what she was trying to tell me. I shook myself from head to tail, ridding my fur of the pond water.

"Yuck, no!" Gloria shrieked. She sternly lectured me, pointing her finger and using a whole string of words I didn't understand, though she did say "bad dog" a few times. I lowered my head, blinking.

"Buddy, come," Hannah said. Her tone was gentle. I followed obediently as we went up to the house.

"Bubby," Clarity kept saying. "Bubby."

As we reached the front steps to the house I paused because of the odd taste in my mouth. I'd had it before—it reminded me of the time when I pulled a thin metal pan out of the trash that was lined with sweet flavors and, after licking it clean, experimentally crunched up the pan itself. The metal tasted bad, so I spat it out. This particular taste, though, I couldn't spit out—it sat on my tongue and invaded my nose.

"Buddy?" Hannah stood on the front porch, regarding me. "What's wrong?"

I wagged and bounded up onto the porch, leading the way into the house when she opened the door.

It was always fun to walk through that door, whether it was going inside or heading out, because it meant we were doing something new.

Later I stood guard while Hannah and Clarity played a new game. Hannah would carry Clarity to the top of the stairs and then watch while Clarity turned around and went down the stairs in a backward crawl. Usually Hannah would say "Good girl," and I would wag my tail. When Clarity got to the bottom step I would lick her in the face and she would giggle; then she would raise her arms to Hannah. "Mo'," she would beg. "Mo', Gramma. Mo'." When she said this Hannah would lift her up and kiss her and then take her to the top of the stairs to do it again.

When I felt satisfied they were safe I went to my favorite spot in the living room, circled, and lay down with a sigh. A few minutes later Clarity came over to me, dragging her blanket. She had the thing in her mouth that she chewed on but never swallowed.

"Bubby," she said. She dropped to all fours and crawled the last few feet to me and curled up against me, pulling her blanket against herself with her tiny hands. I sniffed her head—nobody in the world smelled like Clarity. Her scent filled me with a warm feeling that nudged me into a nap.

We were still sleeping when I heard the screen door

shut and Gloria come into the room. "Oh, Clarity!" she said. I blearily opened my eyes as Gloria reached down and snatched the little girl away from where she'd been sleeping. The place where Clarity had been snuggled against me felt oddly cold and empty without her there.

Hannah came out from the kitchen. "I'm making cookies," she said.

I eased myself to my feet because I knew *that* word. Wagging, I went over to sniff Hannah's sweet-smelling hands.

"The baby was sleeping right up against the dog," Gloria said. I heard the word "dog" and, as usual, it sounded as if I had made her mad. I wondered if this meant no cookies.

"That's right," Hannah said. "Clarity cuddled right up against him."

"I would just prefer it if my child not sleep next to a dog. If Buddy had rolled over, Clarity might have been crushed."

I watched Hannah for some clue as to why my name had just been mentioned. She put her hand to her mouth. "I . . . all right, of course. I won't let it happen again."

Clarity was still asleep, her little head against Gloria's shoulder. Gloria handed the baby to Hannah, then sat with a sigh at the kitchen table. "Is there any ice tea?" she asked.

"I'll get you some." Holding the baby, Hannah went to the kitchen counter. She got things out, but I didn't see any cookies, though I could sure smell them, sugary and warm in the air. I sat obediently, waiting.

"I just think it would be better if, when Clarity and

I are visiting, the dog stays out in the yard," Gloria said. She took a sip of her drink as Hannah joined her at the table. Clarity was stirring and Hannah patted her a little.

"Oh, I couldn't do that."

I lay down with a groan, wondering why people always did this: talked about cookies but didn't give any to a deserving dog.

"Buddy is part of the family," Hannah said. I drowsily raised my head to look at her, but still no cookies. "Did I ever tell you how he brought me and Ethan together?"

I froze at the word "Ethan." His name was mentioned less and less often now in this house, but I couldn't hear it pronounced without thinking about his smell or his hand in my fur.

"A *dog* brought you together?" Gloria replied.

"Ethan and I had known each other as children. We were high school sweethearts, but after the fire—you know about the fire that crippled his leg?"

"Your son may have mentioned it; I don't know. Mostly Henry just talked about himself. You know how men are."

"Okay, after the fire, Ethan . . . there was just something dark inside him, and I wasn't old enough, mature enough I mean, to help him deal with it."

I sensed something like sadness inside Hannah and I knew she needed me. Still under the table, I went over and put my head in her lap. She stroked my fur gently, Clarity's bare feet hanging limply above me.

"Ethan had a dog then, too, a wonderful golden retriever named Bailey. That was his doodle dog."

I wagged at hearing the name Bailey and "doodle dog." Whenever Ethan called me doodle dog his heart would be full of love and he would hug me and I would kiss his face. I missed Ethan more powerfully in that moment than I had in a long time—and I could feel Hannah missing him, too. I kissed the hand petting me, and Hannah lowered her eyes and smiled at my head in her lap.

"You're a good dog, too, Buddy," Hannah said. I wagged some more at being called a good dog. It seemed very possible that this whole conversation could lead to cookies after all.

"Anyway, we went our separate ways. I met Matthew, we were married, and I had Rachel and Cindy, and, of course, Henry."

Gloria made a small noise, but I didn't look at her. Hannah was still stroking my head and I didn't want her to stop.

"After Matthew died I decided I missed my kids and I moved back to town. And one day, when Buddy was probably a year old, he was in the dog park and he followed Rachel home. He had a tag on his collar, and when I looked at it—well, I was pretty surprised to see Ethan's name on it. But not half as surprised as Ethan was when I phoned him! I had been thinking of dropping by to see him, but probably wasn't ever going to do it. Silly, but things hadn't ended well between us and even though it was a long time ago, I felt . . . I don't know, shy, maybe."

"Tell me about bad breakups. I've had plenty of those, for sure." Gloria snorted.

"Yes, I'm sure," Hannah said. She looked down in

her lap and smiled at me. "When I saw Ethan, after all those years, it was as if we had never been apart. We belonged together. I wouldn't say this to my kids, of course, but Ethan was my one, my soul mate. And yet if it hadn't been for Buddy, we might never have even met again."

I loved hearing my name and Ethan's name spoken out loud, and I felt Hannah's love and her sadness as she smiled at me.

"Oh, look at the time," Hannah said then. She stood and handed Clarity to Gloria. The baby stirred, poking a tiny fist in the air and yawning. With a clatter the cookies came out of the hot oven and there was a wave of delicious smell, but Hannah didn't give me any.

As far as I was concerned, having cookies so tantalizingly close to my nose without being given a treat of any kind was the big tragedy of the day.

"I'll be gone for maybe an hour and a half," Hannah told Gloria. She reached up to where she kept some toys called keys and I heard the metallic jangling sound I associated with riding in the car. I watched alertly, torn between my desire for a car ride and my duty to stay by the cookies.

"You stay here, Buddy," Hannah said. "Oh, and Gloria, keep the door to the cellar closed. Clarity loves to climb down any set of stairs she can find and I had to put some rat poison out down there."

"Rats? There are rats?" Gloria said sharply. Clarity was fully awake now, struggling in her mother's arms.

"Yes. This is a farm. Sometimes we get rats. It's okay, Gloria. Just keep the door closed." I picked up a little anger in Hannah and watched her anxiously for signs of what was going on. As was typical in situations like this, though, the strong emotions I sensed were never explained—people are like that; they have complex feelings that are just too difficult for a dog to comprehend.

When she left, I followed Hannah out to her car. "No, you stay here, Buddy," she said. Her meaning was clear, particularly when she slid inside the car and shut the door on me, her keys clinking. I wagged, hoping she might change her mind, but once the car was headed down the driveway I knew there would be no car ride for me that day.

I slipped back inside through the dog door. Clarity was in her special chair, the one with the tray in front of it. Gloria was hunched over, trying to spoon some food into Clarity's mouth, and Clarity was mostly spitting it back out. I'd tasted Clarity's food and didn't blame her one bit. Often Clarity was allowed to put small bits of food into her mouth with her own hands, but when it came to the really bad stuff her mother and Hannah still had to force it on her with a spoon.

"Bubby!" Clarity gurgled, slapping her hands against the tray in happiness. Some of the food splattered on Gloria's face and she stood up abruptly, making a harsh noise. She wiped her face with a towel and then glared at me. I lowered my eyes.

"I can't believe she just lets you wander around like you own the place," she muttered.

I never had any hope that Gloria would ever give me a cookie.

"Well, not while I'm in charge," she said. She regarded me silently for several seconds and then sniffed. "Okay. Come here!" she ordered.

I obediently followed her over to the cellar door. She opened it. "In you go. Go!"

I figured out what she wanted and went through the doorway. A small carpeted area at the top of the stairs was just big enough for me to turn around and look at her.

"You stay," she said, shutting the door. Instantly it was much darker.

The steps that led down were wooden and made a squeaking noise as I descended. I wasn't down in the cellar very often and could smell new and interesting things down there that I wanted to explore. Explore and maybe eat.

TWO

Though the light in the cellar was very dim, the walls and corners were rich with thick, damp odors. Wooden shelves held musty bottles, and a cardboard box, gone soft in the sides, was filled with clothing that held a marvelous jumble of smells from the many children who had been on the Farm over the years. I inhaled deeply, remembering running through summer grasses and plunging through winter snows.

Despite the wonderful scents, though, there was nothing I was interested in eating.

After a time, I heard the easily identifiable sound of Hannah's car coming up the driveway. With a click, the door at the top of the cellar stairs opened.

"Buddy! Come here right now!" Gloria snapped at me.

I hastily made for the stairs, but I stumbled in the gloom and a pain hit my left rear leg, sharp and deep. I stopped, looking up at Gloria, who was framed in the light in the open doorway. I wanted her to tell me that whatever had just hurt me, it was okay.

"I said come!" she said more loudly.

I whimpered a little as I took my first step, but I knew I had to do what she said. I kept the weight off the leg and that seemed to help.

"Would you come on?" Gloria took two steps down, reaching for me.

I didn't crave having Gloria's hand on my fur and I knew she was mad at me for something, so I tried to shy away from her.

"Hello?" Hannah called, her voice echoing upstairs. I put more speed into my gait now, and the leg felt a little better. Gloria turned and she and I entered the kitchen together.

"Gloria?" Hannah said. She put down her paper bags and I went over to her, wagging. "Where's Clarity?"

"I finally got her down for a nap."

"What were you doing down in the cellar?"

"I was, I was looking for some wine."

"You were? Downstairs?" Hannah put her hand down and I sniffed it, smelling something sweet. I was so glad she was home.

"Well, I thought, wine *cellar*."

"Oh. Well, no, I think we have some and it's in the cabinet under the toaster." Hannah was looking at me and I wagged. "Buddy? Are you limping?"

I sat. Hannah took a few steps back and called me and I went over to her.

"Does he look like he's limping to you?" Hannah asked.

"How would I know?" Gloria said. "My expertise is children, not dogs."

"Buddy? Did you hurt your leg?" I wagged with the sheer pleasure of her attention. Hannah leaned down and kissed me between the eyes and I gave her a lick right back. She went over to the kitchen counter.

"Oh, you didn't want any cookies?" she asked.

"I can't have *cookies,*" Gloria said scornfully.

I had never before heard the word "cookies" said so negatively.

Hannah didn't say anything, but I heard her give a tiny sigh as she began to put away the things she'd brought home in her sacks. Sometimes she'd have a bone when she came home, but I could smell that today she hadn't been able to find any. I watched her alertly, though, just in case I was wrong.

"I don't want Clarity to have any, either," Gloria said after a minute. "She's chubby enough."

Hannah laughed, then stopped. "You're serious."

"Of course I'm serious."

After a moment, Hannah turned back to the grocery sacks. "Okay, Gloria," she said quietly.

A few days later Gloria was sitting in the sun in the front yard with her knees drawn up close to her chest. She had small balls of fur between her toes and was touching them with a tiny stick coated with an eye-watering chemical. Each toe was darker after she was done with it.

The smell was so powerful it overcame the strange taste in my mouth, which otherwise had become stronger and more persistent with each passing day.

Clarity had been playing with a toy but was on her feet and tottering away. I looked over at Gloria, who had her eyes narrowed at her toes and the very tip of her tongue sticking out of her mouth.

"Clarity, don't wander off," Gloria said absently.

In the several days that Clarity had been on the Farm she had gone from having a slow, wobbling walk that dropped down to all fours every so often to being able to take off at a near run. She was headed purposefully toward the barn and I followed right behind her, wondering what I should do.

The horse named Troy was in the barn. When Ethan was alive he sometimes rode Troy, which I didn't approve of very much because horses are not reliable like dogs. One time when he was young Ethan fell off of a horse—nobody ever fell off a dog. Hannah didn't ever ride Troy.

We went into the barn, Clarity and I, and I heard Troy snort at our presence. The air was filled with the smell of hay and horse. Clarity marched right over to the kennel where Troy stayed when he was in the barn. Troy moved his head up and down in a quick jerk and snorted again. Clarity reached the bars of the gate and gripped them in her tiny hands. "Horsey," she said excitedly. Her little knees were pumping up and down with glee.

I could feel a rising tension coming off of Troy. The

horse didn't care for me much, and I had noticed from previous visits that when I was in the barn it made him nervous. Clarity reached her hand through the bars to try and pet Troy, who shied away.

I went up to Clarity and touched my nose to her to let her know that if she wanted to pet something there was nothing better than a dog. Her eyes were wide and bright and her mouth was open and she was panting excitedly, her eyes not leaving Troy.

A loop of chain kept the gate shut, but as Clarity leaned against the bars the slack in the loop made for a gap and I knew what she was going to do before she did it. Making happy noises, she slid sideways along the gate up to the gap and then pressed her way through it.

Right into Troy's kennel.

Troy was pacing now, back and forth, swinging his head and snorting. His eyes were wide open and his hooves seemed to be hitting the ground harder and harder. I could smell his agitation; it popped to the surface of his skin, like sweat.

"Horsey," Clarity said.

I put my head into the gap and pushed hard, trying to squeeze through. As I did I felt the pain in my left rear leg again, but I ignored it and concentrated on getting my shoulders through, and then my hips. Panting, I made it into the kennel as Clarity started forward, her hands raised up at Troy, who was stamping and snorting. I could see he was going to step on the baby.

I was afraid of the horse. He was big and powerful and I knew that if he hit me with one of his hooves it would hurt me. My instincts were telling me to back up, to get out of there, but Clarity was in danger and I had to do something, something *now*.

I swallowed my fear and barked at that horse with all the fury I possessed. I tightened my lips, showing my teeth, and lunged forward, putting myself between Clarity and Troy. Troy was making a harsh screaming sound, lifting his front hooves briefly off the ground. I backed up, still barking, pushing Clarity into the corner with my hips. Troy's pacing was more frantic and his hooves were striking the ground close to my face and I kept snarling and snapping my teeth at him.

"Buddy? Buddy!" I could hear Hannah calling frantically from outside the barn. Behind me, I felt Clarity's little hands dig into my fur to keep me from knocking her over. The horse might strike me, but I was going to stay between him and the baby. A hoof whistled past my ear and I bit at it.

And then Hannah was rushing in. "Troy!" She unfastened the loop of chain and swung the gate open and the horse bolted past her and through the big double doors and out into the big yard.

I could feel the fear and anger in Hannah now. She reached down and scooped up Clarity in her arms. "Oh, honey, you're okay, you're okay," she said.

Clarity clapped her hands together, grinning. "Horsey!" she exclaimed happily.

Hannah's other hand came down and touched me and I was relieved to know I wasn't in any trouble.

"Yes, a big horsey, you're right, honey! But you shouldn't be in here."

When we were back outside, Gloria came up to us.

She was walking strangely, taking steps as if her feet hurt her.

"What happened?" she asked.

"Clarity went into Troy's stall. She could have been . . . It was terrifying."

"Oh no! Oh, Clarity, that was so bad!" Gloria reached out and grabbed Clarity, hugging the baby to her chest. "Oh, you must never, ever frighten Mommy like that again, do you understand?"

Hannah folded her arms. "I'm not sure how she got up here without you knowing."

"She must have followed the dog."

"I see." Hannah still felt angry to me, and I lowered my head a little, reflexively feeling remorseful.

"Would you take her?" Gloria asked, holding Clarity out at arm's length.

The pain in my hip stayed with me, after that, not so bad that I was hobbled, but a dull ache that never left. There was nothing wrong with the leg, though, nothing to lick.

At dinner I liked to stay under the table and clean up when things fell on the floor. When there were lots of children around I could usually count on several morsels, but at that time there was just Clarity and, as I've said, her food tasted wretched, though naturally if some fell I ate it anyway. I was lying under there a few nights after the incident with the horse when I noticed that Hannah seemed a little nervous and anxious. I sat up and nosed her, but when she petted me it was in a distracted fashion.

"Did that doctor call for me? Bill?" Gloria asked.

"No. I said I would tell you."

"I don't know why men do that. They ask for your number and then they don't call."

"Gloria. I was . . . I was thinking about something."

"What?"

"Well. First, I want you to know that even though you and Henry are not . . . you're no longer together, and you never got married, you're the mother of my grandchild and I will always consider you family and you are always welcome here."

"Thank you," Gloria said. "I feel the same way."

"And I'm sorry Henry's job has him overseas. He told me he's still looking for a position back here so he can spend more time with Clarity."

When I heard her name, I looked over at Clarity's little feet, which were all I could see of her under the table. She was kicking them, which was how she acted when she was feeding herself her yucky dinner. When Gloria was feeding her, Clarity would twist and turn in the chair.

"Meanwhile, I know that you're hoping to get your singing career back on track," Hannah continued.

"Right, well, having a baby hasn't exactly helped *that*. I still haven't gotten rid of this weight."

"That's why I was thinking. What if Clarity stayed here?"

There was a long stillness. When Gloria spoke again, her voice was very quiet. "What do you mean?"

"Rachel will be back in town next week, and when the school year starts Cindy will be off by four o'clock every day. Between us and all Clarity's cousins, we could give her so much attention and you'd have the chance to pursue your singing. And like I said, any time you wanted to come stay with me, we have plenty of room. You'd have so much freedom."

"So that's what this is about," Gloria said.

"Sorry?"

"I wondered. Inviting me here, telling me I could stay as long as I wanted. Now I know. So Clarity would live with you? And then what?"

"I'm not sure I understand what you mean, Gloria."

"And then Henry sues to end child support, and I'm left with nothing."

"What? No, that's the furthest thing—"

"I know everyone in your family thinks I was trying to trap Henry into asking me to marry him, but I've met plenty of men who do just fine. I don't need to trap anybody into anything."

"No, Gloria, no one ever said that."

With a lurch, Gloria stood up. "I knew. I knew it was something like this. Everyone acting so *nice*."

I could feel the anger coming off of her, and made sure I was well away from her feet. Suddenly Clarity's chair was shaking back and forth and her little feet vanished up into the air.

"I'm packing. We're leaving."

"Gloria!"

I heard Clarity give off a wail as Gloria stomped up the stairs. Clarity hardly ever cried—the last time I could remember was when she crawled into the garden and pulled a green vegetable off a plant that was so pungent it made my eyes water worse than Gloria's toes. Though I could plainly tell it was something no one should ever eat, Clarity stuck the thing in her mouth and gummed it. She had a real look of surprise on her face when that happened, and she cried just like she was crying now—part shock, part hurt, part anger.

Hannah cried, too, after Gloria and Clarity drove off. I tried to comfort her as best I could, sitting with my head in her lap, and I'm pretty sure it helped, though she felt very sad when she fell asleep in her bed.

I didn't really understand what had happened other than Gloria and Clarity leaving, but I figured I would see them both again. People always came back to the Farm.

I slept on Hannah's bed, which I had started doing shortly after Ethan died. For a time she would hold me at night and sometimes she'd cry then, too. I knew why she was crying: she missed Ethan. We all missed Ethan.

The next morning, when I jumped down off Hannah's bed, something felt like it broke in my left hip, and I couldn't help it, I let out a yelp of pain.

"Buddy, what is it? What happened? What's wrong with your leg?"

I could feel her fear and licked her palm in apology for upsetting her, but I wasn't able to put my left rear leg on the floor—it hurt too much.

"We're going right to the Vet, Buddy. You'll be okay," Hannah said.

We made our slow, careful way out to the car, me hopping on three legs and doing my best to look as if it wasn't hurting so I wouldn't make Hannah any more sad. Though I was a front-seat dog, she put me in the back, and I was grateful because it was easier to crawl up there than to try to jump up front with only three legs working.

As she started the car and drove off, I had that awful taste in my mouth again, horrible as ever.

[THREE]

When we got to the cool room and I was lifted onto the metal bed I thumped my tail and shivered with pleasure. I loved the Vet, who was called Doctor Deb. She touched me with such gentle hands. Mostly her fingers smelled of soap, but I could always catch the scent of cats and dogs on her sleeves. I let her feel my sore leg and it didn't hurt at all. I stood when Doctor Deb wanted me to and was lying patiently with Hannah in a small room when the Vet came in and sat down on a stool and scooted it over to Hannah.

"It's not good news," Doctor Deb said.

"Oh," Hannah said. I felt her quick sadness and looked at her in sympathy, though she had never been sad with Doctor Deb before, so I wasn't sure what was happening.

"We could take the leg, but these big dogs don't normally do well with the rear one gone. And there's no guarantee the cancer hasn't already spread—we might be simply making him less comfortable in what little time he has left. If it were up to me, I would just do painkillers at this point. He's already eleven years old, right?"

"He was a rescue, so we don't know for sure. But yes, around that," Hannah said. "Is that old?"

"You know, they say that Labs average twelve and a half years, but I've seen them go a lot longer. It's not that I'm saying he's already at the end of his life span. It's more that sometimes, in the older dogs, the tumors grow more slowly. That would be another factor to consider if we're thinking about amputation."

"Buddy has always been such an active dog. I just can't imagine taking his leg," Hannah said.

I wagged at hearing my name.

"You're such a good dog, Buddy," Doctor Deb murmured. I closed my eyes and leaned into her as she scratched my ears. "Let's start him on something for pain right away. Labradors don't always let us know when they're hurting. They have an amazing pain threshold."

When we got home, I was given a special treat of meat and cheese and then I got sleepy and went to my usual spot in the living room and collapsed into a deep nap.

The rest of that summer it just felt better to keep

my rear leg curled up off the ground and rely on the other three to get around, so that's what I did. The best days were when I'd go into the pond, where the cool water felt so good and where my weight was supported. Rachel came back from wherever she had been and all of her children were there and Cindy's children would come over and they all lavished attention on me as if I were a puppy. I loved lying on the ground while two of Cindy's little daughters tied ribbons into my fur, their small hands soothing as they worked. Later I ate the ribbons.

Hannah gave me lots of special treats and I took lots of naps. I knew I was getting older, because my muscles were often stiff and my vision was dimming somewhat, but I was very happy. I loved the smell of the leaves as they fell to the ground and curled up, and the dry perfume of Hannah's flowers as they became brittle on their stalks.

"Buddy is chasing rabbits again," I heard Hannah say one time when I was sleeping. I awoke at the sound of my name, but I was disoriented and it took me a moment to remember where I was. I had been dreaming very vividly of Clarity falling off the dock, but in my dream, instead of me being a bad dog, Ethan was there, knee-deep in the water. "Good dog," he told me, and I got the sense that he was glad that I had watched over Clarity. When she came back to the Farm I would watch over her again. It was what Ethan would want me to do.

Ethan's smell had slowly left the Farm, but I still felt his presence in some places. Sometimes I would go and stand in his bedroom and it would seem as if he were right there, sleeping, or sitting in his chair and watching me. I took comfort from the feeling. And sometimes I would remember Clarity calling me Bubby. Though I knew that her mother, Gloria, was probably taking good care of the baby, I always felt a little anxious when I thought of Clarity. I hoped she'd soon return to the Farm so I could see for myself that she was all right.

The cold weather came and I went outside less and less. Doing my business, I selected the nearest tree and got it over with, squatting because I could no longer lift my leg properly. Even if it was raining, Hannah would come out and stand with me.

The snow that winter was a delight. It would support my weight just like water, and was colder and felt even better. I would stand out in it and close my eyes and was so comfortable I felt as if I could fall asleep.

The bad taste in my mouth never left me, though sometimes it was strong and other times I forgot it was even there. The ache in my leg was the same way, though there were days when I would wake up from my nap with a start, the pain a sharp, breathtaking stab.

One day I got up to look at the snow melting outside the window and it just didn't seem worth it to go outdoors to play, even though I usually loved it when the new grass would come poking up out of the wet, muddy earth. Hannah was watching me. "Okay, Buddy. Okay," she said.

That day all of the children came over to see me and they petted me and talked to me. I lay on the floor and groaned with pleasure at all the attention and the little hands on me, stroking me and petting me. Some of the children were sad and some seemed bored, but they all just sat there with me on the floor until it was time for them to go.

"You are a good dog, Buddy."

"I will miss you so much, Buddy."

"I love you, Buddy."

I wagged every time someone said my name.

I didn't sleep in Hannah's bed that night. It was simply too delicious to lie there in my spot on the floor and remember all the children touching me.

The next morning I woke up just as the sun was starting to light up the sky. It took all the effort I could muster to struggle to a standing position, and then I limped in next to Hannah's bed. She awoke when I raised my head and placed it next to her on the blanket, panting.

I had a heavy pain in my stomach and throat, and my leg throbbed with a dull ache.

I didn't know if she would understand, but I was looking her in the eye, trying to let her know what I needed from her. This wonderful woman, Ethan's mate, who had so loved both of us—I knew she wouldn't let me down.

"Oh, Buddy. You're telling me it's time," she said sadly. "Okay, Buddy, okay."

When we walked out of the house I limped to a tree to do my business. Then I stood and looked around at the Farm in the light from sunrise, everything painted orange and gold. Water dripped from the eaves, water with a cold, pure smell. The ground beneath my feet was moist and ready to burst forth with flowers and grass—I could smell the new growth, just beneath the surface of the fragrant mud. It was such a perfect day.

I made it to the car okay, but when Hannah opened the rear door I ignored it and shuffled sideways until my nose was pointed at the front door. She laughed a little and opened the door and picked up my rear to help me in.

I was a front-seat dog.

I sat and looked out at the day, which carried with it the promise of warmer breezes. Snow still lurked where the trees were most dense, but it had given up in the yard where Ethan and I had played, rolling and wrestling together. It seemed as if I could hear him, at that moment, telling me I was a good dog. My tail thumped at the memory of his voice.

Hannah reached out to touch me often on that ride in to see Doctor Deb. When Hannah spoke, her sadness came off of her in a gust and I licked the hand that was stroking me.

"Oh, Buddy," she said.

I wagged.

"Every time I look at you I remember my Ethan, Buddy. You good dog. You were his companion, his special friend. His dog. And you led me back to him, Buddy. I know you don't understand, but when you turned up on my doorstep, it led to Ethan and me getting back together. You did that. It was . . . No dog could ever do more for his people, Buddy."

It made me feel happy to hear Hannah say Ethan's name over and over again.

"You're the best dog, Buddy. A really, really good dog. Good dog."

I wagged at being a good dog.

At Doctor Deb's I just sat there when Hannah opened my door. I knew there was no way I could jump down, not with my leg. I gave her a mournful look.

"Oh, okay, Buddy. You wait right here."

Hannah shut the door and left. A few minutes later Doctor Deb and a man I had never seen before came out to the car. The man had cat smell on his hands, plus a pleasant meaty odor. He and Doctor Deb carried me into the building. I did my best to ignore the pain that flashed through me as they did so, but it left me panting. They put me on the metal bed and I was hurting too much to wag, I just laid my head down. The cool metal felt good as I sprawled on it.

"You are such a good dog, a good dog," Hannah whispered to me.

I knew it wouldn't be much longer, now. I focused on Hannah and she was smiling but also crying. Doctor Deb was stroking me, and I could feel her fingers looking for a fold of skin up by my neck.

I found myself thinking of little Clarity. I hoped she would find another dog soon to watch over her. Everyone needs a dog, but for Clarity it was even more of a necessity.

My name was Buddy. Before that it was Ellie, and before that it was Bailey, and before that it was Toby. I was a good dog who had loved my boy, Ethan, and had taken care of his children. I had loved his mate, Hannah. I knew that I would not be reborn, now, and that was okay. I had done everything a dog was supposed to do in this world.

The love was still pouring off of Hannah as I felt

the tiny pinch between Doctor Deb's fingers. Almost instantly, the pain in my leg receded. A sense of peace filled me; a wonderful, warm, delicious wave of it, supporting my weight like the water in the pond. The touch of Hannah's hands gradually left me, and, as I floated away in the water I felt truly happy.

FOUR

Images were just starting to resolve themselves in my bleary eyes when I remembered everything. One moment and I was a newborn puppy with no direction or purpose other than finding my mother's milk, and the next moment I was *me,* still a puppy, but one with a memory of being Buddy, and of all the previous times I'd been a puppy in my lives.

My mother's fur was curly and short and dark. My limbs were dark as well—at least, what I could see of them through my newly opened eyes—but my soft fur was not at all curly. All of my siblings were equally dark colored, though as we bumped into each other I could feel that only one had fur like mine—the rest were as curly as our mother.

I knew that my vision would soon clear, but I doubted that would do much to help me understand why I was a puppy again. My conviction had always been that I had an important purpose and that's why I kept being reborn. Then everything I had ever learned to do added up to helping my boy, Ethan, and I had been by his side and had guided him through the final years of his life. And that, I thought, was my purpose.

Now what? Was I to be reborn over and over, forever? Could a dog have more than one purpose? How was that possible?

All the puppies slept together in a big box. As my limbs grew stronger I explored our surroundings and it was pretty much as exciting as a box could be. Sometimes I'd hear footsteps descending stairs and then a fuzzy shape would lean over the box, speaking with either the voice of a man or the voice of a woman. The way our mother wagged her tail let me know these were the people who took care of her and loved her.

Pretty soon I could see they were, indeed, a man and a woman—that's how I thought of them, as the Man and the Woman.

One day the Man brought a friend to grin down at us. The friend had no hair on his head except for around his mouth.

"They are so cute," the bald one with the hairy mouth said. "Six pups, that's a nice-sized litter."

"You want to pick one up?" the Man responded.

I froze as I felt what seemed like huge hands come down and grab me. I held still, a little intimidated, as the man with mouth hair lifted me up and stared at me.

"This one's not like the others," the man holding me said. His breath smelled powerfully of butter and sugar, so I licked the air a little.

"No, she has a brother that's the same way. We're not sure what happened—Bella and the sire are both AKC poodles, but that one sure doesn't look like a poodle. We're thinking . . . Well, there was this afternoon when we forgot to close the back door. Bella could have gotten out. Maybe another male got over the fence," the Man said.

"Wait, is that even possible? Two different fathers?"

I had no idea what they were talking about, but if all he was going to do was hold me and blow tantalizing odors at me I was ready to be put down.

"I guess so. The Vet said it can happen, two separate sires."

"That's hilarious."

"Yeah, except we're not going to be able to sell the two mystery dogs. You want that one? Free since you're a buddy."

"No, thank you." The man holding me laughed, letting me back down. My mother sniffed the stranger's scent on me and, protective and kind, gave me a reassuring lick, while my brothers and sisters staggered over on their unsteady legs because they had probably already forgotten who I was and wanted to challenge me. I ignored them.

"Hey, how's your son?" the man with the hairy face asked.

"Thanks for asking. Still sick, has this cough. Probably going to have to take him to the doctor."

"He been down here to see the pups?"

"No, they're a little young yet. I want them to get stronger before he handles them."

The two men walked away, dissolving into the blurry gloom beyond my field of vision.

As the days passed I became aware of a young child's voice upstairs, a male, and became alarmed over the prospect of starting over again with a new boy. That couldn't be my purpose, could it? It seemed wrong, somehow, as if I would be a bad dog if I had a boy other than Ethan.

One afternoon the Man scooped up all of us and put us in a smaller box that he carried up the stairs, our mother panting anxiously at his heels. We were set on the floor and then the Man turned the box gently so that we all tumbled out.

"Puppies!" a little boy sang out from somewhere behind us.

I splayed my legs a little for balance and peered around. It was like the living room at the Farm, with a couch and chairs. We were on a soft blanket and naturally most of my siblings immediately tried to get off it, heading off in all directions for the slick floor beyond the edge of the blanket. Me, I stayed put. In my experience, mother dogs liked soft spots more than hard ones, and it's always smarter to stick with Mother.

The Man and the Woman, laughing, grabbed the fleeing puppies and placed them back in the center of the blanket, which should have given them all the hint that they were not supposed to go running off, though most of them tried to do it again. A boy circled around, older than Clarity but still pretty young, hopping excitedly. I was reminded of Clarity's little legs bobbing up and down when she saw that stupid horse in the barn.

Though I was reluctant to love any other boy but Ethan, it was difficult not to be swept up in the joy we all felt at the sight of this little human holding his arms out to us.

The boy reached for my brother, the one who, like me, had longer, flatter fur. I could sense my siblings' distress when the boy snatched him up.

"Be careful, Son," the Man said.

"Don't hurt him; be gentle," the Woman said.

These were, I decided, the mother and father of the little boy. "He's kissing me!" The little boy giggled as my brother submissively licked the boy on the mouth.

"It's okay, Bella. You're a good dog," the Man said, petting our mother, who was pacing around the blanket, yawning anxiously.

The little boy was coughing. "Are you okay?" the mom asked him. He nodded, setting down my brother and immediately scooping up one of my sisters. My other two brothers were at the edge of the blanket and had stopped, sniffing, unsure of the surface.

"I hate the sound of that cough; it sounds like it's gotten worse," the Man said.

"He wasn't bad at all this morning," the Woman replied.

The little boy was breathing loudly, now, coughing

and making a harsh noise. His coughing was getting worse. Both of his parents froze, staring at him.

"Johnny?" the Woman said. There was fear in her voice. Our mother went to her, wagging anxiously. The Man set the puppy he'd been holding on the floor and grabbed the boy by the arm.

"Johnny? Can you breathe?"

The boy bent over, his hands on his knees. His breathing was thick and loud and heavy.

"He's turning blue!" the Woman yelled. My siblings and I flinched at the raw terror in her voice.

"Call 911!" The Man shouted at her. "Johnny! Stay with me, Son! Look at me!"

Whether consciously or not, all of us had found our way to our mother and were at her feet, seeking reassurance. She lowered her nose to us briefly, but she was panting and anxious and went over to the Man and tried to nuzzle him. The Man ignored her. "Johnny!" he shouted, anguished.

Several of the puppies were trying to follow our mother and when she saw this she came back to us, pushing us with her muzzle to keep us on the blanket and out of the way.

The Man laid the boy on the couch. The boy's eyes were fluttering and his breathing was still harsh and painful sounding. The Woman came in with her hands pressed to her mouth, weeping.

I heard the siren and it got louder and then two men and a woman were in the room. They put something on the boy's face and took him out of the house on a bed. The Man and the Woman went with them, and then we were alone.

It is the nature of puppies to explore, so my siblings immediately left the blanket to sniff the far corners of the room. Our mother paced and whined and kept rising up on her rear legs to look out the front window, and two of my siblings followed her around.

I sat on the blanket and tried to understand. Though he was not my boy, I felt a strong concern for the child. It did not mean I didn't love Ethan; I was just feeling a fear.

Because we were puppies we made messes all over the house. I knew when I was older I would have more self-control, but at this point I didn't know I needed to squat until suddenly the need would be upon me. I hoped the Man and Woman would not be angry with me.

We were all asleep when the Man came home by himself. He put us in the basement and I could hear him moving around upstairs and the air carried the scent of soap. We nursed; our mother was finally calm, now that the Man was home.

The next day we were taken to a different basement in a different house. A woman who smelled like cooking and laundry and dogs greeted us with kisses and cooing sounds. Her house had the scent of many, many dogs, though I only saw one: a slow-moving male who walked low to the ground, nearly dragging his big, floppy ears.

"Thanks for this. I'm really grateful, Jennifer," the Man said to her.

"Fostering dogs is what I do," she said. "I just adopted out a boxer yesterday, so I knew I'd be getting more. That's how it always works. Your wife said your son has asthma?"

"Yes. He's apparently deathly allergic to dogs, but we never knew it because Bella is a poodle and apparently Johnny's not allergic to poodles. We had no idea. I feel so stupid. His allergic reaction triggered his asthma attack and we didn't even know he had asthma! I thought we were going to lose him."

Bella, hearing her name, wagged a little. Our mother was distressed, though, when the Man left. We were in a nice-sized box in the basement, but as soon as the Man walked away Bella left it and then sat at the door to the stairs and cried. This distressed the puppies, who sat subdued, not playing. I'm sure I looked the same way—our mother's upset was clear and urgent.

That day, we did not nurse. The woman named Jennifer didn't notice it, but we did, and pretty soon we were all whimpering. Our mother was just too disturbed and saddened to lie down for us, even when her teats became heavy and began to leak a tantalizing odor that made us all dizzy.

I knew why she was so sad. A dog belongs with her people.

Our mother paced all night, crying softly. We all slept, but in the morning we were aching with hunger.

Jennifer came to see why we were crying and told Bella it was okay, but I could hear the alarm in her voice. She left the room and we cried for our mother, but Bella just paced and whined and ignored us. Then, after what seemed like a long time, Bella was at the door, her snout at the crack beneath it, sniffing in with great gusts. Her tail started to wag and then the Man opened the door. Bella was sobbing and jumping up on the Man and the Man was pushing her away.

"You have to stay down, Bella. I need you to stay down."

"She hasn't been nursing the pups. She's too upset," Jennifer said.

"Okay, Bella, come over here. Come on." The Man ushered Bella over to the box and made her lie down. He kept his hand on her head and she stayed and we went at her in a mad rush, pushing and sucking and fighting each other.

"I'm just worried that the puppies' dander is on her and it will get on me and then Johnny will have an attack. He's got an inhaler and everything."

"But if Bella doesn't nurse, her puppies will die," Jennifer said.

"I have to do what's best for Johnny. We're having the entire house steam-cleaned," the Man said.

My belly was getting warm and heavy. It was a glorious thing to feed.

"Well, what if you took Bella and the poodle puppies home with you? You could bathe them, get rid of any trace of the other two puppies. You'd at least save four of them, and it would be best for Bella, too."

The Man and Jennifer were quiet for a long time. Completely full, I staggered away, so sleepy I just wanted to climb on one of the other puppies and nap.

"You'd euthanize the other two, then? I wouldn't want them to starve to death," the Man said.

"They would not suffer," Jennifer said.

A few minutes later I was surprised when the Man and Jennifer reached in and picked up a pair of puppies each. Bella hopped out of the box and followed. My brother, the one who had fur like mine, whimpered a little, but we were both really sleepy. We curled up against each other for warmth, my head on his back.

I didn't know where our mother and our siblings had gone, but I figured they would be back soon.

FIVE

I awoke cold and hungry. My brother and I were pressed up against each other for warmth and when I stirred he opened his eyes. We groggily made our way around the box, relieving ourselves and touching each other several times, communicating to each other what was pretty obvious. Our mother and our siblings were gone.

My brother started crying.

Soon the woman called Jennifer came over to see us. We looked up at her, so tall above us.

"You poor little puppies, you miss your mommy, don't you?"

The sound of her voice seemed to soothe my brother. He stood on his rear legs, his front legs against the side of the box, and strained to raise his small muzzle to her. She bent down, smiling. "It's okay, little one. Everything will be all right, I promise you."

When she left, my brother went back to his whining. I tried to interest him in a wrestling match, but he was really unhappy. I knew everything was fine because we had a woman to watch us and she would bring our mother back soon so we could feed, but my brother was frightened and hungry and apparently couldn't think beyond that.

Soon Jennifer returned. "Okay, time to take care of you. You want to go first? Okay," she said, picking up my brother and carrying him off.

I was alone in the box. I lay down and tried not to think about the empty ache in my stomach. It was easier to ignore my hunger with my brother off with Jennifer. I wondered if maybe I was supposed to take care of my brother but dismissed the thought. Dogs don't take care of dogs; people take care of dogs. As long as we had Jennifer, we would be fine.

I fell asleep and didn't wake up until I felt Jennifer lifting me up into the air. She stared into my face. "Well, that didn't go as well as I had hoped," she said. "Let's hope it goes more quickly with you."

I wagged my tiny tail.

Jennifer and I went upstairs. There was no sign of my brother, though I could smell him in the air. Still holding me, she sat down on her couch, rolling me onto my back in the cradle of her arm. "Okay, okay now," Jennifer said. "Nice and still."

She reached over and picked something up, an odd-shaped thing that she slowly lowered toward my face. What was she doing? I squirmed a little.

"You need to be still now, puppy. This will go okay if you don't fight it," Jennifer said.

Her voice was soothing, but I still didn't know what was going on. But then I caught the delicious scent of warm milk—the thing she was holding was oozing food. The tip of it was soft and when she probed my lips with it I seized it and sucked and was rewarded with a warm, sweet meal.

In a way, it was like being nursed by my mother, except that I was on my back and the thing in my mouth was very large. The milk was quite different, too, more sweet and light, but I wasn't complaining. I sucked and that wonderful warm liquid erased away the ache in my belly.

When I was full I was drowsy and Jennifer held me and patted me on my back and I burped a little. Then she took me down the hall to a soft bed, where the big dog with the huge ears was sleeping, my brother nuzzled up against him.

"Here's another one, Barney," Jennifer whispered.

The big dog groaned, but he wagged his tail and didn't move when I nestled up against him. Though he was a male, his tummy was warm and comforting, just like Mother's.

My brother squeaked out a greeting and then went right back to sleep.

From that point forward, Jennifer fed us in her lap several times a day. I grew to love the feedings and the way Jennifer would talk to me as she cuddled me. It would be easy to love someone like Jennifer.

My brother was distressed when I was fed before he was, and I think Jennifer decided it made more sense to have me go second than to feed me with my brother crying the whole time.

I think I had known it all along, but one day while I was squatting and smelled my urine it occurred to me that we weren't brothers but brother and sister. I was a female dog!

I wondered briefly what had happened to our mother and to my other siblings, but it seemed as if I couldn't really even remember them anymore. We lived here now, my brother and I, a family of two puppies and a lazy dog named Barney. I would have to get used to being a female and being in this odd living situation.

I decided that there were times when all a dog could do was wait and see what would happen next, what choices people would make that would change everything or make it more of the same. In the meantime, my brother and I put our efforts into tugging on Barney's soft, floppy ears.

Jennifer called my brother Rocky and me Molly. As we grew stronger, Barney wanted to have less and less to do with us, becoming impatient with us chewing on his body parts. That was okay, though, because a big gray dog named Che came to stay with us at the house. Che loved to run around the backyard, where the grass was just starting to pop up in the warming spring sun. He was very fast and Rocky and I could not hope to catch up to him, but he wanted us to chase him and when we would give up he would dart over and bow down to get us to play again. And then there was a stocky dog named Mr. Churchill. He was a bit like Barney in size except that he was heavier, and his ears were very short. Mr. Churchill wheezed and waddled when he walked—he was the exact opposite of Che. I am not sure he even *could* run. And after eating he smelled pretty bad.

Jennifer's house, with all the dogs, was just about the most wonderful place imaginable. I sometimes missed the Farm, of course, but being at Jennifer's was like living full-time at a dog park.

A woman came to see Che after a few days and took him with her when she left. "It's wonderful, what you do. I think if I tried to foster dogs I'd wind up keeping all of them," said the woman who took Che.

Che was going to have a new life with a new person, I realized, and I was happy for him, though Rocky appeared completely mystified as to what was going on.

"That's called 'foster failure.'" Jennifer laughed. "It's how I came to have Barney. He was my first foster. I realized, though, that if I didn't get control of myself I'd adopt a few dogs and then that'd be it and I wouldn't be able to help any others."

One day some people came over to Jennifer's house to play with us—a man and a woman and two girls.

"We're pretty sure we want a male," the man said.

The girls were that wonderful age where they couldn't run much faster than a puppy and were always giggling. They picked us up and kissed us and put us down and played with us.

"You said poodle and what, again?" the man asked.

Jennifer said, "Nobody knows. Spaniel? Terrier?"

I knew what was happening: they were here to take either Rocky or me home with them. I wondered why we had to leave this place—if anyone should go it should be Mr. Churchill, who mostly just stood there emitting odors or, when Rocky goaded him into it, would chase us and knock us over with his chest. But I also knew that people were in charge—they decided dogs' fates, and I would have to go where they sent me.

In the end, though, Rocky and I stayed. I was relieved not to lose Rocky and happy not to have to say good-bye to the other dogs, but I didn't understand it, why people would come play with me and then not want to take me with them.

And then one day, I did understand.

Rocky and I were in the backyard with a new brown dog named Daisy. Daisy was very timid around Jennifer—she wouldn't come when called and whenever Jennifer reached down to pet her Daisy would shy away from her hand. Daisy was very thin and had light brown eyes. She would play with Rocky and me, though, and even though she was much larger, she would let us pin her when we were wrestling.

I heard car doors slamming and then a few minutes later the screen door at the back of the house slid open. Rocky and I trotted over to investigate as Jennifer and a boy and a girl came out into the yard, while Daisy slunk over to a place behind a picnic table where she seemed to feel safe.

"Oh my God, they are so cute!" The girl laughed. She was about the age that Ethan had been when he started driving a car. She dropped to her knees and spread her arms wide. Rocky and I obediently ran over to her. She gathered us into an embrace and her scent flowed from her and that's when I made an astounding discovery.

It was Clarity.

I went wild, climbing on her and kissing her and smelling her skin. I was leaping and spinning with joy. Clarity!

Never before had it occurred to me that she might come look for me, that she would know I had been reborn and would find me. But humans drive the cars and decide when dogs eat and where dogs live and clearly this was something else in their power—they could find their dogs when they needed them.

That must be why the family with the little girls left without us. They were searching for their dogs, and Rocky and I weren't them.

I could not get enough of Clarity. My little tail beating the air, I licked her hands, making her laugh. When the boy ran around in the yard Rocky ran with him, but I stayed right with Clarity.

"What do you think, Trent?" Clarity called.

"He's great," the boy replied.

"Molly seems pretty smitten with you," Jennifer said to Clarity. "I'll be right back." Jennifer went back inside her house.

"Oh, you are so cute," Clarity said, smoothing my ears back. I kissed her fingers. "But my mom won't let me have a dog. We're here for Trent."

It was all clear to me now: my purpose was as I had supposed, which was to continue to watch over Clarity. It's what Ethan would have wanted. That's why I was a puppy again—I still had work to do.

And I would. I would watch over Clarity and keep her safe. I would be a good dog.

The boy came over carrying Rocky. "See his paws? He's going to be bigger than Molly."

Clarity stood and I stretched my forepaws up as high as I could on her legs until she picked me up. Rocky struggled to get down from the boy's arms, but I held still, gazing into Clarity's eyes.

"I want him," the boy said. "Rocky, you want to come home with me?" He gently dropped my brother, who jumped on a rubber toy and shook it.

"This is so exciting!" Clarity said. She set me down and I stayed by her heels as she went over to where Rocky was chewing on his toy. When she tried to pet Rocky I thrust my head under her hand and she laughed.

"Molly likes you, CJ," the boy said.

I glanced over at the boy because he'd said my name, but then went back to cuddling with Clarity.

"I know. But Gloria, she'd lose it and start foaming at the mouth. I can just hear her. 'They *lick*. They're *unclean*.' Like our house is so spotless."

"Wouldn't it be fun, though? We'd have a brother and sister."

I felt a wistful sadness coming from Clarity as she held my face in her hands. "Yes, it would be fun," she said quietly. "Oh, Molly, I'm sorry, girl."

Jennifer came back out. "So, are there like papers to fill out?" the boy asked.

"No. I'm not affiliated with any rescue organization or anything. I'm just the neighborhood lady who everybody knows will take in strays and find homes for them. Rocky and Molly are here because a little boy's asthma was aggravated by them."

"You said free to a good home, but could I pay something at least?" the boy asked.

"I accept donations, if you like. And please, if for any reason it's not working out, bring him back."

The boy handed Jennifer something and then reached down and hoisted Rocky up into his arms. "Okay, Rocky," he said. "Ready to go to your new home?"

"You let me know if you have any questions," Jennifer said.

I looked expectantly up at Clarity, but she didn't pick me up. "Oh, look at her," Clarity said. She knelt down and stroked my fur. "It's like she knows I'm leaving without her."

"Let's go, CJ."

We all went to the back door together. Jennifer opened it and the boy went through, still carrying Rocky, and then Clarity, but when I made to follow, Jennifer blocked me with her foot.

"No, Molly," she said, sliding the screen shut, so that I was left behind in the backyard.

What?

I sat down and stared at Clarity, who stared back through the screen. I did not understand.

When they all turned away, I yipped, frustrated that my voice was so tiny. I cried and yipped and put my paws on the door and scratched at it, trying to claw my way through. Was Clarity leaving me? No, that couldn't be! I had to go with her!

Clarity and the boy and Rocky went out through the front door of the house, closing it behind them.

"It's okay, Molly," Jennifer said. She moved into the kitchen.

Clarity was gone. Rocky was gone.

I barked and barked with my useless little puppy voice, grieving, feeling alone in the world.

SIX

Daisy, the big, timid dog, came out from her hiding place behind the picnic table and stood and sniffed me as I barked. She could sense my distress but obviously couldn't understand it.

The back door was getting me nowhere. I went around to the side of the house, but the wooden gate was firmly shut, the knob far out of reach of my tiny teeth. I barked again and again. This yard, which had been so gloriously fun, now seemed a prison. I ran over to Barney and we touched noses, but the slow wag of his tail did nothing to help. I felt desperate. What was happening? How could this be?

"Molly?"

I turned and there was Clarity. She dropped to her knees and I ran to her and threw myself into her arms, licking her face, relieved that I had misunderstood—I thought for a moment she was planning to leave me!

Jennifer and Trent were standing behind her. "She chose me, so what could I do? Molly chose me," Clarity insisted.

I was happy to be Molly and I was happy to be with Clarity and go with her out to her car. Trent drove and she climbed in the backseat with Rocky and me. Rocky greeted me as if we'd been apart for days and days, and then we went about the business of wrestling with Clarity in the backseat.

"So what *is* your mother going to say?" Trent asked. Rocky had seized Clarity's long hair in his teeth and was pulling on it as if he thought it would come off, setting his legs and growling. Clarity was laughing. I jumped on Rocky to get him to cut it out.

"CJ? Seriously."

Rocky and I were climbing all over Clarity, squirming. She struggled to sit upright. "God, I don't know."

"Will she let you keep her?"

"Well, what am I supposed to do? You saw what happened. It's like Molly and I were meant to be together. It's fate. Karma."

"It's not like you can hide a dog in your house," Trent said.

Clarity was looking down and seemed unhappy, so I put my paws on her chest and tried to lick her face. In my experience, being licked by a dog can cheer up just about anybody.

"CJ? You seriously think you can *hide a dog in your house*?" Trent said.

"I could hide a pack of wolves in the house if I wanted. She never looks at anything but the mirror."

"Okay, sure. So for the next ten years you're going to have a dog and somehow your mother won't find out."

"You know what, Trent? Sometimes things aren't practical, but you just do them because it's the right thing."

"Right, that makes sense."

"Why do you do this? You always have to argue."

They were both silent for a moment. "I'm sorry," Trent finally said. "I was just looking out for you."

"It will all work out; I promise."

"Okay."

"But, um, go past my driveway, okay?" Clarity said. "Don't pull in."

The car stopped. Clarity picked up Rocky and passed him up to the front. My brother and I looked at each other. Rocky wagged his tail, his ears back. I had a sense that this was good-bye, that we were going to be apart, now. That was okay, because our fates were always for people to decide and Clarity had decided she needed me and that was that. Going with her was what Ethan would have wanted. What wasn't okay was that Rocky was a front-seat dog and I wasn't, except that Clarity opened the door and we got out together, so there was no more car ride for me anyway.

The car drove off. "Okay," Clarity said. She sounded a little worried. "Let's see how quiet you can be."

She set me down and we approached a house. Some dogs had marked the bushes out front, but they were old scents—there was nothing to indicate there were any other dogs here. Clarity picked me up and carried me swiftly inside, up some stairs, down the hall, and into a bedroom.

"Clarity? Is that you?" a woman called from in the house.

"I'm home!" Clarity yelled. She jumped on her bed with me and started to play. Then she froze as footsteps came down the hall.

"Molly! Shhhh!" she said. She thrust her legs under the covers, raising her knees, and shoved me into the tented space. I sniffed her feet as I heard a door open.

"Ta-daa!" a woman's voice sang out. I knew that voice: it was Gloria, Clarity's mother.

"You bought a fur?" Clarity said, sounding angry.

"You like?" Gloria responded. "It's fox!"

"A *fur*? How could you?"

I decided that the game was for me to get out from the covers. I started to climb toward Clarity's head, and her hand came in and pushed me back down.

"Well, it's not like I killed anything. It was already dead when I bought the coat. And don't worry, I'm sure it was what you call it, free-range."

"Until they trapped it, you mean. God, Gloria. You know how I feel about this."

"If you feel that strongly about it, you don't have to wear it."

"As if I ever would! What were you thinking?"

"Well, I'm sorry, but I need it for my trip—Aspen is the only place left where you can wear a fur without feeling guilty. And, well, probably France."

"Aspen? When are you going to Aspen?" Clarity's hand kept me pinned. I struggled to get out.

"Wednesday. *So,* I was thinking, we should go shopping tomorrow, just the two of us."

"Tomorrow's Monday. It's a school day," Clarity said.

"Well, *school.* It's just a day."

Clarity's legs kicked out from underneath the blankets, which settled softly down on my head. "I need a yogurt," Clarity said.

I popped out from under the covers, but it was too late—Clarity was leaving. "I hate it when you wear those shorts," Gloria was saying as Clarity closed the door. "They make your thighs look so heavy."

Alone on the bed, I quickly determined that the floor was far, far out of range for my little legs. Whimpering my frustration, I paced on the soft blankets, taking the time to sniff deeply at the soft pillow. There were some toys on the bed and I chewed on these a little.

Then the door opened. Clarity was back. I wagged and licked her face when she bent down to me, a sweet milk scent flavoring her breath. Is there anything more glorious than licking someone's face until she giggles?

When Clarity carried me outside, she shoved me deep inside the shirt she was wearing, to keep me warm. She praised me for squatting in the yard and fed me little pieces of cold, salty meat. The flavor was so strong it burned my tongue.

"I'll get you some puppy food tomorrow, Molly, I promise promise promise. Do you want more ham?"

That night I slept in the crook of Clarity's arm. She stroked me with her hand, whispering to me, "I love you, Molly. I love you." I drifted to sleep with her hand still touching me. The day's activities had left me exhausted to the point where I didn't get up once during the night. Clarity woke up when the sun was barely out, putting on her clothes and carrying me with an odd carefulness out to do my business, speaking to me in the barest of whispers. My little bladder had been painfully full. Then she carried me down some stairs to a basement.

"This is my special space here under the stairs, Molly," she whispered. "I called it my clubhouse. See? There's a pillow for you, and here's some water. You just have to be quiet, okay? I'm not going to school, but I have to leave for just a bit. I promise, though, that I'll come back soon. Meantime, don't bark. Be quiet, Molly; be quiet."

I sniffed the little space, which was so low that Clarity had to squat. She handed me some more of the cold, salty meat and petted me in a way that I knew meant she was planning to leave me, so when she abruptly withdrew, sliding boxes to trap me in the space, I nimbly darted out.

"Molly!" Clarity hissed.

I wagged, hoping she understood I didn't want to be in the small space. I felt that I'd made my feelings clear when we'd been at Jennifer's house—I wanted to be with Clarity. She picked me up and pushed me back in and this time I wasn't fast enough to keep the boxes from blocking my exit. What was she doing?

"Be good, Molly," Clarity said from the other side of the boxes. "Remember, stay quiet. Don't bark."

I scratched at the boxes, but Clarity didn't return and I eventually gave it up. I took a brief nap and then found a plastic toy to chew for a little bit, but once I had to squat in the corner the little space under the stairs lost all its charms for me. I yipped, wishing my voice were stronger. Even with the small enclosure bouncing my barks back at me, they sounded tiny and pathetic. Nonetheless, once I was barking it seemed like a good idea to keep it up.

I paused, cocking my head, when I heard someone moving around upstairs, but there was no indication that Clarity or Gloria was coming to my rescue, so I started up again.

Then I heard the unmistakable sound of the door at the top of the stairs opening. Footsteps came toward me, and when they were directly overhead I barked as loudly as I could. Someone was in the basement.

I thought it might be Clarity, but then I heard something strange: a human yowling, somewhere between crying and wailing. It was an awful noise, a noise of pain and perhaps fear. What was happening? I stopped barking, a little afraid. A strong scent—flowery, oily, and musky—flowed into my space from behind the boxes.

Overhead I heard the front door open and shut. There were footsteps and then I sensed someone else standing up at the top of the stairs.

"Gloria? Are you down there?" It was Clarity.

Still the mournful wailing continued. I was silent—no human had ever made a sound like that in my whole life.

Footsteps came rattling down the stairs. "Gloria?" Clarity's voice called.

There was a loud scream—"*Ahhhhh!*" I recognized Gloria.

Clarity screamed, too. "*Aghhhh!*"

I whimpered—what was happening?

"Clarity June, you scared me to death!" Gloria panted.

"Why didn't you answer? What were you doing?" Clarity asked.

"I was singing! I had my earbuds in! What are you doing home? What's in the bag?"

"I forgot something. It's, um, dog food. We're having a food drive at school."

"Do you really think it looks good to give dog food?"

"Mo-*ther*. It's not for the people. It's for their dogs."

"You mean to tell me they can't afford to feed themselves, but they have dogs? What's this country coming to?"

"Are you getting laundry? I'll help you fold," Clarity said. "Let's take it upstairs."

They went up the stairs, leaving me alone again.

I was really, really hungry.

SEVEN

Clarity did come back, and I was as glad to see her as I was the bowl of food in her hand.

"She's finally gone. Oh, Molly, I am so, so sorry."

I buried my face in the bowl, crunching the food until my mouth was dry and then drinking as much water as I could hold. Then Clarity took me out into the backyard, where the sun was shining and bugs were singing and the grass was fresh and warm. I sprawled out, rolling in sheer joy, and Clarity lay down next to me. We played tug-on-a-towel for a few minutes, but I was exhausted from barking all morning and when she picked me up to cuddle me to her chest I immediately fell into a deep sleep.

When I woke up, I was back in the small space. The second I yipped, though, I heard running footsteps and then Clarity shoved aside the boxes. "Shhh, Molly! You need to be quiet!" Clarity said. I thought I understood what she was saying: when I wanted her, I needed to bark and then she would come.

She let me play in the basement and she fed me more food. When I needed to squat on the cement floor, she cleaned it up and wasn't upset that I couldn't yet hold it until I made it outside. She hugged me and kissed me up and down my face, pure adoration flowing from her with such power I squirmed with happiness.

We played and played until I was sleepy. She even woke me up that night to wrestle in the cool air of the backyard, all the bugs gone silent. It was so much fun to be outside when everything was so quiet!

The next morning there were loud noises from upstairs, plus I heard Gloria's voice: "Would you please turn down the music?" I barked and scratched at the boxes that were blocking my exit, ready to get upstairs to play with Clarity.

When I both felt and heard the vibration from a door slamming I quieted down, trying to figure out what was going on. Was I alone again? No, there was still someone upstairs; I could hear walking. Then there was a sigh of air as the door from the outside to the basement opened. The boxes slid away and I jumped out and into Clarity's arms, my heart leaping with joy. Time to have more fun!

"You have to be very quiet," she told me. She carried me out into the backyard and through a gate and then set me down and we went for a walk and then a car ride (front seat!) and then to a park to play all day. We were mostly by ourselves except for a woman with a small black dog named Get Back Here Milo. The black dog ran right over to me and I blinked and sank to the ground submissively, aware that as a puppy I needed to let Get Back Here Milo see I was no threat. "Get Back Here Milo!" the woman called over and over. The black dog pushed me roughly over with his snout and then Clarity reached down and picked me up, holding me the way Jennifer had when she'd fed me the strange milk.

When Get Back Here Milo left, Clarity set me down and played with her face close to mine. I was so happy I yipped and spun.

"She leaves tomorrow," Clarity said to me. "I just need to keep you hidden one more night and then she's gone for a week. Can you go without barking tonight?"

I chewed a stick.

"I don't know what I'm going to do, Molly. She'll never let me keep you." Clarity grabbed me and gave me a fierce hug. "I love you so much."

I felt the affection pouring off of Clarity, but I was really focused on the stick at the moment, so I didn't do much more than just wag my tail.

I was disappointed that when we got home Clarity took me right down stairs and placed me into the small space under the stairs, sliding the boxes back. I voiced my displeasure with a volley of barks and she appeared instantly.

"I need you to not bark, okay, Molly? My mother will be home any minute."

She slid the boxes back. Truthfully, I was tired from playing all day, so I settled down for a nap. I woke up, though, when I heard the front door slam. "I'm home!"

Gloria's voice boomed through the house. "Wait until you see what I bought at Neiman's!"

Though I had been smelling and hearing Gloria for a few days, I hadn't yet had a chance to greet her. I thought she would probably be as glad to see me as Clarity had been. I yipped a couple of times and then waited, but all I heard was talking. I barked some more and then got the expected results when the door opened overhead and footsteps came down. Clarity shoved the boxes aside.

"Please, Molly, *please*. Please be quiet."

Clarity fed me and took me inside her jacket down the street and then we walked and walked. It was dark and cool by the time we returned. Clarity pushed me back into the small space.

"Okay. Go to sleep, okay, Molly? Go to sleep."

I tried to slip out as she was pushing the boxes back across the entrance, but I wasn't fast enough. She ran up the stairs, which rattled, and shut the door and then it was quiet.

I slept a little, but then I woke up and remembered I was all by myself. I whimpered. I knew that upstairs Clarity was probably lying in her bed, feeling lonely because I wasn't with her, and that made me sad. I knew she thought that I liked to lie on the nice pillow under the stairs, but actually I wanted to be with her. I barked. There was no response, so I barked again, and then again.

"Clarity! What's that sound?" Gloria shrieked. I heard running, and then the door at the top of the stairs opened.

"I think it came from down here!" Clarity shouted.

I wagged my tail as she came down the stairs. "Go back to bed, Gloria. I'll take care of it."

"It sounded like an animal!" Gloria replied.

I heard Clarity moving around on the other side of the boxes. I scratched at them. I heard Gloria walking through the house and then I could sense her at the top of the stairs.

I barked.

"There it is again!" Gloria hissed. "It's a dog; there's a dog in the house!"

Clarity shoved the boxes aside and I tumbled into her arms, licking her face. "No, it's . . . Oh my God, it's a fox!" she yelled. "Stay back!"

"A fox? What? Are you sure?"

"Foxes do bark, Gloria," Clarity said.

"How did it get in the house? What's a fox doing here?"

"The basement door must have blown open in the wind. It probably came because it smelled your stupid coat."

Clarity was smiling at me now. We played tug-on-a-towel and she wasn't pulling very hard.

"That can't be right," Gloria said.

"They have very sensitive noses! I'm going to try to scare it out of the house and down the street," Clarity said.

"Are you sure it's a fox? A fox, as in, the animal?"

"I know what a fox looks like. It's a little one."

"We should call the police."

"Like cops would come for a fox. I'm just going to shoo it outside. Stay back in case it makes a run for the stairs."

I heard Gloria gasp and slam the door at the top of the stairs. Clarity picked me up and ran out the back door and into the cool night. She took me right out the gate and didn't set me down until we were around the corner.

I didn't understand the game we were playing, but after shaking and squatting I was ready to keep going. Clarity paced with me up and down the street and then a car came around the corner and stopped. The window rolled down and I smelled Rocky! I put my feet on the metal side of the car and tried to peer in. I smelled Trent then, too.

"Thanks for doing this, Trent," Clarity said.

"It's okay," Trent said.

Clarity picked me up and handed me through the window. I crawled across Trent's chest, licking him in greeting, and then sniffed along the seat. Rocky wasn't in the car, but he had been. We were both front-seat dogs.

I went home with Trent that night and Clarity did not come with us. I was distressed when we drove off, and I whimpered, wondering where Clarity was, but when we arrived at Trent's house Rocky was there! We were overjoyed to see each other and he and I wrestled in the living room and in the backyard and in Trent's bedroom. Trent had a younger sister named Carolina who played with us and Trent played with us and even his parents played with us. I fell asleep in the middle of it all, suddenly so fatigued I simply had to lie down even though Rocky was chewing my face.

As soon as Rocky and I awoke the next morning

we recommenced the play. He was a little bigger than I was and obviously very attached to Trent, because sometimes he'd break off wrestling and run over to Trent to be stroked and praised. It made me miss Clarity, but every time it occurred to me that I should be worried about her Rocky would climb on me and we'd be back at it. I comforted myself that she had to come back to get me, and eventually she did.

Later the back gate clanged and Rocky and I tore over to see who it might be, and there she was. We both jumped up on her and I finally growled at Rocky for acting as if he was as important to her as I was.

Clarity and Trent stood in the backyard to watch me play with my brother. I tried to show her I could pin Rocky when I wanted to, but he wouldn't cooperate.

"She gone yet?" Trent asked.

"Not yet. Her flight isn't until one o'clock. I told her I had to leave early for school."

"*Are* you going to school?"

"Not today."

"CJ, you can't keep skipping school."

"Molly needs me."

I froze at the sound of my name and Rocky jumped on my back.

"You've had Molly for three days. What about the other times?"

"I just don't feel like school is relevant in my life."

"You're a high school student," he said. "School *is* your life."

"I'll go Monday," Clarity told him. "I just want to spend time this week with Molly, while Gloria's gone."

"And when Gloria gets back, what's the plan then?"

"I don't know, Trent! Sometimes people don't plan everything, it just happens, okay?"

Clarity and I went for a car ride and I sat in the front seat. We went to a park that had a lot of grass but just one dog in it, an unfriendly brown canine who was only interested in walking with his owner on a path. Then we went home and, thankfully, I wasn't shoved back into the tiny place under the stairs but had the run of the house. I could smell Gloria, but she was not around.

I slept in Clarity's bed. I was so excited I kept waking up and licking her face. She would bat my nose away, but there was no heat in the gesture. Finally she was content to just let me gnaw gently on my fingers when I felt the need, and that's how we spent the night.

The next day it rained and we played inside, only going out for me to do my business in the wet grass. "Molly! Come here!" CJ called to me at one point. I trotted down the hall, Gloria's smells getting stronger and stronger. CJ was grinning and nodding at me, and I watched her curiously. She pushed open a door and Gloria's overpowering odors flooded out.

"See the dog in the mirror?" CJ asked.

I heard the word "dog" and figured she wanted me to go through the door. I walked in and immediately stopped dead: there was a dog in there! It looked like Rocky. I bounded forward, then pulled back in surprise as it jumped aggressively at me. It was not Rocky—in fact, it didn't smell like any dog at all. I wagged my tail and it wagged. I bowed down and it bowed down at the same time.

It was so strange, I barked. It looked like it was barking, too, but it didn't make a noise.

"Say hi, Molly! Get the dog!" CJ said.

I barked some more, then approached, sniffing. There was no dog, just something that looked like a dog. It was very strange.

"You see the dog, Molly? See the dog?"

Whatever was going on, it wasn't very interesting. I turned away, smelling under the bed, where there were dusty shoes.

"Good dog, Molly!" CJ said. I liked being praised, but I was glad when we left the room. There was something a bit disquieting about the dog-thing with no smell.

The morning after that, everything was moist and deliciously fragrant and I sniffed at several worms but didn't eat any because after you've done that a few times you learn they're never going to taste any better than they smell.

We had just gotten home when the doorbell rang. I ran to the front door and barked. I could see a shadow on the other side of the glass in the door.

"Look out, Molly. Stay back," Clarity said. She opened the door a crack.

"Are you Clarity Mahoney?" the woman on the other side of the door asked. I pushed my face to the crack and tried to squeeze out, but Clarity kept me inside. I wagged my tail so the person would know I wasn't serious about all the barking; I was just doing my job.

"I go by 'CJ,'" Clarity said.

"CJ. I'm Officer Llewellyn. I'm a truant officer. Why aren't you in school today?"

"I'm sick." CJ turned her head and coughed. The

woman outside looked down at me and I wagged harder. Why didn't we all go outdoors and play?

"Where's your mother?"

"She's out shopping. For my prescription," CJ said.

They just stood there for a long moment. I yawned.

"We've left several messages for her and she hasn't called back," the woman said.

"She's very busy. She sells real estate."

"Well, okay. I want you to give her this, okay?" The woman handed Clarity a piece of paper. "You've missed a lot of school, CJ. People are worried about you."

"I've been sick a lot, I guess."

"Give that to your mother. I'll be expecting her call. Tell her she can call anytime, leave me a message if I'm not there. Understand?"

"Yes."

"Good-bye, CJ."

Clarity closed the door. She seemed afraid and angry. She went into the kitchen and put some things on the table. "Molly, we need ice-cream bars," she told me. She put a cold, deliciously sweet treat in a bowl for me.

Clarity sat at the table and ate and ate. I sat, too, staring at her intently, but she didn't give me any more treats. When she was done she put some papers in a tub under the sink and I could smell the same sweet smell on them and couldn't understand why she didn't set them down to lick. People are like that; they discard the most delicious things.

A little while later Clarity went into her bathroom and stood on a small, flat, square box, bigger than a dog bowl but not as high off the ground. "Two point

70 | W. BRUCE CAMERON

six pounds? God! I'm such an idiot!" she hissed unhappily. I picked up on her anguish, but she didn't
seem to notice me trying to comfort her.

She made a ragged sound and then knelt down in
front of the water bowl and vomited. I paced behind
her, distressed because I could feel her pain and upset.
I could smell the sweet scent from the treats she'd
eaten earlier, and then she pulled the handle and the
smell went away with a whoosh. I wagged my tail as
hard as I could, trying to climb on her and lick her,
and after a while it seemed to do some good, though
she was still a little upset.

A couple of days later we settled into a routine.
Every morning Clarity would leave me alone in the
basement for hours at a time, blocked into the little
space under the stairs. She would come home and
play with me and clean up any messes and feed me for
a short time in the middle of the day and would run
down the stairs calling, "Molly!" in the afternoon and
then stay home until the next morning. She was, I decided, doing school. My boy, Ethan, had done school,
too. I didn't like it any better with her doing it.

Clarity and I played a game every night: She would
block me in the space using the boxes but would stay
outside where I could sense her. If I cried or barked,
she would slide the boxes and say, "No!" very harshly.
If I sat quietly, she'd slide the boxes back and give me
a treat. We'd go longer and longer periods of time
with me sitting quietly, and every time I got a treat. I
came to understand that when I was under the stairs
she wanted me to be quiet as long as she was on just
the other side of the boxes.

I didn't like being alone in there and could think of a lot of other games that were much more fun to play.

When I had to be there all night I was pretty sure it was a mistake, especially when I heard Clarity go upstairs. Every time I barked, though, Clarity came down and said, "No!" And when I finally just gave up and lay down, she woke me up and gave me a treat. I wasn't sure what to make of any of it.

Then one day Clarity said, "Okay, here she comes. Let's do this, Molly." She led me down and put me under the stairs. I sat quietly. Then I heard voices and footsteps and knew that Gloria had come home.

I sat quietly.

Clarity gave me a big treat and took me for a long walk. I smelled a rabbit!

When it was dark Clarity put me in the space and I lay down with a heavy sigh. I was quiet, though, and got a big treat and a walk in the early morning.

"You be good. Stay quiet. I love you, Molly. I love you," Clarity said. Then she left. I napped for a bit, and then I heard Gloria walking around upstairs. I didn't know if Gloria knew I was supposed to be fed treats for being quiet.

Clarity hadn't shoved the boxes all the way across the space and, when I put my nose to it, I found I could move the bottom box just enough to stick my head through. I wriggled and pushed and strained and then I was through!

Though I was big enough to climb stairs, it was not easy work to get to the top. The door there was open and just as I reached the highest step the doorbell rang. I heard Gloria move across the floor to open the front door.

I trotted into the living room, stopping to sniff at a suitcase on the floor that hadn't been there before.

"Yes?" Gloria said, standing in the doorway. Air flowing in from outside brought the scent of wonderful grasses and trees but also the strong flowery smell that was Gloria, so overpowering it threatened to choke off everything else.

"Miss Mahoney? I'm Officer Llewellyn. I'm the truant officer in charge of CJ's case. Did she give you the citation?"

I trotted over to say hi to Gloria. The officer on the porch glanced at me as I approached.

"Citation. Clarity? What are you talking about?"

"I'm sorry. I need to talk to you. Your daughter has been absent from school too many times this semester."

Gloria was just standing there, even though I was right by her side. I put a paw on her leg.

She looked down at me and screamed.

EIGHT

Gloria jumped out onto the porch and I followed her, wagging my tail at both women.

"That's not a fox!" Gloria yelled.

The woman bent down and petted me. She had warm, gentle hands that smelled of soap and also nuts of some kind. "A fox? Of course not, it's a puppy."

"What's it doing in my house?"

The woman stood. "I can't answer that, ma'am; it's *your* house. The dog was here when I saw your daughter last week."

"That's impossible!"

"Well . . . look," the woman said, "here's another copy of the citation, along with a notice to appear." She handed Gloria some papers. "You'll need to come to court with your daughter. Understand? Because she's a minor, you are legally liable."

"What about the dog?"

"Sorry?"

I sat at the word "dog." Gloria seemed upset about something, but I thought the nice lady might be good for a treat. I liked nuts of all kinds, even the salty ones that burned my tongue.

"Take the dog with you," Gloria said.

"I can't do that, ma'am."

"So you mean to tell me you're more concerned about a high school student skipping a few classes than a woman trapped by a dog?"

"That's . . . yes, that's right."

"That's the stupidest thing I ever heard of. What kind of police officer are you?"

"I'm a truant officer, Miss Mahoney."

"I'm going to file a formal complaint with the police commissioner."

"You do that. Meanwhile, I'll see you in court." The woman turned and walked away, so no treats.

"What do I do about the dog?" Gloria yelled at her.

"Call Animal Control, ma'am; that's what they do."

"All right, I will," Gloria said. I made to follow her back into the house but cringed when she yelled, "No!" at me. She slammed the door, shutting me out.

I wandered out into the front yard. It was another nice day. Maybe that rabbit would be outside looking for me. I trotted down the sidewalk, sniffing at the bushes.

The front yards of the houses on the street reminded me of the home Ethan lived in before he moved to the

Farm: they were big enough to play in and often were bordered by shrubs. The air was full of the sweet smell of flowers and all of the growth was lush and full. I smelled dogs and cats and people but no ducks or goats. An occasional car cruised past, stirring the air and adding its metallic and oily odors to the riot of scents.

I felt a little like a bad dog, wandering free without a leash, but Gloria had set me loose, so I reasoned it must be okay.

After an hour or so of sniffing and exploring, I heard footfalls coming toward me, and a man called out, "Here, puppy!" My initial inclination was to trot right over to him, but I stopped when I saw the pole in his hand, a loop dangling from the pole. He advanced on me, holding the loop out. "Come on; that's a good girl," he said to me.

I could feel that loop of rope around my neck as if it were already there. I danced back.

"Now don't run away," he said softly.

I ducked my head and made to run past him, but he lunged and then I was twisting on the end of that pole. "Gotcha!" he said.

I was afraid. This was not right. I didn't want to go with the man, who pulled me with his pole over to a truck. The line around my neck tightened, forcing my head toward the truck tire, and then he scooped me up and with a clang I was in a metal cage in the back of the truck.

"Hey!"

The man turned at the sound of approaching footsteps.

"Hey!"

It was Clarity.

"What are you doing? That's my dog!"

The man held his hands out to Clarity, who stood before him, panting. I put my paws on the cage, wagging, delighted to see her.

"Now wait, just wait," the man said.

"You can't take my dog!" Clarity said angrily.

The man crossed his arms. "I *am* taking the dog. We've had complaints, and it was running loose."

I yipped so she'd know I was right there waiting to be let out.

"Complaints? Molly is just a puppy. Who complains about a puppy?" Clarity said. "What was she, making people too *happy*?"

"That's not your business. If it is your dog, you can pick it up at the shelter anytime after noon tomorrow." The man made to move away.

"But wait! Wait! She's just . . . " The tears were flowing down Clarity's face now. I whimpered, wanting to kiss her sadness away. She put a hand to her mouth. "She won't understand if you take her. She's a rescue dog who has already been abandoned once. Please, please. I don't know how she got out, but I promise you it won't happen again. Promise, promise. Please?"

The man's shoulders slumped. He took in a deep breath and then let it out slowly. "Well . . . All right, look. Okay, but you need to get her chipped and vaccinated and in a few months spay her. Deal? And then get a license. It's the law."

"I will. I promise."

The game of truck was over. The man opened the

cage and Clarity reached in and pulled me out. She hugged me and I kissed her face, then looked at the man to see if he wanted a kiss, too.

"All right," the man said.

"Thank you, thank you," Clarity said.

The truck drove off. Clarity stood and watched it go, still holding me. "Complaints," she muttered.

As she carried me to her house, I could feel her heart beating loudly in her chest. We went through the front door and she stooped, setting me down. A piece of paper was right in front of my nose on the floor and I sniffed it, smelling the woman who had been on the porch a little while ago. Clarity picked up the paper and looked at it.

"Clarity? Is that you?"

Gloria came around the corner and stopped, staring at me. I wagged and started to go to her to say hello, but Clarity reached down and picked me up.

"*What*? What are you doing?" Gloria demanded.

"This is Molly. She's . . . she's my dog." Clarity's hands were trembling.

"No, she is not," Gloria said.

"Not which part? Not Molly? Or not a dog?" Clarity asked.

"Out!" Gloria yelled.

"No!" Clarity shouted back.

"You cannot have a dog in my house!"

"I am keeping her!"

"You can't say anything to me right now. Do you know what trouble you're in? I had a visit from the delinquency officer. You've been missing so much school that they came out here to arrest you."

Clarity set me down.

"No! Do not put that animal on my carpet."

With all the shouting, I shied away from Gloria.

"It's a dog. She won't do anything, she just peed outside."

"A dog—are you sure it's not a *fox*?"

"Why? Do you need another *coat*?"

I wandered over to the couch, but there was nothing underneath it but dusty smells. In fact, most of the odors in the house were coming from Gloria.

"It's going to lift its leg on the couch! I'm calling someone," Gloria shrieked.

"Did you even bother to read this?" Clarity said. She rattled the paper in her hand and I watched alertly, wondering if she was going to throw it. "This is a summons for *you*, you know. You have to appear in court, too."

"Well, I'm going to tell them you are completely out of control."

"And I'm going to tell them why."

"Why what?"

"Why I was able to skip so much school. You go on trips all the time and leave me without any adults in the house, including when I was twelve years old. By myself!"

"I don't believe this. You *asked* to be left alone. You hated the babysitter."

"I hated her because she was a drunk! One time she fell asleep in her car in the driveway."

"We're not having this conversation again. If you're going to imply that I was in any way a negligent mother then I'll just call Social Services and you can live in an orphanage."

I turned in circles a few times and lay down on the soft rug. The shouting made me anxious, though, and within a few seconds I was back on my feet.

"Sure, that's how it works. You just leave me in a box on the front porch and they come by on Tuesdays to pick it up and take me to be an orphan."

"You know what I mean."

"Yes. You're going to call Social Services and tell them you don't want to be a mom anymore. So then there will be a hearing. And the judge is going to want to know where you were all last week—Aspen—and where you were when you went to Vegas when I was thirteen, and where you were when you went to New York for a *month*. And you know what he's going to say? He's going to say that you need to go to jail. And everyone in the neighborhood will know. They'll see you getting into a patrol car in handcuffs with your fur coat over your head."

"My mother left *me* alone when I was a lot younger than you. I never complained."

"The same mother who beat you with garden tools? Who broke your arm when you were eight years old? I don't think you would."

"My point was, I was fine. You were fine."

"Well, my point was, they arrested your mom and they'll arrest you, too, Gloria. The laws are a lot more strict now. You don't have to actually send your kid to the emergency room to wind up in jail."

Gloria was staring at Clarity, who was breathing

hard. "Unless," Clarity said in a low voice, "you let me keep Molly."

"I don't know what you mean."

"I'll tell the judge that I lied to you. That I told you I was going to school, but actually I was skipping. I'll say it wasn't your fault."

"It *wasn't* my fault!"

"Or I can tell him about you leaving me all the time on your little trips with your boyfriends. That's the deal. I keep Molly and I'll lie to the judge. If you try to make me get rid of her, I'll tell him everything."

"You're as horrible as your father."

"Oh darn, Gloria. That one doesn't even upset me anymore. You used it on me too often. So what do you want to do?"

Gloria left the room. Clarity went over to me and petted me and I curled up on the rug and fell asleep. When I woke up, Gloria was no longer in the house. Clarity was in the kitchen and I arose with a yawn and went in to see what she was doing. A delicious odor was in the air.

"Want some, Molly?" Clarity asked me. She sounded sad, but she fed me toast. "No honey butter for you, though," she said. "That's people-only food."

She stood up from the table and opened a bag and soon the air carried with it the tantalizing smell of more toast. She dropped a toy on the floor and I chased it, my nails scrabbling on the smooth floor.

"You want the lid? Okay, you can have the lid," she told me.

I licked the toy, which had an amazing sweet scent to it, but there was nothing to eat on it. I chewed it.

Clarity got up from the table and made more toast, and then more, and then more, while I happily chewed on the toy. Then she stood up. "Out of bread," she said, throwing a plastic sack into the trash can. I wagged, thinking she would come over to play with the toy, but instead she went to the counter and I heard her open a plastic bag and then she made more toast. She kicked the toy and it slid across the floor and I jumped on it. Every time she got up to make more toast, she would kick the toy and I would chase it. I found that if I put my front paws on it I could slide on it until I hit the wall. What a great game!

"All gone. Come on, Molly," Clarity said. I followed her into her bedroom. "You want to sleep on this pillow? Molly?" Clarity patted a pillow and I jumped on it and shook it in my teeth.

Clarity didn't want to play, though. She lay on her back with her eyes open. I put my head on her chest and she ran her fingers through my fur, but there was a change overcoming her, a darkening of her mood. I cuddled with her, hoping I could lift her out of her sadness, but when she moaned I knew I was failing. I went to lick her face, smelling butter and toast and the same sweet, sugary tang that had coated the toy, but she rolled away from me. "Oh God," she said softly.

Clarity went into her bathroom and I heard her making a choking noise and I smelled the sweet toast. She was vomiting again. Her head was in the water bowl, which she refreshed a few times before standing up and looking at her teeth in the mirror. Then she stood on the small box. "A hundred six point five," she moaned. "I hate myself."

I decided I despised that box for how it made her feel.

"Let's go to bed, Molly."

Clarity didn't take me down to the basement—she let me sleep on her bed. I was so excited to be out of that space and back in bed with her that I of course had trouble sleeping, but she put her hand on me and petted me until I got drowsy. I turned around and curled up against her and, as I drifted off, her love flowed into me and my love flowed into her. This was more than just watching over someone out of loyalty— I loved Clarity, loved her as completely and totally as any dog could love a person. Ethan had been my boy, but Clarity was my girl.

I woke up later because I heard Gloria and a man talking outside the house. The man laughed and then I heard a car start and drive away and the front door of the house opened and closed. Clarity was still asleep. I heard someone coming down the hall—my time under the stairs, listening to footsteps, told me it was Gloria.

The door to the hallway was open and Gloria stopped in it, staring in at me on the bed. Her complex scents drifted into the room. I wagged a little.

That's all she did: just stared at me from the darkened hallway.

NINE

Clarity had lots of friends who would come over to play with me and gradually I came to understand that her name was now CJ. People can do that, change the names of things, though I was still Molly. Gloria's name was Gloria and also Mo-*ther*. Only Gloria called CJ Clarity anymore.

It worked the other way, too—sometimes the names would stay the same, but the people would change. That's how the Vet, which was another name for Doctor Deb, was now what CJ called Doctor Marty. He was as nice as Doctor Deb, with hair between his nose and his lip, and strong hands that touched me very gently.

My favorite of all of CJ's friends was Trent, the boy who took care of Rocky. Trent was taller than CJ and his hair was dark and he always smelled like Rocky. When Trent came to visit he usually brought my brother, and the two of us would tear around in the backyard, wrestling with each other. We would play until we collapsed with exhaustion, sprawled out on the lawn. Often I would lie panting on top of my brother, holding his leg in my mouth out of sheer affection.

Rocky was stockier than I was and taller, too, but he usually let me pin him when I wanted. When I had him down I always noticed that the darker brown of his muzzle matched the color of my legs—he was otherwise a lighter brown color. I found that as the days became warmer I could measure my growth by assessing Rocky's—my brother was no longer a gawky puppy, and neither was I.

Rocky was completely devoted to Trent. In the middle of play he would suddenly break off and run over to Trent to be petted. I'd follow him, and CJ would pet me, too.

"You think he's maybe schnauzer-poodle?" CJ asked Trent. "A schnoodle?"

"I don't think so. Maybe a Doberman-poodle," Trent said.

"A Doodle?"

I wagged at my favorite name and gave CJ a friendly nudge with my nose. Ethan had called me a doodle dog; it was a special name that carried with it all the love a boy could have for a dog. Hearing CJ say it reminded me of the connection between my boy and CJ, my girl.

"Or a spaniel of some kind," Trent speculated.

"Molly, you could be a schnoodle, a spoodle, or a Doodle, but you're not a poodle," CJ told me, holding me close and kissing my nose. I wagged with pleasure.

"Hey, watch this. Rocky? Sit! Sit!" Trent commanded. Rocky stared at Trent alertly, sitting down and holding still. "Good dog!"

"I'm not teaching Molly any tricks," CJ said. "I get enough orders in my own life."

"Are you kidding? Dogs want to work. They crave it. Don't you, Rocky? Good boy, Sit!"

Well, I knew what that word meant. This time, when Rocky sat, I sat, too.

"Look, Molly figured it out by watching Rocky! You are such a good dog, Molly!"

I wagged at being a good dog. There were other commands I knew, too, but CJ didn't say any of them. Rocky rolled on his back for a tummy rub and I put my teeth on his throat.

"Hey, so . . . ," Trent said. Rocky froze, then struggled out of my grip. I'd felt it, too—a sudden whiff of fear from Trent. Rocky pushed his muzzle at Trent's hand, while I checked on CJ, who was smiling up at the sky, unaware of any danger.

"Maybe . . . CJ? Maybe we should go to prom together this year."

"What? No, are you kidding? You don't go to prom with your *friends*. That's not what it's for."

"Yeah, but . . . "

"But what?" CJ rolled over, brushing her hair back from her face. "God, Trent, ask someone pretty. What about Susan? I know she likes you."

"No, I'm . . . Pretty?" Trent said. "Come on. You know you're pretty."

CJ slugged him lightly in the arm. "Ya goof."

Trent was frowning and looking at the ground.

"What?" CJ asked.

"Nothing."

"Come on; let's go to the park."

We went for a walk. Rocky held us up, sniffing and marking the bushes, while I stuck close to CJ's side. She reached into her pocket and pulled out a little box, but it wasn't a treat. There was a flare of fire and then a smelly smoke was coming out of her mouth. I knew that odor: it was in all of CJ's clothing and was often on her breath.

"So what's probation like? The whole house arrest thing?" Trent wanted to know.

"It's nothing. I just have to go to school. It's not even real probation. Gloria acts like I'm some kind of, like, felon." CJ laughed, then coughed out more smoke.

"You get to keep the dog, though."

Both Rocky and I looked up at the word "dog."

"I'm moving out the second I turn eighteen."

"Yeah? How are you going to manage that?"

"I'll join the army if I have to. I'll go to a *nunnery*. I just have to survive until I'm twenty-one."

Rocky and I found something deliciously dead to sniff, but CJ and Trent kept walking and our leashes pulled us away before either one of us could roll in it. Sometimes people let their dogs take the time to smell everything important, but most of the time they walk too fast and the wonderful opportunities are lost.

"What happens at twenty-one?" Trent asked.

"That's when I get the first half of the trust fund my daddy left me."

"Yeah? How much?"

"Like a million dollars."

"No *way*."

"Way. There was a settlement with the airline after the crash. It's enough to pay for college and for me to move to New York to take my acting to the next level."

A squirrel was hopping along in the grass a few houses ahead of us. It froze, realizing its fatal mistake. Rocky and I lowered our heads and charged, straining against our leashes. "Hey!" Trent said, laughing. He ran with us, but with him and CJ holding us back the squirrel was able to make it to a tree and dashed up, chattering at us. Otherwise we most surely would have caught it. We chased that same squirrel on the way back home. Did the stupid thing *want* to be caught?

Every so often CJ would say, "Want to go to the Vet?" Roughly translated, this meant "We're going for a car ride in the front seat to see Doctor Marty!" I always responded enthusiastically, even when I came home one day wearing a stupid collar, a plastic cone that magnified all sounds and made it difficult to eat and drink. It had taken me a long time to get used to the idea, but eventually I had learned that people like to put their dogs in stupid collars from time to time.

When I next saw Rocky, he was wearing the same kind of collar! It made wrestling difficult, but we managed.

"Poor Rocky's singing soprano now," Trent said.

CJ laughed, smoke coming from her nose and mouth.

Soon after the stupid collar came off we started doing "art building," which was where we'd go to a quiet place and I'd munch on a chew toy while CJ sat and played with smelly sticks and papers. Everyone at Art Building knew my name and petted me and sometimes fed me—it was so different from at home, where CJ hugged me and cuddled me and Gloria just pushed me away if I tried to greet her in any fashion.

Gloria never touched CJ, either, which was why it was good I was there. In a way, being held by CJ was my most important function. I could feel the lonely ache inside her melting away as we lay together on her bed. I would wag and kiss her and even nibble lightly on her arm, so happy to be with my girl.

When CJ wasn't home I lived downstairs. Trent came over and he and CJ put a dog door in the basement door, so that I could go out into the backyard if I wanted. I loved going in and out through that dog door—there was always something fun to do on the other side!

Sometimes when I was out in the yard I could see Gloria standing at the window, watching me. I always wagged. Gloria was mad at me for some reason, but I knew from experience that people can't stay mad at dogs forever.

One day when CJ came home it was late enough that the sun had set. She hugged me for a long time and was sad and upset. Then we went into her bathroom and she vomited. I yawned and paced anxiously—I never knew what to do when this happened. CJ and I both looked up at the same time and there was Gloria standing in the doorway, watching us.

"You wouldn't have to do that so often if you didn't eat so much," Gloria said.

"Oh, mo-*ther*," CJ replied. She stood and went to her sink and drank water.

"How did your auditions go?" Gloria asked.

"Terrible. I didn't get *anything*. It's like, you have to have been doing drama this whole year or they won't even consider casting you."

"Well. If they don't want my daughter in their summer play, it's their loss. It hardly matters—no one ever got to be an actress by being in plays in high school."

"That's right, Gloria. Who ever heard of an actor *acting*?"

"I am just saying that I never sang in high school and it didn't slow me down one bit."

"I am noticing all the record companies beating down our door lately."

Gloria crossed her arms. "I had a very promising career until I got pregnant with you. Once you have a baby, it's all different."

"What are you saying, you couldn't sing anymore because you'd had a baby? Did you deliver me through your esophagus?"

"You've never thanked me, not once."

"I'm supposed to thank you for giving birth? Seriously? Do they make cards for that, like: 'Thanks for letting me hang out in your uterus for nine months'?"

I launched myself up and landed with expert placement at the foot of the bed.

"Get off!" Gloria snapped.

Guiltily I jumped down and slumped to the floor, my head lowered.

"It's okay, Molly. You're a good girl," CJ soothed. "What do you got against dogs, Gloria?"

"I just don't see the attraction. They're messy and foul smelling. They lick. They don't do anything useful."

"You'd feel different if you just spent time with one," CJ replied, petting me.

"I have. My mother had a dog when I was little."

"You never told me that."

"She used to kiss it on the mouth; it was disgusting," Gloria continued. "She was always loving it up. It was fat and it just lay in her lap all day and didn't do anything useful, just sat and watched me clean the house."

"Well, Molly's not like that."

"You spend all your money on dog food and vet bills when there are so many nice things we could buy."

"Now that I have Molly, I don't need anything else." CJ scratched my ear and I leaned into it, groaning a little.

"I see. The dog gets all the credit and your mother gets nothing." Gloria turned away and walked out the door. CJ got up and shut it and then cuddled with me on the bed.

"We're getting out of here as soon as we can, I promise, Molly," CJ said. I licked her in the face.

I was a good dog who was taking care of Ethan's child, but it wasn't just because it was what he would want. I loved CJ. I loved falling asleep in her arms and walking with her and going to do art building.

What I didn't love was the boy named Shane who started coming over all the time. Gloria was very often not home in the evening, so Shane and CJ would cuddle on the couch. Shane's hands smelled of the same smoke that permeated CJ's clothing. He always said hello to me, but I could tell he didn't really like me—the way he petted me was too perfunctory. A dog can always tell.

I didn't trust people who didn't like dogs.

One evening Trent and Rocky came over when Shane was there. Rocky was very alert, staring up at Trent, who didn't sit down. I could feel Trent's anger and sadness, and obviously Rocky could, too. I tried to engage Rocky in a little wrestling, but he wasn't interested—he was focused on Trent.

"Oh, hey, just thought I'd come by, and . . . ," Trent said. He kicked at the carpet a little.

"As you can see, she's busy," Shane said.

"Yeah," Trent said.

"No, come in; we're just watching TV," CJ said.

"No, I'd better go," Trent said.

After he left I went to the window and looked out it and saw him standing next to his car, gazing at the house for a long minute before he opened the door and drove off.

Rocky was in the front seat.

The next day CJ didn't come home from school right away, so I chewed sticks in the backyard and watched some birds hopping from tree to tree. Barking at birds seldom does any good, because birds don't understand they are supposed to be afraid of dogs and will just go about their business. I had eaten dead birds before and they were not satisfying at all, and I probably wouldn't eat a live one if I caught it, though

I wouldn't mind trying it to see if its being alive improved the taste any.

I was startled when Gloria slid open the back door. "Here, Molly. Want a treat?" she called.

I cautiously approached, wagging my tail and keeping my rear end lowered submissively. Gloria usually did not talk to me unless I was in trouble for something.

"Well, come on," she said.

I entered the house and she closed the door behind me. "You like cheese?" she asked.

I wagged and followed her into the kitchen. She headed toward the refrigerator, so I watched her alertly, and was rewarded with the usual rush of delicious odors that swam out on the flood of cold air.

She rustled something. "It's all moldy, but that's okay for dogs, right? You want this?"

Gloria held out a big hunk of cheese at the end of a metal fork. I sniffed it, then very, very tentatively chewed at it, waiting for her to get angry. "Hurry up," she said.

I pulled the cheese off the fork, dropped it to the floor, and then ate it in a few gulps. Okay, so maybe she wasn't angry at me anymore!

"Here," Gloria said. With a clang, she dropped a huge hunk of cheese into my food bowl. "Make yourself useful. Ridiculous we spend so much on premium dog food when you could be cleaning up our throwaways."

I'd never before been given more than a little bit of cheese at a time, so to have all this at once was an unexpected luxury. I picked up the heavy block, unsure as to how to begin. Gloria left the kitchen, so I just concentrated on eating the cheese a bite at a time. By the time I was finished, I was drooling a little, and lapped up most of my water.

Gloria came through the kitchen a little while later. "Finished?" she said. She went to the rear door and slid it open. "Okay, out," she ordered. I got the drift of what she was saying and hurriedly moved through the door out into the backyard. I felt better out there.

I didn't know when CJ would be home, and I missed her. I went through the dog door into the basement and curled up on my pillow, wishing she were there with me.

I fell asleep, but when I woke up I felt sick. I paced for a while, panting. I was drooling and was thirsty and my legs were trembling. Eventually all I could do was stand there, shaking, too weak to move.

I heard CJ's footsteps and knew she was home. She opened the door at the top of the stairs.

"Molly? Come! Come upstairs!" CJ called.

I knew I had to do what she asked. I took a step, dizzy, my head low.

"Molly?" CJ came down the stairs. "Molly? Are you okay? *Molly!*"

This time when she said my name it was a scream. I wanted to go to her to let her know it was okay, but I just couldn't budge. When she came to me and picked me up it sounded like my head was buried under the covers—everything muffled and quiet.

"Mom! There's something wrong with Molly!" CJ yelled. She carried me up the stairs and past Gloria, who was sitting on the couch. CJ ran with me out to the driveway.

When CJ set me down to open her car door I vomited explosively in the grass. "Oh God, what's that? What did you eat? Oh, Molly!"

I was a front-seat dog for the car ride but couldn't even lift my head to the window when CJ opened it. "Molly! We're going to the Vet. Okay? Molly? Are you okay? Molly, *please*!"

I could feel the pain and fear in CJ, but I couldn't move. It was getting dark in the car, darker and darker. I felt my tongue flop out of my mouth.

"Molly!" CJ shouted. "Molly!"

TEN

When I opened my eyes I could see nothing but
a fuzzy light, my vision blurred and indistinct.
It was a very familiar sensation—that and having unresponsive limbs and a head too heavy to hold up. I
shut my eyes. It did not seem possible that I could be
a puppy again.

What had happened to me?

I was hungry and instinctively groped for my
mother. I couldn't smell her, or smell anything, really. I
groaned, feeling myself slide helplessly back to sleep.

"Molly?"

I jerked awake. The film left my vision and CJ swam
into focus. My girl put her head next to mine.

"Oh, Molly, I was so worried about you." Her hands
stroked my fur and she kissed my face. I wagged, my

tail banging softly on the metal table. I felt too weak to raise my head, though I did lick CJ's hand, relieved I was still alive to take care of her.

Doctor Marty came up from behind her. "Her last seizure was very short and was more than four hours ago. I think we're out of the woods."

"What was it?" CJ asked.

"I don't know," the Vet said. "She obviously got into something she shouldn't have."

"Oh, Molly," CJ said. "Don't eat bad things, okay?"

I licked her face as she kissed me again. I was relieved that I was not a puppy, that I was still with my girl.

CJ and Gloria got angry at each other the first night I was home.

"Six hundred dollars!" Gloria shouted.

"That's what it cost. Molly almost died!" CJ yelled back.

Usually when they fought I would pace and yawn anxiously, but I was simply too fatigued. I lay there while Gloria went down the hall to her room, and when she shut her door it made a very loud noise, her various smells wafting around the house.

That summer Trent wasn't around much, but CJ and I would sleep until the sun was high in the sky and then have breakfast together and then often lie in the backyard. It was glorious. CJ would cover herself in an oil that smelled bad and tasted worse, though I would still lick her occasionally out of sheer affection. I loved taking naps with CJ.

Sometimes she lay outside almost all day, only going inside to use the bathroom and stand on the small box she had in there. I didn't understand why she stood on that thing so often. It never made her happy to do so.

I always went with her on these trips, so I was at her side when CJ slid open the back door and saw Gloria lying on a blanket next to where we'd been basking in the sun. "Gloria! What are you doing in my bikini?"

"It fits me just fine. Better, even."

"God, it does not! It's gross."

"I lost eleven pounds. And when I lose weight, it stays off."

CJ made a loud noise of frustration, her fists clenched, then turned back to the house. "Come on, Molly," she said. She sounded angry at me, so I padded silently next to her, my head down guiltily. She went straight to her room and went into the closet where she washed herself with water. I lay on the rug, panting because I could hear her crying. My girl was unhappy.

That day she didn't throw up, but many days she did. She was always very unhappy when this happened, too.

One day CJ took me for a car ride and I sat on the front seat. We went to Trent's and I played with Rocky in his backyard, which wasn't as big as CJ's but had the added attraction of having Rocky in it.

"Thank you so much for doing this," CJ said.

"Oh, it's no big deal at all. Rocky appreciates the company—he misses me while I'm at work," Trent replied. "Did I tell you they made me an assistant manager?"

"Really? So do you get to wear a special paper hat?"

Rocky stopped playing and trotted over to Trent.

"Well . . . no. But I mean, I'm only in high school and yet they trust me . . . aw, never mind." Trent sighed.

"Wait, no. I'm sorry. It was just a stupid joke. I'm proud of you."

"Sure you are."

Rocky was nuzzling Trent.

"No, seriously, I am," CJ said. "It shows how good you are at everything. That's why you're class president. You can accomplish anything you want."

"Not everything."

"What do you mean?"

"Nothing."

"Trent?"

"Just tell me about your trip."

"I'm really excited," CJ said. "I've never been on a cruise before. Two weeks!"

"Try not to push Gloria overboard. I'm pretty sure there's a rule against it, even if there shouldn't be."

"Oh, once we're on the boat I don't think we'll even see each other."

"Good luck with that," Trent said.

I wasn't surprised when CJ left me there—often she would drop me off to play with Rocky, and sometimes Rocky came over to our house to play with me. After a few nights, though, I began to worry, nosing Trent for reassurance.

"You miss CJ, don't you, Molly?" Trent said to me, holding my head in his hands. I wagged at her name— *yes, let's go back home to CJ.*

Rocky didn't like all the attention I was getting from Trent and jumped on my back. I turned on him and showed my teeth and he fell over, exposing his throat to me, so I had no choice but to straddle him and chew on his neck.

One night I heard Trent say, "CJ!" as if she was there, but when I ran into his room (Rocky jumping on me the whole way) he was by himself. "Molly, you want to talk to CJ on the phone? Here, Molly, the phone."

He held out a plastic toy. I sniffed at it. Okay, it was a "phone." I'd seen them before but had never been invited to play with one.

"Say hi," Trent said.

I heard a tinny, weird noise. I looked at the phone, cocking my head. Trent brought the phone up to his face. "She knows it's you!" he said. Trent sounded happy.

People often are happy when they talk to their phones, though in my experience talking to a dog is much better.

Trent's behavior was very strange, I thought. I felt weary from having been fooled into thinking CJ was in his room. I went to the foot of the bed and collapsed, sighing. After a moment, Rocky lay down next to me, his head on my stomach. He could sense my mood—I felt sad, even with him there. I missed my girl.

Somehow, though, I knew CJ would be coming back. She always came back to me.

One day Trent didn't go to work. He went to his basement and played, grunting as he picked up heavy things and set them down. Then he took a shower and spent a long time putting on different clothes in his room. Rocky picked up on his nervousness well before I did and started panting a little. When Trent went out to the living room and started pacing, stopping every so often to look out the window, Rocky was glued to his heels. I got bored with it and sprawled out on the living room rug.

I heard a door slam outside. Trent's nervousness spiked. Rocky put his feet on the window to look out. I got up, curious. The front door opened.

"Hi, Rocky! Hi, Molly!" It was my girl. I was so excited to see her I whimpered, circling at her feet and licking her face when she bent down to pet me. When she stood up I tried to leap up and kiss her face all the way up there, and she grabbed my head and hugged me. "Molly, you're a doodle-schoodle, but not a poodle," she told me. Everywhere her hands touched me my skin underneath my fur contracted with pleasure.

"Hi, CJ," Trent said. He reached for her and then stopped. She laughed and jumped to him and hugged him.

Rocky was so wound up he ran around the house, leaping on the furniture. "Hey, get down," Trent said, but he was laughing, so Rocky kept doing it, tearing around like a crazy dog. I stayed with CJ.

"Want something to eat? I've got cookies," Trent offered.

Rocky and I froze. Cookies?

"God, no," CJ said. "I'm fat as a pig. They had all this food; it was amazing."

Trent made Rocky and me go outside to wrestle, but I missed CJ, so after a while I scratched at the door and Trent's mother let us back in. Trent and CJ were sitting next to each other on the couch, and I curled up at her feet. CJ was holding her phone in her lap.

"Here's our stateroom," CJ said.

"What? It's huge."

"It was perfect. We had this living area and we each had our own bedroom and bathroom. I don't know if you've noticed, but Gloria and I get along best when we don't see each other."

"God, that had to be, like, really expensive."

"I guess."

"Does your mom really make that much money?"

CJ looked at him. "I don't know; I guess so. She's always going out at night for showings, so I know business must be pretty good."

I sighed. Across the floor Rocky had a chew toy and was watching me as he gnawed on it, waiting for me to try to make a move for it.

"Who is that guy?" Trent asked.

"Him, oh, he's nobody."

"There's another one of him."

"He was just a shipboard romance. You know."

Trent was quiet. Rocky sensed something and went across the room to put his head in Trent's lap. I seized the opportunity and pounced on the chew toy.

"What's the matter?" CJ asked Trent.

"Nothing," Trent replied. "Hey, it's getting kind of late and I have to work tomorrow."

We left and after that it seemed as if we didn't see Trent and Rocky as much as we used to, though we saw a lot more of Shane, whom I didn't care for very much. He wasn't ever mean to me; there was just something off about him, something I didn't trust. Often Gloria and CJ would talk about Shane and CJ would say, "Oh, Mo-*ther*," and walk out of the room.

CJ would be unhappy and Gloria would be unhappy. I didn't understand because there seemed to be so much to be happy about, like bacon, or the days when just the two of us would lie in the backyard, CJ's fingers lightly touching my fur.

What I didn't like very much was Bath. Always before in my lives, Bath meant standing outside and being sprayed with water and rubbed with a slippery soap that smelled as bad as Gloria's hair and lingered in my fur long after being rinsed off. To CJ, Bath meant staying in the house, standing in a small box with very smooth sides. I felt like a bad dog as she poured hot water on me from a dog dish that had a handle sticking out of it. She would rub me with foul-smelling soaps and I would stand miserably under the assault, eyes closed and head lowered. The delicious scents I had accumulated over time—dirt and old foods and dead things—would wilt before the bowl after bowl of warm, stinky water. If I tried to escape, my nails would scratch fruitlessly at the walls, unable to gain purchase, and then CJ would grab me.

"No, Molly," CJ would say sternly.

Bath was the worst sort of punishment, because I never knew what I had done wrong. But when it was over, CJ would wrap me in a blanket and pull me to her, and that was the very best. Being held so tightly made me feel safe and warm and loved. "Oh Molly dog, oh Molly dog, you are a schnoodle schnoodle dog," CJ would whisper to me.

Then she would take that blanket and rub me up and down until my skin felt so alive and buzzing that when she let me go I would race around the house, shaking myself of any remaining water and leaping over chairs and on the couch and running with first one shoulder and then another scooting along the carpet, drying and massaging myself.

CJ would laugh and laugh, but if Gloria was there she always yelled at me, "Stop!" I didn't know why she was mad, but I chalked it up to her always being mad, even when punishment Bath was over and we could all celebrate how great it felt to run around and jump on the furniture.

When the daily routine of locking me in the basement became more regular I knew CJ was back to doing school, and I could hear Gloria moving around upstairs before she, too, left the house. I would wander out through the dog door and lie in my usual spot, missing CJ. Sometimes when I slept it felt as if her fingers were still touching me.

We still did art building on a regular basis. Sometimes other people would be there and they would pet me, and sometimes it would just be CJ alone in the building with me. One night when it was just the two of us there was a tapping on the door, an odd sound that made me growl and raise the fur on the back of my neck.

"Molly! It's okay," CJ said. She went to the door and I followed. I smelled Shane on the other side, but that didn't make me any more comfortable.

"Hey, CJ, open up," Shane said. There was another man with him.

"I'm not supposed to let anyone in," CJ said.

"Come on, babe."

CJ opened the door and the two men hustled in. Shane grabbed CJ and kissed her. "Hi, Molly," he said to me. "CJ, this is Kyle."

"Hey," Kyle said.

"You got that key?" Shane said.

CJ crossed her arms over her chest. "I told you . . ."

"Yeah, well, Kyle and I would like to pass our art history mid-terms, okay? Come on. You know the whole thing is a joke anyway, like we're ever going to need to know any of it in real life. We'll make a copy of the test and be gone."

I couldn't tell what was going on with CJ, but I could see she wasn't happy. She handed something to Shane, who turned and tossed it to Kyle.

"Right back," Kyle said. He turned and walked away. Shane grinned at CJ.

"You know I could be expelled for this? I'm already on probation," CJ said.

"Relax; who is going to tell: Molly?" Shane reached out and petted my head. He was a little too rough. Then he grabbed CJ.

"Don't. Not here."

"Come on. No one else in the entire building."

"Stop it, Shane."

I heard anger in her voice and I growled a little. Shane put his hands out, laughing. "Okay. God. Don't sic the dog on me. I was just kidding around. I'll go hang with Kyle."

CJ went back to playing with her papers and her wet sticks. After a while Shane came back and dropped something on the table next to her, bouncing it with a metallic ring. "Okay, we're out," he said.

CJ didn't reply to him.

A few days later Gloria and CJ were watching television and I was asleep when there was a knock at the door. I got up, wagging, thinking it would be Trent, but it was two men who wore dark clothes and had metal objects on their belts, so I knew from experience they were police officers. CJ let them into the house. Gloria stood up. I wagged and nosed the officers in a friendly fashion.

"Are you Clarity Mahoney?" one of them asked CJ.

"Yes."

"What's going on?" Gloria asked them.

"We're here about the break-in at the art department at the high school."

"Break-in?" CJ said.

"Laptop computer, some cash, a silver picture frame," the officer said.

Gloria gasped.

"What? No, that's not . . . ," CJ said. I felt the fear rising in her.

"What have you done?" Gloria said to CJ.

"It wasn't me. It was Shane."

"We need you to come with us, Clarity."

"She's not going anywhere!" Gloria declared.

"'CJ', I go by 'CJ.'"

I went to her side.

"Let's go," the officer said.

"No daughter of mine is going with the police! I'll drive her down myself," Gloria said.

"It's okay, Gloria," CJ said.

"It is not okay. They can't come in here like the Gestapo; this is our home."

It seemed to me that the officers were getting angry. "Yes, well, we need your daughter to come down to the station now."

"No!" Gloria shouted.

The police offer reached to his side and pulled out two metal rings. "Turn around, CJ."

Everyone left after that. CJ didn't even pet me before departing, which made me feel like a bad dog. The house was very empty and alone with them gone.

I went downstairs to my pillow in the basement, full of the need to curl up in a safe place.

I got up when I heard the front door open, but I didn't go upstairs because I could hear that it was just Gloria and not CJ. Gloria shut the door at the top of the stairs.

I waited all night for my girl to come home, but she didn't. Nor did she come home the next day. I had a chewy bone to gnaw on, but otherwise, I was hungry because there was no dinner, not all day. Water I could get in the backyard, especially when it rained that morning, but I was sad and lonely and hungry.

I eventually gave voice to my feelings, barking out my fears and empty belly. A lone dog answered me from somewhere far away, a dog I'd never heard before. We both barked for a while, and then he stopped abruptly. I wondered who that dog was and if we would ever play together. I wondered if he had eaten that day.

A day lasts much, much longer when you're hungry and worried about the person you are supposed to take care of. Eventually, though, the sky darkened, and I went through the dog door and curled up in a tight ball under the stairs, my stomach aching and empty. I was starting to become afraid, and my fear kept me from sleeping very much.

Where was CJ?

ELEVEN

Most of the next day I spent lying in a pool of shade in the yard, watching some birds hop around in the wet grass. The only time I wasn't thinking of my hunger was when I saw Gloria standing at the glass doors, staring at me as I lay in the backyard. Whenever Gloria looked at me I felt like a bad dog. Otherwise, I was starving.

Wherever CJ was, I knew she wouldn't want me to go without dinner. Several times I restlessly went into the house to check my food bowl, but it was always empty and there was nothing else to eat unless you counted some socks I found in a basket. I didn't eat the socks, because I had chewed up similar items before and knew they would offer no real satisfaction. I licked the bowl anyway, imagining I could faintly taste some food there.

Cruelly, I could sometimes smell food on the air, delicious odors that I associated with people cooking. Somewhere, someone was grilling meat. It was probably far away, but I knew my nose would lead me to it if I got out of the yard.

There were two gates in the yard. The one next to the garage was tall and made of wood, but the one on the other side, through which CJ seldom went, was made of the same steel as the fence and was, in fact, even a little shorter. With a running start, I could probably clear it.

The idea wouldn't leave my mind. I would leap over the fence and follow my nose and find the cooking meat and a person would give me something to eat.

Though the whole concept made me drool, just thinking about leaving the yard made me feel like a bad dog. CJ would need me to be here. I couldn't protect her if I ran off in search of a meal.

Whimpering, I went back through the dog door to check my food bowl again. Still nothing. With a moan, I curled up, the sick emptiness in my belly too strong to allow sleep.

I was in the basement when I heard Trent calling my name. I ran out the dog door and he was standing in the yard, whistling for me. I was so happy to see him I barreled right into him, and he laughed and wrestled with me. I could smell Rocky all over him.

"Hi, Molly! Are you okay? You miss CJ, don't you."

I heard the back door slide open and Gloria was

standing there. "Are you here to take him with you?" she asked.

"Molly is a she," Trent said. I sat at my name. "Have you been feeding her?"

"Have I been feeding her?" Gloria said. I felt a small jolt of emotion—alarm, maybe—go through Trent.

"You haven't *fed* her?"

"Don't speak to me with that tone. I assumed there was food out for her somewhere. No one told me any different."

"But . . . I just can't believe you'd let a dog go hungry."

"And that's why you're here. For the dog. Right." An ugly emotion was coming off of Gloria, something like anger.

"Well . . . yeah. I mean . . . "

"You're here because you think feeding the dog will get you in good with Clarity. I know you've got the hots for her."

Trent took a deep breath and then let it out very slowly. "Come on, Molly," he said quietly.

I followed Trent to the backyard gate, looking over my shoulder at Gloria when he stopped to open it. She was standing with her hands on her hips and staring me in the eyes. It made me frightened, the way she looked at me.

Trent took me to Rocky's house and fed me. I was really hungry and growled at Rocky when he tried to get me to play before I was ready. When I was finished my belly was pleasantly full and I felt sluggish and just wanted to nap, but Rocky had a rope in his mouth and was running around in the yard as if I could never catch him, which of course was untrue. I ran over to him and grabbed the other end of the rope and we pulled each other around the yard. Trent was watching and he laughed, and when he did Rocky looked over at him, and I took advantage of the lapse in attention and yanked the rope away and took off, Rocky in hot pursuit.

That night Rocky and I lay together on the floor of Trent's room, utterly exhausted. I'd momentarily forgotten about CJ in the battle for the rope, but now, in the dark room, I missed her and felt sad. Rocky sniffed me and nuzzled me and licked my mouth, eventually resting his head on my chest.

Trent left the next morning, and the way he did so—getting more and more hurried as he dressed, gathering papers—led me to conclude he was doing school. Rocky and I wrestled, played more with the rope, and dug a couple of holes in the backyard. When he returned home Trent fed us and spoke crossly to us as he played with the dirt, filling in the holes we'd made. Apparently we, or at least Rocky, were bad dogs for something, but we didn't know what. Rocky stood with his head low and his ears down for a while, but then Trent petted him and everything was okay.

We were wrestling and Trent was in the house when the side gate clanged. Rocky and I barked, running over with our fur up, but I dropped my ears and charged joyously when I saw my girl standing there. "Molly!" she called happily. "Hi, Rocky!"

Rocky kept shoving that stupid rope in the way as CJ dropped to her knees and put her arms around me and kissed my face. Then Rocky whipped his head up and ran over to where Trent was coming out of the back door. Rocky greeted Trent as if he'd been gone as long as CJ, which was ridiculous.

"Down, Rocky. Hi, CJ."

CJ straightened up. "Hi, Trent."

Trent kept walking right up to CJ and hugged her. "Oh!" CJ said, laughing a little.

They got out the leashes for a walk! The leaves were falling from the trees and Rocky and I strained, dying to pounce on them as they skipped along in the breeze, but the leashes kept us in check.

I was so happy CJ was back, and, I realized, also really happy to be with Rocky and Trent. It was not up to me because I was just a dog, but as far as I was concerned we should just live here, at Trent's house. If Gloria didn't move in with us that would be okay with me as well.

There was a click and a flash of flame and then CJ's mouth was full of the smoke from the small stick. "They won't let you smoke in there. God," she said. "The minutes went by so slowly you could practically hear them."

"What was it like? Was it horrible?"

"Juvie? Not really. Just, I don't know, strange. I lost about four and a quarter pounds, though, so that's something good." CJ laughed. "The guys are on the other side and we never see them, but we can hear them, all right. There's a lot more of them than us girls. Most the girls in there were in trouble for doing something for their boyfriends, if you can believe it."

"Like you," Trent said quietly.

We were having such a great walk! When Rocky

passed trees and bushes he had to stop to mark them, and I usually squatted in the same place because I could remember the same compulsion, though it wasn't as important to me now.

"I didn't know Shane was going to *steal* stuff."

"You knew he was going to steal the test."

"He was going to copy the test, not steal it. And it's art history, not like math or something. God, you, too?"

Trent was quiet for a moment. "No, not me. Sorry."

Rocky leaped on a blowing leaf and picked it up and tried to tease me with it, but once it was in his mouth it was just a leaf.

"So because I was on academic probation, I'm now on academic suspension. Big woo. And you've never seen so much paperwork. I'll bet you international spies don't have a file as thick as mine."

"Suspended for how long?"

"Like, just this semester."

"But that means you won't graduate with the rest of us."

"That's okay. The outfits are ugly, anyway. Those hats? Come on. No, I'll graduate at mid-year without pomp. It's all been worth it for how mad it makes Gloria that she won't be able to sit with all the parents and call attention to herself when they say my name."

"And that's it? Suspension?"

"Also community service. I picked the coolest thing— training dogs, service dogs."

I looked up at her at the word "dog." She dropped her hand to my head and petted me and I licked her fingers. "Good dog, Molly," she said.

At the park they unsnapped our leashes and Rocky and I took off, gloriously happy in the cool air, free to race around the park, wrestling and running just as we did in the backyard. We could smell other dogs, but none came.

Dashing alongside my brother, I felt as full of energetic joy as when Bath punishment was over and I was allowed to jump on the furniture. Sometimes Rocky would stop and turn and look to see if Trent was still there. Rocky was a good dog. I could tell CJ was still there because the acrid smell of the smoke wafted off of her even when she wasn't actively putting fire in her mouth.

Many people emitted the same smoky odor and I'd never much cared for it, but I loved the way it mingled with CJ's unique scent because it was CJ. Still, I sometimes wished she still smelled the way she did as a baby, when I would sniff the top of her head, drinking her in. I loved that smell.

Rocky and I found a rotting squirrel corpse in the corner of the yard—I loved that smell, too! Before we could roll in it properly, though, Trent called us and we raced back. They put the leashes back on us—time for another walk!

At Rocky's house, Trent and CJ stood by CJ's car. I waited by the door, a little anxious that CJ might have forgotten that I was a front-seat dog.

"Good luck with your mom," Trent said.

"She doesn't care. She wasn't even home when the taxi dropped me off."

"Taxi? I would have picked you up."

"No, you would have had to cut school. I don't want to corrupt everyone with my criminal influence," CJ said.

We took a car ride with me in the front seat. When we got home, a man was sitting with Gloria on the couch. I went over to sniff him, wagging, and he petted my head. Gloria stiffened and pulled her hands up. I didn't sniff Gloria. CJ remained standing by the front door, so after greeting the man I went back over to be with her.

"Clarity, this is Rick. He has been very helpful during these difficult times you've put me through," Gloria said.

"I have a teenage daughter," Rick said. He held out his hand and CJ touched it.

"I go by 'CJ.' Gloria calls me Clarity because that's the one thing she'll never have."

"Gloria?" The man turned to look at Gloria, so I did, too, though in truth I pretty much avoided her eyes. "She calls you by your first name?"

"I know," Gloria said, shaking her head.

"See, that's the first problem right there," the man said. He seemed nice enough to me. His hands smelled like grease and meat and also Gloria.

"She asked me to call her Gloria and not Mom because she didn't want strange men in the grocery store knowing she had a daughter my age," CJ explained. "She's very concerned about what strange men think about her, as you might have figured out."

Everyone was quiet for a minute. I yawned and scratched behind my ear.

"Okay, well, good to meet you, CJ. I'm going to take off now; your mom has some things to talk to you about."

"It's so very special that you're here to tell me that," CJ said.

We went to CJ's room. I curled up in my usual spot. It was wonderful to be back home with my girl. I was pleasantly tired from wrestling Rocky and couldn't wait for CJ to crawl into bed so I could lie there with her and feel her hand on the fur on my neck.

The door opened and Gloria came in.

"Can you at least knock?" CJ said.

"Did they knock on your prison cell?" Gloria responded.

"Yes, and they had to ask permission to enter, what do you think?"

"I know that's not true."

I stood up and shook, yawning anxiously. I didn't like it when Gloria and CJ spoke to each other—the emotions were too strong and dark and confusing.

"So what's the deal with the guy?" CJ asked. "He acts like he's auditioning to be my stepfather."

"He's a very successful businessman. He knows a lot about managing people."

"I knew he'd be successful or you wouldn't be making out with him on the couch when I came in."

"He has given me a lot of advice on how to handle out-of-control children. I'm worried about you, Clarity June."

"I could tell how worried you were when I got home eight hours late from being released and saw you drinking wine in the living room."

CJ sat on the bed and I jumped up next to her. I could barely smell her, with Gloria's odors wafting through the room.

When I glanced at her, Gloria was staring at me, so I looked away. She made an exhaling noise. "So okay," she said. "The first thing is, you're grounded for the rest of the year. That means no dating, no boys over, no talking on the phone. You can't leave the house for any reason."

"So when the court calls to find out why I'm not doing community service, I'll just tell them, 'Gloria says I'm grounded.' They'll be okay with that. There's one guy from death row they can't execute because he's still in trouble with his mom."

Gloria stood there for a moment, frowning.

"Well, obviously," she finally said, "you can do that."

"And Christmas shopping? You aren't going to ground me from that, are you?"

"No, I'd have to make an exception for that, of course."

"And obviously Thanksgiving at Trent's."

"No. Absolutely not."

"But you said you're going to someone's house— Rick's, I suppose. You want me alone on *Thanksgiving*?"

CJ's hand scratched absently at my ear and I leaned into it. I wanted Gloria to leave now.

"Well, I suppose you could come to Rick's with me, though his children will be with their mother," Gloria said slowly.

"No way. Are you serious?"

"Fine, then. You can go to Trent's, since I already gave permission."

"And what about Jana? You told me you wanted me to hang out with Jana because her father is on the board of the country club."

"That's not what I said at all. I said that Jana was the type of person I wanted to see you spending more time with. And yes, Jana could come over."

"What if she wants to take me to the club for lunch?"

"I think we should handle these things as they come up. It's too hard to figure them all out now. If you get a special invitation of some sort, we'll talk about it. I am ready to make exceptions where they are called for."

"I can see that Rick has been a real help to you with this parenting stuff."

"That's what I said. And . . . there's something else."

"More punishment besides getting grounded with exceptions? Come on, Mom, I've already been to Juvenile Hall, isn't that enough?"

CJ's hand had stopped stroking me. I nuzzled it to remind her there was a deserving dog here who needed more petting.

"I don't think you understand just how humiliating it was for me to have you hauled out of here in handcuffs," Gloria said. "Rick says it's a wonder I don't have post . . . post something."

"Postpartum depression? Little late for that."

"That's not it. That doesn't sound like it."

"I'm sorry this whole ordeal was such a nightmare for you, Gloria. That's all I was thinking about, as I was sitting in the back of the cop car with you standing there in the front yard, was how much worse you had it than me."

Gloria stiffened and she turned and looked at me. I edged my eyes away quickly.

"Rick says it's your lack of respect for me that is causing all this. And it all started when you brought home that dog."

It worried me to hear the word "dog" coming out of Gloria's mouth.

"I think it started when I realized you were my mother."

"So you're going to have to get rid of it," she continued.

"*What?*"

I looked anxiously at CJ, feeling her shock.

"Rick says your bluff won't work. Nobody is going to believe you if you say you were left here by yourself when I took an occasional break, not if I say I had a babysitter, which by the way I always offered to provide one and you said no. And I took you on a cruise, which is proof right there that sometimes you got to go with me. Do you know how much money that cruise cost me? You've got to learn who is in control of the house, and that's me."

"I'm not going to get rid of Molly." I cocked my head at my name.

"Yes, you are."

"No. Never."

"Either you get rid of the dog or I'm taking away your car. *And* your credit cards. Rick says it's ridiculous for you to have a card on my account."

"So I'm getting my own account?"

"No, you have to earn it! When Rick was your age he had to get up early to do something with chickens every day, I forget what."

"Okay, I'll raise chickens."

"Shut up!" Gloria shouted. "I am so tired of your smart mouth! You are not to speak to me again this way, not ever! You have to learn that this is my house and we live by my rules."

Gloria jabbed a finger at me and I cringed. "I will not have that dog in my house. I don't care where you take it and I don't care what happens to it, but I will make your life a living hell, you and the dog both."

CJ sat on her bed, breathing hard. She was distressed. I moved as quietly as possible over to the bed, nuzzling her hand and doing everything I could not to be seen by Gloria.

"You know what? Fine," CJ said. "After tomorrow, you won't see Molly again."

TWELVE

The next morning we took a car ride and went to visit a dog named Zeke and a cat named Annabelle. Zeke was a small dog who loved to race around in his backyard at top speed with me chasing him. When I'd get tired of chasing him he'd bow and wait for me to decide to go at it again. Annabelle was all black and sniffed at me and then dismissed me in that way that cats sometimes do, walking languidly away. Also at the house was a girl named Trish and her parents. Trish and CJ were friends.

We only stayed for two days there and then we were on to another house with no dogs or cats, and then another house with two cats but no dogs, and then another with an old dog and a young dog and no cats. Also, at every house there was at least one girl CJ's age plus other people. For the most part, the people were very nice to me. Sometimes CJ had her own room, but usually she stayed in a room with one of her friends.

It was glorious to meet all these new dogs! Nearly all of them were friendly and wanted to wrestle, except for when they were very old. I was also, for the most part, interested in the cats. Some cats are timid and some are bold, some are mean and some are nice, some rub up against me and purr and others ignore me completely, but all of them have delicious breath.

I loved our new life, though I sometimes missed Trent and Rocky.

At one house there was a boy who reminded me of Ethan. He had dark hair like Ethan and his hands smelled like the two rats he had in a cage in his room. He was the same size Ethan had been on the day I first met my boy so long ago, and he loved me instantly and we played tug-on-a-stick and fetch the ball in the front yard. The boy's name was Del. He didn't have a dog of his own. Rats are a poor substitute for a dog, even if you have two of them.

At one point I realized with a jolt that I'd been playing with Del all day long and hadn't seen CJ since breakfast. I felt like a bad dog. As I went to the door and sat, hoping someone would open it for me so I could go inside and check on my girl, I found myself thinking about Ethan. I loved CJ as much and in the same way as I had loved Ethan. So had I been wrong that my purpose was to love Ethan? Or did I now have a new purpose, to love and protect CJ? Were these separate, distinct purposes, or was it all tied up in some even larger purpose?

I never would have pondered any of this if I hadn't been playing with Del all day. His resemblance to Ethan just made me miss my boy.

Del's sister was Emily. She and CJ liked to talk together in low whispers, but they always would pet me when I went over to see if they might be talking about what treats I should get.

At dinner I liked to sit under the table. A steady rain of delicious morsels would come down from where Del sat and I would eat them silently and wait for more. Sometimes CJ's hand would reach down to touch my head and I gloried in the food and the love. Del and Emily had a mother and a father, but they never dropped any food.

When the doorbell rang, Del jumped up and ran to get it and I stayed with CJ. Del came skipping back a minute later.

"There's a boy here to see CJ," he said.

The front door was left open and I could smell who it was: Shane. I was not happy. The only time my girl ever shut me out of her life was when Shane came around. I didn't understand why I couldn't stay with her, like when Trent visited.

When CJ got up from the table I naturally accompanied her, but sure enough, she shut the door on me, so I went back to my station under Del's legs. Del rewarded me with a tiny piece of chicken.

"Emily. How long is she planning to stay?" Emily's mother asked.

"I don't know. God, Mom, she was kicked out of her own house."

"I'm not trying to say Gloria Mahoney's a good mother," Emily's mom said.

"Mahoney? Is she the one who came to the Halloween party dressed as a stripper?" the father asked.

"Stripper?" Del chirped brightly.

"Las Vegas showgirl," Emily's mother corrected sternly. "I didn't realize she was so effective at grabbing your attention."

The father made an uncomfortable noise in his throat.

"She's always embarrassing us," Emily interjected. "One time she brought a date home and the two of them sat down to watch what we were watching on TV, and then right there in front of us—"

"Enough!" Emily's mom said loudly.

There was a silence. I licked Del's pants so he'd know I was still there.

"What I am trying to say," the mom said in quieter tones, "is that I know that CJ has a difficult home situation, but . . . "

"She can't live here," the father said.

"She's not. It's just temporary! God, Dad!"

"I like her," Del said.

"This isn't about liking her, Son; it's about what is right," the father said.

"I like her, too," the mother said. "But she's a girl who makes bad choices. She's suspended from school, she's been to jail—"

"It was juvie and it wasn't her fault," Emily said. "I can't stand this."

"Yes, and the boy who is responsible is standing on our front porch," the mother replied.

"What?" the dad said. I looked over at his legs, which had jerked under the table a bit.

"Plus . . . I heard her in the bathroom last night. She was throwing up," the mother said.

"So?" Emily said.

"That boy is not coming in here," the father said.

Del tossed me a piece of broccoli, which I didn't want but ate just to keep the treats coming.

"She was throwing up *on purpose,*" the mother said.

"Oh, Mother," Emily said.

"How do you do that?" Del asked.

"She sticks her finger down her throat. Don't you ever try it," the mother warned.

"I don't see what's the big deal," Emily said.

The front door slammed.

"Del, not a word of what we've been talking about," the father said.

CJ came around the corner and she was upset. "I'm sorry," she apologized. I sprang out from under the table and ran to her side. She wiped tears from her face. "I need to be excused," she said in a low voice.

I followed her back to the bedroom she was sharing with Emily. CJ threw herself on the bed and I jumped up with her and she held me and I felt some of her sadness going away. Helping CJ be less sad was one of my most important jobs.

I only wished I was better at it. Sometimes the dark feelings were buried so deep in CJ they felt as if they'd be there forever.

Later that night Emily and CJ sat on the floor and ate pizza and ice cream and fed me little bits of it.

"Shane says if he can't have me no one will," CJ said. "Like we're on a soap opera or something."

I saw Emily's eyes grow larger. (I was mostly watching Emily because she didn't eat her crusts and CJ did.)

"But you broke up!"

"I know; I told him that. But he said he loved me in a special way no one else can, and that he would wait forever no matter how long it took. That's how intelligent he is—I told him forever is actually forever, so we didn't have to guess how long it would take."

"How did he even find you?"

"He's been calling like everybody, asking where I was staying," CJ said. "God! He can't open a book, but he can work the phones to track me down. He'll probably be in a call center someday, selling life insurance over the phone. Oh wait, that would be hard work. Forget it." She took what I was sad to see was the last piece of pizza. "You want this?"

"God no, I was full like three pieces ago."

"I didn't eat much dinner."

"I don't blame you." Emily tossed me a piece of crust and I snagged it out of the air and dispatched it with a single chew, ready to do the trick again.

"You want any ice cream?" CJ asked. I heard the question in her voice as she picked up the carton, and wondered if maybe she was thinking of giving me some ice cream. The thought made my mouth water and I licked my lips.

"No, get it out of my sight."

"I'll probably gain like ten pounds," CJ said.

"What? I wish I had your legs; mine are thunder thighs."

"No, you look great. I'm the one with the big butt."

"I'm seriously dieting after New Year's."

"Me, too."

"Oh, stop, you look amazing right now," Emily said. I was staring at her, willing her to pick up another piece of crust and toss it.

"I go to community service tomorrow," CJ said. "It's training service dogs."

"It sounds like fun."

"I know, right? The list was like, pick up trash along the highway, or pick up trash in the park, or pick up trash at the library—and then at the end of the list, work for this service dog place. I thought, which one will look better on my résumé? I mean, who knows, maybe I'll want to go into waste management; then all the trash experience would help me with my career."

Emily laughed.

"God, I can't believe I ate all that," CJ said, falling back with a groan.

The next morning CJ woke up before anyone else, showered, and took me for a car ride (front seat!). We arrived at a big building and I smelled dogs as soon as my paws touched the parking lot. I heard them, too, several dogs barking.

A woman greeted us. She said, "Hi, I'm Andi," and then she dropped to her knees and reached for me, her long black hair draping my face. "Who is this?" she asked.

She was older than CJ but younger than Gloria and she smelled like dogs.

"This is Molly. I'm CJ," CJ said.

"Molly! I had a Molly once. She was a good dog." The affection pouring off of Andi was intoxicating. I licked her and she kissed me right back. Most people don't like to kiss a dog's lips. "Molly Molly Molly," she crooned. "You are so beautiful; yes, you are. What a great dog."

I liked Andi.

"What is she, a spaniel-poodle mix?" Andi asked, still kissing me and petting me.

"Maybe. Mother was a poodle, but the father nobody knows. Are you a spoodle, Molly?"

I wagged at my name. Andi finally stood up, but she kept her hand down within reach and I licked it.

"It's a godsend you're here; I really need the help," Andi said as we walked inside the building. There was a big open space with kennels on either side and lots of dogs in the kennels. They all barked at me and each other, but I ignored them because I was a special-status dog, allowed to be out free while the rest of them were in cages.

"I don't really know anything about training dogs, but I'm willing to learn," CJ said.

Andi laughed. "Well, okay, but what you're really going to do is free me up so I can do the training. The dogs need to be watered and fed and their kennels cleaned, and they need to be walked outside."

CJ came to a halt. "So, wait, what is this place?"

"Technically we're a dog rescue, that's our main function, but my grant is letting me use the facility to research cancer detection. Dogs have a sense of smell that's as much as a hundred thousand times more intense than ours, and some studies show that they can detect cancer on people's breath before any other diagnosis has been made. Since early detection is the fastest way to a cure, this could be really important. So I'm taking the methodologies from the studies and trying to put them into practice."

"You're training dogs to smell cancer."

"Exactly. I'm not the only one doing this, of course, but most trainers are working with dogs to detect specimens in the lab. They let the dog sniff a test tube. I'm thinking, what if it could work in the field, like at a health fair, or a community center?"

"So you're training the dogs to go from person to person and see if they detect cancer."

"Right! But my part-time employee got a full-time job and my full-timer is out on maternity. I've got some volunteers, of course, but they're mainly interested in walking the dogs and not so much cleaning the kennels. That's where you come in."

"Why do I get the feeling you're trying to tell me my job is going to be picking up dog poo," CJ said.

Andi laughed. "I'm trying *not* to tell you that, but there it is. My aunt is a clerk for the judge, which is how I got approved for community service. At first I posted a very detailed description of the position and nobody picked me, small wonder. Then I changed it to be just working with dogs. I figure, though, you have to do community service and it's sort of a punishment for your crimes, right? In the end, it's not supposed to be all fun. So, what did you do?"

CJ let a few moments go by with no sound but dogs barking. "I let a guy talk me into doing something stupid."

"You mean you can get arrested for that? Wow, I'm in big trouble, then," Andi said. They both laughed and I wagged my tail. "Okay, you ready to get started?"

It was a strange day. CJ would put me in the outdoor pen with a dog to play with and be gone for several minutes. Then she'd come out and walk the other dog and me on leashes around the block. Her shoes got wetter and wetter throughout the day, as did her pants, and both were fragrant with dog urine. It was so much fun!

At the end of the day, CJ was rubbing her back and sighing. We stood and watched Andi play with a big brown male dog. There were several metal buckets and Andi would lead the dog to each one and the dog would sniff the inside of the bucket. At one of them, Andi would say, "Smell that? Now drop!" and the dog would lie down and Andi would give him a treat. Andi came over to us when she saw us watching, the dog by her side.

I edged up to the dog and we sniffed each other's rear ends. "This is Luke. Luke, you like Molly?"

We both looked up at our names. Luke was a serious dog, I could tell. He was focused on the game he had been playing with Andi. He wasn't like Rocky, who was interested only in fun and in loving Trent.

"That's six hours total with the lunch break, right?" Andi said.

"Yeah. Six blissful hours. One hundred ninety-four to go."

Andi laughed. "I'll sign the form at the end of the week. Thanks, you did a good job."

"Maybe I have a future in dog poop," CJ said.

We took a car ride with me in the front seat! We went to Emily's house. When we pulled in the driveway, Gloria was standing there talking to Emily's mother. CJ stiffened when she saw her mother. Gloria fluttered a hand to her own throat.

"Oh great," CJ muttered. "Just great."

[THIRTEEN]

I'll let you two talk," Emily's mother said when we approached. She went inside the house. I stayed by CJ's side, and CJ didn't move at all, just stood there. Gloria's powerful arsenal of scents wafted over me, obliterating everything else.

"Well," Gloria said, "don't you have anything to say to me?" Gloria was, as usual, very unhappy.

"I see you got a new Cadillac," CJ said. "Nice car."

"Not that. I've been worried sick about you. You never once called to tell me where you were. I could barely sleep."

"What do you want, Gloria?"

There was a motion at the big front window. It was Del, who had pulled aside the drapes and was looking out. As I watched, his mother's hand appeared, grabbing him and pulling him away.

"I have just one thing to say to you, and then that's it, no discussion," Gloria said.

"Sounds like a fair debate," CJ said.

"I have, at great expense, consulted an attorney who practices family law. She says that I can file a motion of judgment with the court and force you to move home. She also says that I do not have to be held prisoner in my own house to a dog. So I am going to file for that, too. You have no choice and the judge could even give you a curfew. So that's it. It will cost a lot of money to go to court and you'd lose, so I came to tell you that. There's no sense spending the expenses for court when we could take a nice trip or something for the same money."

It looked like nothing interesting was going to happen for a while, so I lay down with a yawn.

"Well?" Gloria said.

"I thought I wasn't allowed to talk."

"You can speak about what I just told you; I'm just not going to stand here and argue with you. You're a minor and the law is on my side."

"Okay," CJ said.

Gloria sniffed. "Okay what?"

"Okay, let's do what you said."

"All right. That's better. You've been very disrespectful and I have no idea what these people think that you've been living here with them. I am your mother and I have rights under the Constitution."

"No, I meant let's do what you said and go to court."

"What?"

"I think you're right," CJ said. "Let's let a judge decide. I'll hire a lawyer. You said there were provisions
for withdrawing money from Dad's trust for my
welfare. So I'll get a lawyer, and we'll go to court.
You'll fight for custody and I'll fight to have you declared unfit to be a mother."

"Oh, I see. Now I'm the horrible mother. You went
to jail, and you got suspended, and you lie and you
disobey, and I have devoted my life to you, but I'm the
bad one."

They were both angry, but Gloria was shouting. I
sat up and anxiously put a paw up on CJ's leg because
I wanted to leave. She petted me but didn't look at me.

"I hope someday you have a child as awful as you,"
Gloria said.

"Trent said you didn't feed Molly at all."

"You're changing the subject."

"That's true; we were talking about what a bad
child I was. So what do you think? Should I call a
lawyer? Or do you recognize that Molly is my dog
and that I'm keeping her? I mean, I can keep living
here." CJ gestured toward the house and, as she did
so, a shadow backed away from the front window. It
looked too tall to be Del.

"I don't want you living with other people. It looks
terrible," Gloria said.

"So what do you want to do?"

That evening we moved back into our room at CJ's
house. Trent came over with Rocky and I was overjoyed to see my brother, who sniffed me up and
down, suspicious of all the new smells. When we

went outside, snow was falling and Rocky ran around in it, kicking up his heels and rolling in it until he was all wet. Trent came out and rubbed Rocky all over with a towel and Rocky groaned with pleasure. I wished I had rolled in the snow, too.

After that, things were back to normal, except that CJ didn't leave to do school—instead, I got to take a car ride with her most mornings to play with Andi and her dogs!

The first morning we returned to Andi's place, she greeted me by throwing her arms wide and kissing me and hugging me. I loved her affections and her wonderful dog smells. Then she stood.

"I thought maybe you'd given up," Andi said to CJ.

"No, I just had . . . There were family issues I needed to deal with. You didn't call the court or anything, did you?" CJ replied.

"No, but I wished you'd called *me.*"

"Yeah, I'm . . . I should have. For some reason I never think to call people."

"Well, okay, let's get to work."

The dogs at Andi's building weren't allowed to go out into the snow except for walks on leashes, so while CJ cleaned out their kennels my job was to play with the dogs in a fenced area inside the big room in the building. A lot of the dogs didn't want to play, though. A couple of them were too old to do anything but sniff me and then lie down, and a couple just didn't know how to play, snarling and snapping at me while I danced out of the way. Those dogs seemed sad and frightened and were put in another inside pen, one at a time, while CJ cleaned their kennels.

This left me with a lot of time to watch Andi play with Luke, her big brown male, and two females, one yellow and one black. The game was this: Some old people sat in metal chairs sitting far away from each other, and Andi would lead the dogs one at a time up to sniff them. The people didn't play with the dogs, though—sometimes humans like to just sit, even if there's a dog right there. Then Andi would put the dogs in their kennels and the people would all stand up and change position, sitting in new seats.

She told all the dogs they were good dogs, but she really got excited with Luke. Every time Luke was led to a man with no hair, Luke would carefully sniff, then lie down and cross his paws and put his head on his paws. Andi would give him a treat right there on the spot. "Good dog, Luke!" she would praise.

I wanted a treat, too, but when I dropped down and crossed my front paws Andi didn't even notice and CJ was unimpressed. That's how life is—some dogs get treats for doing almost nothing and some dogs are good dogs and get no treats at all.

At one point CJ came to get me and we went out to the outdoor pen. Several inches of snow were on the ground and I crunched through it to find a good place to squat. CJ put the burning stick in her mouth and exhaled smoke.

I heard the back door open and ran over to see who it was. A flash of alarm coursed through CJ, so the fur went up on my neck.

"I thought. You. Might be out here." It was the bald man in front of whom Luke was always lying down. He made a gasping sound while he talked to CJ. I nosed her hand because she still felt scared to me. "Could. I have. A cigarette?"

"Sure," CJ said. She fumbled in her jacket.

"Would you. Light it. For me? I cannot. Get. Enough. Suction," the man said. He stroked his bald head.

CJ lit fire and handed the stick to the man. He lifted it to his throat, not to his mouth like CJ did. There was a weak sucking sound and then smoke came out of a hole in his throat.

"Ah," the man said. "So good. I only. Allow. Myself one. A week."

"What happened? I mean . . . "

"My hole?" The man smiled. "Throat. Cancer."

"God, I'm really sorry."

"No. My fault. I didn't. Have to. Smoke."

They stood together for a moment. CJ was still upset, but her fear was slowly draining from her and dissipating like the smoke coming from her mouth.

"Your age," the man said.

"Sorry?"

"Your age. When I. Started. Smoking." He smiled at her. I decided I didn't need to stand guard over CJ anymore and went over to sniff his hand and see if maybe he had any treats. He leaned over. "Nice dog," he said. His breath smelled like smoke, but it also had an odd metallic tang to it that I instantly recognized from when I was Buddy and had a bad taste in my mouth that I couldn't get rid of. The bald man probably had the same taste in his mouth, because it was on his breath.

The man went inside and CJ stood in the cold air and stared off into space for a long time. The stick in her hand was still smoldering. She leaned over and poked it into the snow and then threw it in the trash can and we went inside together.

Andi was playing with the yellow dog. I was off leash and CJ was distracted, so I trotted over to where the bald man from outside was sitting in a chair. I went to him and bowed down, crossing my front paws as I'd seen Luke do.

"Look at that," Andi said. She came up to me. "Hey, Molly, did you learn to do that from Luke?"

I wagged. However, I did not get a treat. Instead, Andi led me back over to be with CJ.

I really liked Andi. I loved the way she greeted me with all the hugs and kisses a dog could ever want. But I thought it was unfair of her to give Luke a treat but not me.

When we got home, Gloria was glad to see CJ but ignored me as usual. I had learned to stay away from Gloria, who never spoke to me or fed me or even looked at me, most of the time.

"I think we should have a Christmas party this year," Gloria said. She had a pad of paper in her hand and waved it at CJ. "Something really fancy. Catered. With champagne."

"I'm seventeen, Gloria. I'm not supposed to drink champagne."

"Oh, well, *Christmas*. You can invite whoever you want," Gloria continued. "Are you seeing someone special?"

"You know I'm not."

"What about that nice young man, Shane?"

"And that's why you're not my go-to source for deciding who is a nice young man."

"I'll invite Giuseppe," Gloria said.

"Who? What happened to Rick?"

"Oh, Rick? He turned out to be not what I thought."

"So now you're dating Pinocchio's father?"

"What? No, Giuseppe. He's Italian. He's from St. Louis."

"That's where Italy is? No wonder I do so badly in geography."

"What? No, I mean real Italy."

"Are you helping him buy a house or something?"

"Well, well, yes. Of course."

I went into the kitchen to check to see if anything edible had fallen on the floor, and that's when I saw a man standing outside, peering in through the glass doors. I barked the alarm.

The man immediately turned and ran away. CJ came into the kitchen. "What is it, Molly?" she asked. She went to the door and slid it open and I raced out into the yard. The man's scent was on the air and I followed it quickly to the closed back gate. I knew that smell, knew who it belonged to.

Shane.

CJ called me back into the house. "Come on, Molly; it's too cold," she said to me.

The next time we went to Andi's, she came over to us as CJ was stomping the snow off her feet. "Hey. I want to try something today."

"Sure," CJ said.

It was the same game Andi played every day. It did

not seem like much fun to me when there were ropes to tug on and balls to chase, but people are like that—their idea of play is usually less fun than a dog's. People were sitting in chairs spaced wide apart from one end of the big room to the other. Andi had CJ hold my leash and we went to the person at the far end, a woman who had on fur boots that smelled like cats. "Hi, what's your name?" she said, holding her hand down for me to lick. Her fingers had a tangy taste to them.

"This is Molly," Andi said. I wagged at hearing my name.

We went together to the next person, and the next, at each occasion taking the time for them to pet me and talk to me but not to give me any treats even though I could smell that one man had something with cheese on it in one of his pockets.

Then we came to a woman whose hands smelled like fish. She leaned over to pet me and I picked up that same scent, the one that was similar to what I couldn't get off my tongue when I was Buddy, the same scent the bald man who talked to CJ had on his breath.

"Hello, Molly," the woman said.

I felt the slightest bit of tension in Andi as we started to move on, and that's when I got it: the game, it had to do with this smell. I turned back to the woman and lay down, crossing my paws.

"That's it!" Andi said, clapping her hands. "Good dog, Molly, good dog!"

Andi gave me treats. I decided I loved this game and wagged, ready to play again.

"So Molly just figured it out?" CJ asked.

"Well, there's more to it than that. I think that all dogs can detect the odor, but that doesn't mean they necessarily connect it to signaling us that they've done so. But Molly has been watching Luke—did you see how she crossed her paws, just like he does? I've never heard of a dog learning this from watching another one, but there it is; there can't be any other explanation." Andi knelt down and kissed me on the nose. I licked her face. "Molly, you are a genius, a true genius dog."

"You're a goodle, Molly," CJ said. "Part genius, part poodle. A goodle dog." I wagged, loving the attention.

"If you don't mind, I'd like to involve Molly in the program. You, too, if you're interested," Andi said. "It would count toward your community service."

"What, and give up shoveling dog poo? I'll have to think about it."

From that day forward, whenever we were with Andi, CJ would lead me to meet people and I would signal whenever I picked up that odd, bad odor. It didn't happen very often, though. Most of the time, people just smell like people.

But sometimes, they smell like food! For Happy Thanksgiving CJ and I went to Trent's house and the air and people's hands were so redolent with meat and cheese and bread and other wonderful smells that Rocky and I were nearly delirious. People ate all day, tossing us morsels to snatch out of the air.

Trent had a father and a mother. For the first time,

I wondered why CJ didn't have a father as well. Maybe if Gloria had a mate she wouldn't be unhappy all the time.

There was nothing I could do about that, though. I had to content myself with eating Happy Thanksgiving food.

And I was *very* content.

CJ was happy, too. At one point in the day we all gathered against a wall that smelled strongly of smoke and the people all put their arms around each other, full of love. Rocky and I were told to sit and there was a lot of laughter and bright flashes.

When we were leaving, CJ hugged and kissed Trent's mother. "This was the most wonderful Thanksgiving I've ever had," CJ said.

"Please come every year. You're one of the family," Trent's mother said.

I smelled tears on CJ's face, but she was happy and as we drove away she held my head in her lap, stroking me. As I drifted off to sleep, I was thinking about how much the people in Trent's house hugged each other. I hoped we'd go back there often, because the hugging seemed good for my girl.

At Merry Christmas time, CJ and Gloria put a tree in the living room and hung cat toys from it. I could smell that tree from anywhere in the house. And one evening people came over and hung lights and cooked food. CJ put on clothes that swished loudly when she moved, and so did Gloria.

"What do you think?" Gloria asked, standing in CJ's doorway. She twirled noisily. It didn't seem possible, but Gloria was even more fragrant than usual. My nose crinkled involuntarily at the flood of odors drenching the air.

"Very nice," CJ said.

Gloria laughed happily. "Now let me see you."

CJ stopped brushing her hair and spun. Then she stopped and stared at Gloria. "What?" she said.

"Nothing, it's just . . . Have you put on some weight? It fits different than when we bought it."

"I quit smoking."

"Well . . . "

"Well what?"

"I just don't know why you couldn't control your-self with the party coming up."

"You're right, I should have kept sucking poison because it would help me fit in my new dress for a party."

"I never said that. I don't know why I bother to try to talk to you," Gloria said. She was angry and walked away.

Then friends arrived. Trent came but did not bring Rocky, for some reason. Mostly they were people Gloria's age. I wandered around, smelling warm deli-cious things, and after a while people started feeding me treats—not for doing any tricks but just for being a dog. They were the best sort of people, in my opinion.

One woman leaned over and fed me a piece of meat with melted cheese on it. "Oh, you are such a pretty dog!" she said to me.

I did what I was supposed to do: I lay down on the floor, crossing my front paws.

"How cute! She's doing a curtsey!" the woman said.

CJ came around the couch to see me and I wagged. "Oh my God," CJ said.

FOURTEEN

CJ was anxious and scared. "Sheryl, can I talk to you for a minute? Privately?"

The woman was still petting me, but I was watching CJ to see what was wrong. "Sure," the woman said.

I started to follow them down the hallway, but then CJ turned and said, "Stay, Molly."

I knew "Stay," but it was my least favorite thing to do. I sat for a minute, then got up and went down to sniff under the door where they had gone. They were in there for about ten minutes, and then the door popped open and the woman came out with a hand to her mouth. She was crying. CJ was upset, too, and felt sad.

The woman got her coat and Gloria came up holding a glass. "What happened?" She looked between CJ and the crying woman. "What did you say to her?"

CJ shook her head. The woman said, "I'm sorry. I'll call you," to Gloria and then was out the door. Gloria was very angry. Trent came up from behind her, looking from Gloria to CJ and then moving past Gloria to stand by CJ. I lifted my nose to touch his hand as he passed.

"What happened?" Gloria said.

"Molly signaled the way she's been trained. For cancer. She signaled Sheryl had cancer."

"Oh God," Trent said.

Some people had come down the hallway and I heard one of them say, "Cancer? Who has cancer?"

"And you had to tell her *now*?" Gloria hissed. She then turned, jerking her head when she saw the people behind her. "It's nothing," she said.

"What happened?" a man asked.

CJ shook her head. "Just a personal conversation. I'm sorry."

The people stood for a moment and then turned away.

"You only care about yourself," Gloria said.

"How does that make sense?" Trent responded, his voice loud.

"Trent," CJ said. She put a hand on Trent's sleeve.

"Do you know how much money this party cost?" Gloria said.

"The *party*?" Trent said.

"Trent. Don't," CJ said. "Just . . . you know what, Gloria? Give my excuses to your friends. Tell them I've got a headache and I'm going to my room."

Gloria made a loud noise and then turned and stared at me hatefully. I glanced away from her eyes.

She spun and strode off down the hallway, where the people had silently withdrawn. When she got to the end of the hallway she stopped, straightened her back, and tossed her hair. "Giuseppe?" she called into the living room. "Where did you get to?"

"I'll get your coat," CJ said to Trent.

His shoulders slumped a little. "You sure? I mean, I could stay with you for a while. Talk."

"No, it's okay."

CJ went into Gloria's bedroom and came out with Trent's coat. He put it on. He was sad. CJ smiled at him. "Hey, in case I don't see you, Merry Christmas."

"Yeah, same to you."

"CJ, you do get that your mom's wrong, don't you? That you might have upset Sheryl, but you gave her really important information. And if you had waited because you didn't want to disturb the party, you'd have a hard time ever telling Sheryl at all because, well, it would look *crazy* that you had waited."

"I know."

"So don't let her get to you, okay? Don't let Gloria into your head."

They stood and looked at each other for a minute. "Okay, Trent," CJ finally said.

Trent turned and went to the door and we followed. Then he paused and looked up. "Hey, mistletoe."

CJ nodded.

"Well, come on then," Trent said. CJ laughed as he held out his arms. Trent pressed forward and kissed her and I jumped up and put my front feet on her back so I would be part of whatever was going on.

"Whoa," CJ said.

"Okay, well, good-bye. Merry Christmas," Trent said.

I tried to slip out the door with him, but CJ held me back. Then she shut the door and looked at it for a minute, while I looked at her, wondering what we were doing.

I would have been happy to circulate under the feet of all the loud people in the living room and eat treats, but CJ went up to her room, snapping her fingers for me to follow. She took off her loud clothes and put on what she usually wore: a soft shirt that went to her knees. She got into bed with the lights on, holding a book.

Books are okay to chew on, though they are fairly tasteless and it always makes people unhappy when a dog does so. They are one of those toys that dogs aren't supposed to play with.

I curled up on the floor next to her bed and fell asleep, though I was conscious of the hum of people talking below me and, later, the front door opening and shutting a few times. Then there was a knocking sound and I woke up. The bedroom door pushed open.

"Hello, CJ," said a man. I recognized his scent from downstairs. When he had reached down to feed me a piece of fish, his watch slid down his wrist with a heavy sound.

"Oh, hi, Giuseppe."

The man laughed and came into the room. "Call me Gus. The only person who calls me Giuseppe is your mother. I think because she believes I'm from Italian royalty." He laughed again.

"Huh," CJ said. She smoothed the blankets down over her legs.

The man shut the bedroom door behind him. "So what are you reading?" he asked.

"You're drunk, Gus."

"Hey, it's a party." The man sat down heavily on the bed, his feet on the floor right by me. I sat up.

"What are you doing? Get out of my room," CJ said. She felt angry.

The man put his hand on the blanket. "I loved that dress you were wearing. You have great stems. You know what stems are? Legs."

The man pulled on the blanket. CJ pulled back. "*Stop*," she said.

"Come on," the man said. He stood back up, reaching for CJ with both hands. I felt the fear coming off of her and I leaped up and put my paws on the bed and thrust my face at the man and snarled the way I'd gone after Troy the horse when he'd been about to stamp on the baby.

The man threw himself back and stumbled against the shelf on the wall, books and photographs falling to the floor. He twisted and with a crash fell on the carpet, lying on his side. I barked and lunged forward, my teeth still bared.

"Molly! It's okay. Good girl." I felt CJ's hand on my fur, which was stiff along the ridge of my back.

"Hey," the man said.

CJ found my collar and pulled me back. "You need to leave, Gus."

He rolled and got on his knees. The door flew open and Gloria was standing there. "What happened?"

she demanded. She looked at Gus, who was crawling on the floor. He put his hands on the bedpost and hauled himself to his feet. "Giuseppe? What happened?"

He pushed past her out into the hallway, his footsteps heavy. Gloria turned to face her daughter. "I heard the dog; did it bite him?"

"No! Of course not."

"Well, what is going on?"

"You don't want to know, Gloria."

"Tell me!"

"He came in here and started touching me, okay?" CJ shouted. "Molly was protecting me."

I turned my head at my name. Gloria turned rigid and her eyes grew large, then narrow and small. "You are such a liar," she hissed. She turned and ran away just as the front door slammed. "Giuseppe!" she called.

For the next several days Gloria and CJ never seemed to be in the same room. When they sat down for the part of Merry Christmas where they tore papers and had boxes, they didn't talk to each other very much. CJ started eating her meals in her bedroom and sometimes it would just be a tiny amount of vegetable and sometimes it would be wonderful plates full of noodles and sauces and cheeses, or pizza and chips, and ice cream. Then she would go into the bathroom and stand on that small box and make a sad noise. Every few hours, every single day, CJ would go stand on that small box. I started thinking of it as the sad box, because that's how CJ always felt when she was on it.

Trent came over with Rocky and we all played in the snow. It was the only time CJ seemed truly happy.

I did not feel like a bad dog for snarling at the man. CJ had been afraid and I did it without even thinking. I was worried that I'd be punished for it, but I never was.

Soon CJ started doing school again. She and Gloria were talking to each other more often, but I could still feel a tension in the room between them. When CJ was in school, I would go down to my old place under the stairs and wait for her to come home, leaving only to go out though the dog door and play or bark at dogs I could hear yapping off in the distance.

We no longer went to see Andi every day, but sometimes we'd go for a visit and it was always wonderful to see her. People do that—just when the routine is established, they'll change it. On these occasions, after the usual greeting of hugs and kisses, we played the game with people sitting in chairs and also a new game with people sitting or sometimes standing in a long line.

"This is what my grant is for, to see if a dog could signal positive on people in a group," Andi said. "Only Luke has been able to figure it out."

Luke looked up at his name.

We went up and down the line of people and the first couple of times we did so I could tell that Andi and CJ wanted something from me, but I wasn't sure what I was supposed to do. And then I caught an odor coming off of a woman with no hair and with hands that smelled like harsh soap—there it was, the unmistakable metallic smell on her breath. I signaled and was given a biscuit.

That seemed to be the game, though I couldn't be sure because Andi kept leading me to other people who didn't have the same scent, as if I was supposed to signal for them as well. When I did so, though, Andi would stand with her arms crossed and not give me a biscuit. It was very puzzling.

One day I was out in the backyard in heavy new snow, bounding through it, having to leap up with every step because of how deep it was. I heard the sliding door open and saw Gloria standing there. "Want a piece of roast beef?" she called.

I hesitantly took a step toward her, then stopped. I could hear the question in her voice but didn't know if it meant I was in trouble or not.

"Here," she said. She tossed something into the snow a few feet in front of me and I went over to it, having to locate it by smell because it had sunk so far. It was a delicious piece of meat! I raised my head and looked back at Gloria, giving my tail an experimental wag.

"Want another one?" She pitched a piece of meat near me and I jumped on it, snorting, until I found it and ate it in a quick gulp.

When I looked up, Gloria had gone back inside. What, I wondered, had that been all about?

Then I heard Gloria calling from the front yard, "Yoo-hoo, Molly! Dog, want another treat?"

Treat! I bounded over to the gate and found it open. The walk had been shoveled by the man who came by on winter mornings with a truck to clear away the snow. I trotted around the side of the house. Gloria was standing in the driveway.

"Treat," she said. She tossed another piece of meat and I snagged it out of the air. She opened her rear car door. "Okay, want to get in? Treat?"

Her meaning was clear. I hesitantly made my way over to the open door. She pitched some meat onto the rear floor and I jumped in and she shut the door while I gulped down the treat. Then she got in the car, started it, and we drove off down the driveway.

I didn't mind that I wasn't a front-seat dog. I didn't think I would like it with Gloria driving. I stared out the window at the snowy trees and yards for a while, then circled around and lay down on the seat for a nap.

I woke up and shook when the car stopped and Gloria turned it off. She twisted around in her seat. "Careful now. Remember, I fed you a treat? You be nice, Molly."

I wagged at my name. I sniffed at Gloria's hands as they came around my throat, but there was no meat in them. With a sudden click, my collar dropped off and landed on the seat. I lowered my nose to it.

Gloria got out of the car and opened my door. "Come along. Heel. Be a good dog. Don't run off."

We were approaching a building that reeked of dogs. Gloria pushed open the front door and slapped her leg and I followed her inside. Inside was a small room with an open door through which I could hear what had to be more than a dozen dogs barking.

"Hello? Hello?" Gloria called.

A woman came out through the open door and smiled. "Yes, can I help you?"

"I found this poor dog abandoned in the streets," Gloria said. "There's no telling how long he's been living like that, alone and far, far away from his family. Is this where you drop off lost dogs?"

FIFTEEN

I had been in places like this before. In fact, it was a little like where CJ and I went to play with Andi and Luke, except there were far more dogs and the ceiling was low and there was no big area for people to sit in chairs—just cramped aisles filled with dog cages.

I was put in a cage with a cement floor and only a few feet between the gate and the door to a doghouse. The doghouse had a piece of carpet in it that smelled of many dogs, just as the air around me smelled of dogs and was filled with the constant sound of barking.

When the woman came with water or food I rushed to the gate, wagging, hoping she would let me out. I wanted to run, to play, to have people pet me. The woman was nice, but she would not let me out.

Most of the other dogs also rushed to their gates when the woman was nearby. A lot of them barked, and some of them sat quietly, being as good as they knew how. The woman did not let them out.

I did not understand what was happening or why I was in this place of barking dogs. I missed CJ so much I found myself pacing, whimpering a little, and then I'd go into the doghouse and lie on the small piece of carpet, but I wouldn't sleep.

The barking that assaulted my ears was full of fear, with some anger, some pain, some sadness. When I barked, my voice carried with it my heartbreak and my plea to be let out of this place.

At night most of the dogs quieted down, but then one of them would start barking, often a brown and black dog in the kennel next to mine, tall and thin with no tail, and that would stir up the other dogs and pretty soon we'd all be barking again. It was very difficult to sleep under such circumstances.

I pictured myself lying at the foot of CJ's bed. Sometimes in the night I would get too hot and jump down on the floor, but now, missing her so much, I wanted to be lying on that bed no matter how hot it was. I yearned for the touch of her hands on my fur and the familiar and wonderful scent of her skin.

The next morning I was let out of the cage and taken down the hallway and put up on a table, just like at the Vet's. A man and a woman petted me, and the man looked in my ears. The woman took a stick and held it near my head, but the man had his hands on both sides of my face so I couldn't get a good look at it to see if it was a toy.

"Got a hit," the woman said.

"I knew she'd be chipped," the man said.

I was returned to my cage. I was so disappointed I could barely summon the energy to go back and lie down on the carpet. I chewed a little on the doghouse, but even that didn't make me feel better. I sighed, lying down with a groan.

A few hours later the man came back. "Hello, Molly," he said to me. I sat up and wagged, loving to hear my name. He slipped a rope around my neck. "Come on, girl; someone's here to see you."

I smelled CJ the second the man opened the door at the end of the hall. "Molly!" she called. I dashed up to her and she fell to her knees and put her arms around me. I kissed her face and her ear and ran around and around her, the rope trailing behind me and getting all tangled. I gave voice to my relief, crying and crying. She laughed. "Good dog, Molly, you sit, now."

It was hard to sit, but I knew I needed to be a good dog. I sat, wagging my tail, while my girl stood and talked to the man.

"I've been so worried," she said. "I think she got out of the gate when the man came over to shovel the walk after that big snow we had."

Back down the hall, the tall black and brown dog started barking and everyone joined in. I hoped their people would come to take them home soon, too.

"The woman who dropped her off said she was running down the street."

"That's so not like Molly. How much is it total?"

"Sixty dollars."

I wagged at hearing my name. CJ reached down to pet me. "Wait, the woman?"

"Some rich lady," the man said.

"Rich?"

"Well, you know. She had a new Cadillac, dressed expensively, nice hair. Lots of perfume."

"Blond hair?"

"Yeah."

CJ drew in a deep breath. She was looking for something in her purse. I watched attentively because she often kept cookies in there. "Look, was this her?" CJ leaned over the counter.

"I don't think I should say."

"The woman in the picture is my mother."

"What?"

"Yeah."

"Your mother dropped off your dog? Without telling you?"

"Yeah."

There was a silence. CJ was both angry and sad.

"I'm sorry," the man said.

"Yeah."

I was put in the front seat for the car ride. "I missed you so much, Molly. I was so scared something was going to happen to you!" CJ said. She held me to her and I licked her face. "Oh, Molly, Molly," she whispered. "You silly schnoodle not a poodle." She felt sad even though we were back together. "I'm so, so sorry. I didn't know she'd do something like this."

Though there were many interesting things to see out the window, I looked at CJ and licked her hand and put my head in her lap, just like I used to do when

I was a little puppy. It felt so good to be near her I slipped into a quick and exhausted sleep.

I sat up when the car slowed and turned sharply, filling with familiar scents. We were back home. The car became quiet and CJ reached for me, holding my head in both hands. "It's not safe for you here, Molly. I don't know what I am going to do. I can't trust Gloria not to hurt you. I'd die if anything happened to you, Molly."

I wagged a little. CJ let me out of the car and I stepped through the melting snow to the front door—it felt so good to be home. CJ opened the door and walked in and then gasped, the fear rising up in her in a flash.

"Shane!"

CJ's friend Shane was sitting in the living room. He stood, but I didn't go over to him and I didn't wag my tail. There was something wrong about him being here, alone in our house.

"Hi, CJ."

"How did you get in?"

Shane went down on one knee and clapped his hands. "Hiya, Molly." He smelled like smoke. I remained by CJ's side.

"Shane? I said how did you get in?"

"I stuck a rake up through the dog door and turned the dead bolt," he said, laughing.

"What are you doing here?"

"How come you never call me back?"

"You have to get out of here right now. You can't come in my house!"

CJ was angry. I watched her carefully, wondering what was going on.

"You left me no choice. You've been completely ig-noring me."

"Yes, that's what people do when they break up, Shane. They stop talking to each other. You can look it up."

"Okay if I smoke in here?"

"No! I need you to leave."

"Well, I'm not leaving until we talk this thing out."

"What *thing*? Shane, you . . . " CJ took a deep breath. "You called me like thirty times in a row at two in the morning."

"I did?" Shane laughed.

I heard a car pulling into the driveway and went to the window to see who it was. The car door opened and it was Rocky! Trent got out, too. Rocky ran over to lift his leg on a tree.

"Somebody's here," CJ said.

"Should I wait upstairs?"

"What? Are you crazy? I want you to leave."

There was a light knock on the door. I ran over to it and put my nose to the crack, sniffing. Rocky was on the other side doing exactly the same thing. CJ crossed over and opened the door.

"You found her!" Trent said. Then he stopped.

"Hey, Trent," Shane said.

Rocky and I were sniffing each other. I jumped up and joyously grabbed a fold of skin on the back of his neck and yanked on it.

"Sorry, maybe I should come back at a different time," Trent said.

"No!" CJ said.

"Yeah, we're in the middle of something kind of personal," Shane said.

"No, you were in the middle of leaving," CJ said.

"CJ, we *need to talk*," Shane said.

"It sounds like she wants you to leave," Trent said.

Rocky stopped moving. I bit at his face, but he was watching Trent, his muscles rock hard and still.

"Maybe I don't want to leave!" Shane said loudly.

I could feel the anger in Trent then. CJ reached out and put a hand on his wrist. Rocky's ears were up and the fur was rising on the back of his neck.

It occurred to me at that moment that Rocky's purpose was to love and protect Trent, just as mine was to love and take care of CJ.

"Shane," CJ said. "Go. I will see you tomorrow."

Shane was staring at Trent.

"Shane!" CJ said more loudly.

Shane blinked and then looked at her. "What?"

"I'll see you tomorrow, out where you skateboard. Okay? After school."

Shane stood there for a moment, then nodded. He picked up his coat and slung it over his shoulder. As he left he pushed past Trent, who continued to stare at him until he was out the door.

"You're going to see him tomorrow?" Trent asked. He absently petted Rocky on the head. I licked Rocky's mouth.

"No! I'm not going to be here tomorrow."

"What do you mean?"

"Molly and I are leaving. Today, this afternoon. We're going to California."

CJ went to the stairs and headed up to her room and Trent, Rocky, and I all followed.

"What are you talking about?" Trent asked.

CJ went to a closet and pulled out a suitcase. I knew that suitcase; when CJ left me at Trent's house for days and days she had pulled it out of the closet. Rocky was ready to play again, but seeing that suitcase made me anxious and I stuck close to CJ's feet as she began opening things and pulling out her clothes and putting them inside it. "Molly didn't run off. Gloria dumped her off at Animal Control."

"What?"

"I showed the guy at the shelter her picture. Can you believe it?"

"Yeah, well, I'd believe just about anything about your mother."

"So that's it. We're going to California. We'll live on the beach until I get a job. And then when I'm twenty-one I'll get my dad's trust and I'll go to college."

"You're not thinking this through, CJ. College? You haven't finished high school."

"I'll get a GED. Or I'll go to school out there, I don't know."

"I'll go with you," Trent said.

"Oh sure, that'll work."

"You can't go live on a beach; what are you thinking?"

CJ didn't answer, but I could feel her getting angry. Trent watched her for a few minutes. "What about the other thing?" he finally asked quietly.

CJ stopped and looked at him. "What do you mean?"

"The . . . eating."

CJ stared at him, taking a deep breath. "God, Trent, every single day of my life I wake up with this little voice in my head asking what I'm going to eat that day. I can't have your voice in my head, too. I just can't."

Trent looked down at the floor. He seemed sad. Rocky went over to nuzzle him. "Sorry," he said.

CJ pulled out another suitcase and put it on the bed. "I need to get out of here before Gloria sees I got Molly back."

"Hey, let me give you what money I have on me."

"You don't have to do that, Trent."

"I know that. Here."

I yawned anxiously. I loved being with Rocky and Trent but not if CJ was going to take the suitcases and go somewhere without me.

"You're my best friend in the world, Trent," CJ said softly. They hugged each other. "I don't know what I'd do without you and Molly."

There was a loud bang that I recognized as the sound of the front door being shut. "Clarity?" Gloria's voice sang out. "Is that Trent's car?"

CJ and Trent stared at each other. "Yes," CJ called. Her voice sank to a whisper. "Can you keep Molly quiet?"

I wagged.

"Yes," Trent said. He knelt in front of me, stroking my ears. "Molly, shhh," he said very softly. I wagged. Rocky, jealous, shoved his face in front of mine.

CJ went out to the hallway and leaned over the railing. I started to follow, but Trent gently held me back. I strained, feeling a whimper building inside me. I didn't want to let CJ get even two feet away from me, not with those suitcases out. "No," Trent said to me, his voice very muted. "Stay still, Molly."

"Honey, Giuseppe is taking me to the movies and then out to a late dinner, so don't wait up for me."

"Giuseppe," CJ said. Her voice sounded flat with anger.

"No, don't start with me, Clarity June. I've put all that unpleasantness behind me and I expect you to do the same."

"Good-bye, Gloria."

"What's that supposed to mean? Why do you say it like that?"

I couldn't help it, I whined a little, shuffling my feet.

"What was that?" Gloria asked.

CJ turned to look at me. I whimpered again, straining to get to her. "That's Rocky. Trent brought him over to see me. He knows I'm just heartbroken about Molly."

"Do we have to be overrun with dogs all the time?"

"No, Gloria, it won't happen again."

"Thank you. Good night, CJ."

"Good-bye."

CJ came back into the room and shut her door. I bounded to her, licking her face. "Molly, I was four feet away from you, you crazy dog. Hey, you know what you'd be if you're a cocker spaniel poodle? You'd be a cocker doodle doo dog. Yes, you would." CJ kissed me on the face.

Trent carried the suitcases down the stairs and put them in the back of the car while I staked claim to the front seat. Rocky came over to sniff me but didn't try to get in with me, which I wouldn't have allowed anyway.

Trent seemed sad when he gave me a hug. I licked his face. I knew I'd see him and Rocky in a day or two.

Trent leaned in the front window, which CJ lowered after she got in the car. She put my window down, too, so I could breathe in the cold air.

"You know where you're going?" he asked.

"I put it into my phone," CJ said. "We'll be fine, Trent."

"Call me."

"Well, I mean, won't she be able to trace my cell phone calls?"

"Right, she'll just ring up her contacts at the FBI."

CJ laughed. Trent hugged her through the window. "You be a good dog, Molly," he said to me.

I wagged at being a good dog.

"Here we go, Molly," CJ said.

SIXTEEN

We took a long car ride. I elected to curl up on the front seat with my head within easy reach of CJ's hand, and she'd touch me every so often. The love flowed through that hand and eased me into untroubled slumber. It was so much better than being in the place of the barking dogs. I hoped I would never have to go there again. I just wanted to be right where I was, a front-seat dog with my girl, CJ.

We stopped at a place with outdoor tables and wonderful food smells. "It's not too bad out here if I keep my coat on," CJ said as she tied my leash to a table leg. "You'll be okay, right, Molly? I'm just going in there for a second. Don't look at me like that; I'm not leaving you. You're a good dog."

I understood that I was a good dog. I made to follow her as she turned, but the leash stopped me. I strained against it as CJ went through some glass doors and into the building. I didn't understand, and whimpered. If I was a good dog, I should be going with CJ!

"Hello, Molly."

I looked around and there was Shane. I did not wag.

"Good dog." Shane crouched next to me and petted my head. He smelled like smoke and oils and meat. I wasn't sure what to do.

I wagged when I saw CJ. She was holding a bag and standing on the other side of the glass doors, looking at us. Shane waved his hand. CJ came out slowly.

"Hi, babe," Shane said, standing up.

"I guess it would be stupid to ask if you've been following me," CJ said. She set the bag down. I could smell food in it and really, really wanted to poke my head in for a sniff.

"I saw Trent putting suitcases in your car. So you're not going to meet me at the park tomorrow."

"A cousin of mine is sick. I've got to go visit her. I'll be back in a couple of days."

"The point is, you made a commitment to me. Now you're breaking your promise."

"You're right, I'm in breach of contract."

"This isn't funny. This is what you do all the time," Shane said.

"I would have called you."

"That's not the point. I told you I need to talk to

you and you've been blowing me off. And now this, leaving town without even telling me—you gave me no choice *but* to follow you."

I nuzzled CJ's hand to remind her I was here and that I could put the contents of the bag to good use if she wasn't going to.

"What do you want to talk about, Shane?" CJ said quietly.

"Well, *us*." Shane stood up. "I'm having, like, insomnia. I even feel a little sick to my stomach, sometimes. And you don't respond to my messages, how is that supposed to make me feel? Pretty angry, is what. You can't do this to me, babe. I want it to be back the way it was. I miss you."

"Wow," CJ said. She sat at the table and finally, finally, started taking food out of the bag. I sat, being quiet and good.

"Wow what? Hey, can I have some of your fries?" Shane reached out and grabbed some delicious-smelling food and put it in his mouth. I tracked his hand, but he didn't drop anything.

"Help yourself," CJ said.

"You get any ketchup?"

CJ pushed the bag to him and Shane started rooting around in it. "Wow what?" he repeated.

"I just realized something about myself. About how talented I am," CJ said.

"Yeah?"

"I have this ability to find friends who think only about themselves."

Shane halted his food halfway to his mouth. I gave him all of my attention.

"Is that all we are? Friends?" he asked quietly.

CJ exhaled and looked away.

"You know that's not true, babe," Shane said, tantalizing odors swirling out on his words. "It's like you're perfect for me. Everyone says we're great together. Hey, get more ketchup, okay? You only got one packet. That's not enough."

CJ sat for a moment looking at him, then wordlessly got up and went into the building. As soon as she was inside, Shane reached over and looked in her purse, pulling something out that wasn't edible—CJ's phone. He didn't talk to it, though. He stared at it. "Santa Monica?" he said out loud. "Holy . . . " He tossed the phone in the purse and sat back.

CJ came outside and handed him something. Her hand reached down and stroked me. "I'll give you some dinner in a minute, Molly," she said. Having "dinner" and "Molly" in the same sentence made me happy.

"So this cousin, where did you say she lives?" Shane said.

"What?"

"I said where are you going."

"Oh. St. Louis."

"Right. We both know that's a lie."

"Sorry?"

"You don't have a sick cousin. You're taking off so you don't have to deal with me like an honest person."

"And your special talent is being accidentally hilarious."

Shane's anger flashed hot, popping off his skin. He brought his hand down on the table in a hard slap. I jumped up, startled and uncertain what he was doing.

I felt some fear in CJ. What was going on? The fur on my back involuntarily rose—I could feel the prickling of my skin as it did so.

"This ends here," Shane snapped.

"What does?"

"The lying. The manipulating. The selfishness."

"What do you mean?"

"We're getting in our cars and driving back to Wexford. I'll follow you and Molly will ride with me so I know you won't try anything stupid."

I looked up at him. CJ sat for a long time without saying anything or eating. "Okay," she finally said. Her fear had left.

"Good." Shane's anger was receding as well. Whatever had happened between the two of them appeared over.

CJ pushed the sack away from her.

"You're not going to eat that?" Shane asked.

"Knock yourself out."

Shane began eating CJ's meal. I watched mournfully. "Give me your keys; I'll put Molly in your car," CJ said.

"I'll do it," Shane said.

"No, I have to be the one."

"I don't trust you."

"If you do it she won't understand. I have to do it. She won't want to go with you—dogs are good at judging character. I want her to sit in there for a minute and get used to the idea before we go."

"Judge of good character." Shane snorted.

"Are you going to give me the keys or not?"

Shane, chewing, reached into his pocket and tossed

something at her that jangled with the distinctive sound of keys. CJ started to pick them up and dropped them in front of me. I leaned forward for a sniff, smelling smoke and some long-dead animal.

"You have a *rabbit's foot* on your keys now?" CJ said.

"Yeah. It reminds me how lucky I am to have you."

CJ made a noise and scooped up the dead-animal thing with the keys. She untied me. "Come on, Molly."

"I'll be there in a sec," Shane said.

"No rush." CJ led me over to a car and opened the door. I could smell Shane inside, plus other odors, but no dogs. "Okay, Molly, get in!"

This didn't make a lot of sense to me, but I jumped in as instructed, glad it was the front seat. CJ leaned over and the window on my side of the car slid all the way down. "Okay, Molly, you're a good girl," CJ said. "This is all going to work out okay."

CJ shut the car door. I watched, mystified, as she went back to sit with Shane. What were we doing? I stuck my head out the open window, whining softly.

CJ stood and went back into the building. Shane continued to eat without looking up or indicating he was saving any dinner for me.

Then I jerked my head, startled. The back door of the building had opened and now CJ was there, moving quietly away. What was going on? I lost sight of her around the building and whimpered.

I heard the distinctive sound that was her car starting up and whimpered even more loudly. Shane stood up, taking the bag and putting it in the trash. He yawned, looked at his wrist, and then stared at the doors to the building. He cocked his head, rubbing his jaw.

CJ's car came around the corner, speeding right past Shane, who stared at it, frozen. It drove a few dozen yards down the road and the front door opened.

"Molly!" CJ yelled.

Shane turned to look at me. I barked out the window.

"Molly!" CJ yelled again.

Shane lowered his head and ran right at me. I pulled my head out of the window and circled around in the front seat. It seemed very probable that Shane was going to open the door and let me out to be with my girl.

"Molly!" CJ screamed. "Come here! Now! Mol*ly*!"

I turned and scampered across the car seat and flew straight out the open window just as Shane arrived at his car. "Got you!" he said, grabbing me. I felt his hand on my back and I ducked my head and twisted and then broke free. "Stop! Bad dog!" he yelled.

Shane started chasing me. I streaked across the parking lot and bounded through CJ's open door, across her lap, and into the seat next to her, panting. CJ shut the door and drove off.

She was looking up at the top of the front window. "You're just not very bright, are you, Shane," she said. She was driving slowly and after just a few moments pulled over and stopped. She was still looking at the top of the window.

I turned and looked out the back window and there was Shane, running after us. I could tell by his face that he was angry. CJ rolled down her window and very, very slowly began driving again.

Shane stopped running, putting his hands on his knees. CJ stopped her car. He looked up, then started walking toward us. He got closer, then closer still, so close that with the wind at his back I could easily smell the food he'd just been eating. I would have liked to lick somebody's fingers at some point.

The car started rolling again. CJ reached into her purse and picked up the dead-animal keys. She held them out the window, waving them, then tossed them over the top of the car and into the tall grass on the side of the road. Then she drove away. I watched through the back window as Shane walked up to where we'd been and stared into the field, his hands on his hips.

I could have found the keys easily, but people aren't especially good at locating lost things. That's one of the reasons why they have dogs. In this case, though, something told me that CJ had thrown the keys for reasons that had nothing to do with a game of find-and-bring-back.

CJ soon stopped the car and poured food into a bowl for me. I knew she wouldn't forget to feed me, but frankly, what Shane had been pulling from the bag had smelled a lot more interesting.

It was the longest car ride I can ever remember taking. In the night CJ parked the car under a light and slept on the front seat and I slept with my head resting on her legs. We drove through a very snowy place and then a windy and dry place.

Most of the time when CJ ate, someone would hand her a bag of food from a building. Sometimes we ate at an outside table. The meals were exotic and delicious. This was one of the best car rides I'd ever taken!

I was in a deep sleep when the car stopped and shut off. I shook myself, blearily looking around. We were with a lot of other cars. The sun was not yet very high in the sky. "We're here, Molly!" CJ said.

We got out of the car and the smell hit me and, just like that, I knew exactly where we were.

When I was a dog who Worked doing Find and Show, I would often come with my people, Jakob or Maya, to this very place. It was the ocean. CJ led me down to the water and let me off the leash and laughed and I leaped into the water, a couple of days' worth of pent-up energy inciting me to run though the waves in lunges.

We played there for a while and then walked up to some outdoor tables. CJ gave me water and food and sat with me in the sun as it got warmer.

"Nice day," a man said. "Pretty dog."

He reached down to pet me. His hands smelled like mint.

"Thanks," CJ said.

"Where're you from? I'm going to guess Ohio."

"What? No, I'm from here."

The man laughed. "Not with that coat you're not. My name's Bart."

"Hi," CJ said. She looked away.

"Okay, I get it, you don't want company. It's just such a nice day, I wanted to say hello to you and your dog. Be careful the cops don't catch your pooch on the beach; they'll ticket you if they do." The man smiled again and then went over to a table and sat by himself.

For the next couple of days we would sleep in the car and then CJ would go to stand under some flowing water and take me with her into a small building where she would change her clothes. Then we would drive around, mostly to restaurants, by the smell of them. CJ would tie me up in the shade and go inside and sometimes come right out and sometimes stay in for a while. By the end of the day her hair and clothing was rich with wonderful cooking odors.

CJ always took me to the ocean to run and play, but she didn't ever swim herself.

"Oh, you are such a good dog, Molly," CJ said. "It's a lot harder to get a job than I thought it would be, even for minimum wage."

I wagged at being a good dog. We were, as far as I was concerned, having one of the most wonderful times ever. We were either in the car or outside every day!

Several nights later, as we were settling in to go to sleep, it began to rain. CJ usually left the windows cracked open, but when the rain started to come in she rolled them up, which was why I didn't smell the man. I saw him only when he emerged from the rain under the tall street lamp. It was as if the night and the rain came together and suddenly made a wet, dark man. I sat perfectly still, watching him. He had long hair on his head and face and was carrying a big bag over his shoulder. He was looking right at us.

I felt the fear rise in CJ and knew she saw him, too. A low growl came from my throat.

"It's okay, Molly," CJ said. I wagged. The man looked around slowly—he seemed to be examining the other few cars in the parking lot. Then he turned to look at us again.

CJ inhaled sharply as the man strode deliberately toward us.

SEVENTEEN

The man came right up to the car and when his hand reached out to touch the door I hit the window in full snarl, barking and snapping. I was letting him know if he tried to get in the car he would be met with teeth. And I *would* bite him; I could feel it in my mouth.

Rain was pouring off of the man's long hair, flowing down his face as he bent over to see us. He was ignoring me and was instead watching CJ. CJ was so afraid a small cry came from her lips. I could hear her heart beating.

I was enraged that anyone would frighten my girl. Incensed, I scratched at the glass, hurling myself at it again and again, wanting to get through it. My bark had the same savage quality to it that I'd brought to the barn to protect Clarity from Troy.

The man smiled and knocked at the window. I bit at the glass where his knuckle was rapping. Then he straightened and looked around.

"Go away!" CJ yelled.

The man didn't react. After a minute, he walked off, disappearing into the gloom.

"Oh my God. Oh, Molly, you are such a good dog," CJ said, throwing her arms around me. I licked her face. "I was so scared. He looked like, like a zombie or something! But you protected me, didn't you? You're a guard dog, a guard dog and a poodle— a goodle! I love you so much."

There was a huge bang and CJ screamed. The man was back and he had a stick and he had hit the window with it. He was smiling—all I could see in the rain and the dark were his crooked, yellow teeth, his eyes hidden by the brim of his hat. He hit the window again and I put my face to the glass and now I could see his eyes and I stared at them, my mouth in a snarl, drool flying. He was frightening my girl and I let the rage flow into me and I desired nothing more but to bite that man.

He laughed, looking in the window. He pointed his finger at me and then shook it, the way Gloria did when she talked to me. And then he straightened and vanished into the wet darkness.

I'd always thought of sticks as being something to play with, but now I understood a stick could also be a bad thing, if you were in a scary place and the person holding it wasn't trying to play with you.

The rain made a loud roar on the car all night. CJ didn't sleep at first, but gradually the fear left her and she put her head down. I pressed up against her as I dozed to let her know she was being protected by her dog.

The next morning it was very bright outside. The wet ground smelled really interesting, but CJ wanted to go to the place where we could sit at outdoor tables. When we got there the nice man we'd met a few days before greeted us and leaned down to pet me. He was taller than most men I'd ever met. His hands smelled like mint again. "Let me buy you breakfast," he said.

"No thank you," CJ said. "I just want coffee."

"Come on. What do you want, an omelet?"

"I'm good."

"She'll have a veggie omelet," the nice man said to the woman who brought food.

"I said I was fine," CJ said as the woman left.

"Hey, sorry, but you look like you're hungry. You an actress? Model, you're probably a model. You're pretty enough. I'm Bart. My parents named me Bartholomew, I'm like, thanks for that. So I pick 'Bart,' but are you ready for it? My last name is Simpson. So yeah, I'm Bart Simpson. Doh! What's your name?"

"Wanda," CJ said.

"Hi, Wanda."

We all sat comfortably together for a few minutes, enjoying the smell of bacon coming from the kitchen.

"So was I right? Modeling, that's why you're so thin," the man said.

"Actually, I'm thinking of becoming an actress."

"Well, good for you. I represent actresses; that's what I do. I'm a talent agent. You have an agent?"

I sat up because the woman brought out food and set it in front of CJ, who started to eat it but then stopped and gave me toast!

"No, I'm good when it comes to representation, actually," CJ said. "But thanks."

"What did I tell you? You were hungry. Look, I know what's going on."

CJ stopped eating and looked at the man.

"I go for a walk on the beach in the morning. I've seen you get out of your car, like you're just pulling up, except I came down here the other night and I saw it parked there. You think you're the first actor to sleep in a car? There's no shame in it."

CJ started eating again, but more slowly. "I'm not ashamed," she said softly. She tossed a piece of cheesy food at me and I expertly snagged it out of the air.

"What you should do is come home with me, now."

"Oh. Like, as a reward for the omelet?" CJ said.

The man laughed. "No, course not. I have more than one bedroom. Just until you're on your feet."

"Actually, we're on vacation and I have to leave tomorrow."

The man laughed again. "You really *are* an actress. What are you worried about, that you won't be able to get what you need? Whatever it is, I can get it for you."

"What?"

"I'm trying to protect you here, help you out. What's with the hostility?"

"Drugs? Is that what you're talking about? I'm not

on drugs." I could feel CJ getting angry, but I didn't know why.

"Okay, my mistake. Most of the girls are, to tell you the truth; I mean, this is LA."

"Most of the girls. So you've got what, a harem? A stable?"

"I said I represent—"

CJ stood up. "I know what you *represent*. Bart. Come on, Molly." She gathered my leash.

"Hey, Wanda," the man called after us. CJ did not stop walking. "You know you're going to see me again, right? Right?"

We spent that day sitting on a blanket on the sidewalk. There was a box on the blanket and every so often someone would stop and drop something in the box and nearly always they would talk to me. "Nice doggy," they usually said. CJ would say, "Thank you." I loved seeing all the people.

We stayed on that blanket until the sun went down, and then CJ fed me. "I've got enough to get you some more food tomorrow, Molly," she said. I wagged to show her that I'd heard my name and was happy I was eating.

As we got back to the car, CJ slowed. "Oh no," she said.

The ground around the car was covered with small pebbles. Curious, I went to sniff them. They glinted in the light from the street lamps.

"No, Molly, you'll cut your feet!" CJ pulled the leash and I understood that I had done something wrong. I looked at her. "Sit," she said. She tied the leash to a post so that I couldn't follow her to the car.

The windows were open, and she stuck her head in. I whined because if we were getting in the car I didn't want to be forgotten.

A car slowly approached us. A beam of light came from the side of it and landed on CJ, who whirled around to look at it.

"Is that your car?" a woman said out of her window. CJ nodded. The woman got out of her side and a man got out of the other and I saw they were both police officers.

"They take anything?" the policewoman asked.

"I had clothes, stuff like that," CJ answered.

The policeman came over to pet my head. "Nice doggy," he said. I wagged. His fingers smelled spicy.

"We'll take a report," the policewoman said. "Insurance will pay for the glass and maybe the contents, too. Depends on your deductible, and the like."

"Oh. Well, I'm not sure it's worth it."

"No problem," the policewoman said. "See some ID?"

CJ handed something to the policewoman. The policeman stood up and took whatever it was and went back to sit in his car. CJ came over to me. "Good dog, Molly," she said. She seemed a little afraid, for some reason.

The policewoman was walking around the car. CJ unclipped my leash. The policeman stood up. "She's in the system," he said.

The policewoman looked at CJ, and CJ turned and ran! I didn't know what we were doing, but I was more than happy to gallop along beside her.

We hadn't gone very far before I heard footsteps behind us. It was the policeman. He caught up to us. "How long you want to do this?" he asked as he ran next to us.

CJ faltered, then stopped. She put her hands on her knees and I licked her face, ready to take off again.

"I'm doing a 10K this weekend, so I appreciated the opportunity to do a quick wind sprint," the policeman told her. He reached down to pet me and I wagged. "Want to tell me why you took off like that?" he asked.

"I don't want to go to jail," CJ said.

"You're not going to jail; we don't put people in jail for running away from home. But you're a minor and you're in our system, so you're going to have to come with us."

"I *can't*."

"I know it looks that way now, but believe me, you don't want to be a street person. What do they call you?"

"CJ."

"Well, CJ, I am going to have to cuff you because you took off on us like that."

"What about Molly?"

"We'll call Animal Control."

"No!"

"Don't worry; nothing's going to happen to her. They'll hold her until you can pick her up. Okay?"

We went back to the car and the people stood around and talked. Eventually a truck came with a cage on the back. I didn't want to go for a car ride in that cage, and shrank to the ground when a man got out of the truck with a pole that had a loop on the end.

"No, wait, it's okay. Molly, come here," my girl said. I dutifully went to her. She knelt down and took my head in her hands. "Molly, you're going to have to go to the shelter for a few days, but I will come get you. I promise, Molly. Okay? Good dog."

CJ seemed sad. She led me over to the truck, and the man with the pole opened the cage door. I looked up at her. *Really?*

"Come on, Molly. Up!" CJ said. I jumped up into the cage, then turned around. CJ put her face next to mine and I licked the salty tears on her face. "You'll be okay, Molly. I promise."

The car ride in the cage was not fun. When the truck stopped, the man opened the cage and slipped the loop at the end of his pole over my neck and we went into a building.

I smelled them and heard them before he even opened the door: dogs. Inside the building the floor was slick and I couldn't get a good purchase on it and the barking was so loud I couldn't hear my nails as they scrabbled for traction. The din was amazing, an absolute riot of dogs. He took me back into a room and had me walk up a ramp until I was on a metal table. Two other men were there and they held me.

"She's friendly," said the man with the pole.

I felt a hand grab the fur behind my head and then there was a small, sharp pain. I wagged, my ears low, to let them know that though they had hurt me, it was okay.

"So that's the first thing we do, is inoculate them.

Won't hurt them if it's redundant, and that way we avoid a distemper epidemic," one of the men said. Because it was so loud, he had to shout. "So that'll be your job as part of the induction process."

"Got it," said the third man.

"The owner's over at the women's shelter. She's a minor," said the man with the pole.

"Yeah, well, she's got four days."

I was led down a narrow corridor. The floor here was just as slippery—it was very unnerving. The hall was lined with cages and every one of them had a dog in it. Some of them were barking and some of them were crying. Some of them were at the gate and some of them were cowering in the back. The place stank with fear.

I had been in places full of barking dogs before but never as loud as this.

A strong chemical smell wafted on the air. It smelled like the machine in the basement where CJ liked to put her clothes to get them wet. And I could smell cats, too, though I couldn't hear any because of all the noise from the dogs.

I was put in a small cage. There was no doghouse, but there was a small towel on the slick floor. The man shut the cage door. There was a drain in the floor and I sniffed it. Many dogs had marked it with their scent. I chose not to do so at that time.

Across the hall from me, a large black dog was throwing himself at his cage door and growling. When he saw me he met my eyes and snarled. He was a bad dog.

I curled up around the towel. I missed CJ. The

heartbroken barking and crying and howling went on and on.

After a while, my voice joined theirs. I couldn't help it.

EIGHTEEN

I was scared and, despite the constant din from all the dogs, I had never felt so alone. I curled up on the towel on the floor in as tight a ball as I could manage. I was given food and water, served in paper bowls. The dog in the cage across from me ripped up his bowl, but I did not.

After a long time had passed, a man came to get me. He led me out of the cage and put straps on my face so that I could only open my jaws a small amount. He took me into a cold room with the same slippery floor. It was quieter in there, but I could still hear barking.

I could smell many dogs in the room, and their scent carried with it fear and pain and death. This was a place where dogs had died. The man led me over to a hole that was covered with a metal grate. I stood, my legs trembling. I tried to press into the man for comfort, but he backed away from me.

I recognized the scent of the other man—he had been in the room the day before. I wagged my tail at him a little, but he did not say my name.

"Okay, this the first time you've been in here?" the man who had led me in said.

"No, I loaded out the bodies of the ones we euthanized yesterday," the man I knew said.

"Okay, well, this is the aggression test. They fail this, they're short-tracked. That means they only get the four days before we put them down. Otherwise, we give them longer if we're not crowded."

"Are you ever not crowded?"

"Ha, yeah, you're catching on. Sometimes we're not completely packed, but usually it's like this." The other man went to a counter and grabbed a bowl full of food. "What I'm going to do, here, is let her smell this and get used to the idea that it's her food. Then I start to pull it away using this plastic hand. Okay? If she turns to snap at the hand, that's aggression. If she growls, that's aggression."

"How does the dog know it is a hand?"

"It's shaped like a hand and it's kinda flesh colored. It's a hand."

"Well, all right. Looks more like just a wedge of white plastic to me."

"So growl at it."

Both men laughed.

I did not know what was happening, but I had never felt so miserable. The man in front set the food down in front of me. I started to salivate—were they planning to feed me? I was hungry. I put my nose down and the man came at me with a big stick.

I'd learned from being with CJ in the car that when times were scary sticks could be bad, so as the man poked the stick at my nose I growled, too frightened to do anything else.

"Okay, that's it," the man with the food said. "Aggressive. Short track."

"But the owner said she was coming back," the other man objected.

"They all say that. Helps them to feel better when they're dropping off Fido. But you know what? They never do."

"Still . . ."

"Hey, I know you're new, but you're going to have to get used to it real fast or you're not going to last. It's an aggressive dog. So, that's it."

"Yeah, all right."

I was led back to my cage. I curled up, my eyes closed. After a time I was able to fall asleep, despite the physical assault of the barking.

A day went by, and then another. I felt anxious and sick. I was becoming accustomed to the noise and the smells but never to being without my girl. When I barked, it was with the pain of separation.

Another day went by and this one was the worst one because it really did seem as though my girl had forgotten all about me. I needed CJ to come get me now.

The din was so loud that I sensed the presence of a woman outside my cage door without hearing her.

She opened the door and patted her knees. Slowly, unsure, I approached her, my ears down, wagging. She hooked a leash onto my collar and led me past the other cages, the dogs howling and barking and snarling and whimpering at me.

The woman took me to a door and when it opened CJ was there. Sobbing, I jumped up, trying to lick her face.

"Molly!" she said. "Oh, Molly, Molly, are you okay? I am so sorry; Molly, are you okay?"

For several minutes we hugged and kissed each other. My girl. She hadn't forgotten about me after all. I felt the love pouring out of her and it made my heart soar.

CJ led me over to a car and I joyously followed. She opened the back door, but I was so happy to be leaving I sailed inside and then I got to see why I wasn't going to get to be a front-seat dog—Gloria was there, sitting in my usual spot. She looked at me and I wagged because I was even glad to see her, so elated was I to be leaving the place of barking dogs.

"Good dog, good dog," CJ said as she slipped behind the wheel and started the car.

We drove to a place that was every bit as loud as the place with all the dogs, but these were all people noises. I heard cars and busses and shouting and other sounds and every so often a giant thundering noise that would seem to shake the very air.

CJ got a box out of the trunk and opened a metal mesh door at one end of it. "Go into the crate, Molly." I looked at her questioningly. "Crate," she repeated. I lowered my head and went inside. "Good dog, Molly. This is your crate."

When I was inside I could see out through the metal grate, but the rest of the crate was solid. "You're going to go for a plane ride, Molly. It will be okay." CJ poked her fingers through the grate.

It was one of the strangest days of my life. Several times the crate was tilted one way or another, and eventually I was put in a room and there was another dog in it I could smell but not see. The dog started barking, but I was all barked out and just wanted to sleep, though a teeth-rattling roar soon filled the room, vibrating my crate and making my body feel heavy, as if I were on a car ride. The dog barked and barked and barked, but I had heard worse recently and wasn't annoyed. The vibrations seemed to drive fatigue into my bones and I was soon asleep.

After some more tilting and moving, I was in a place with a lot of people and the same loud noises. CJ appeared and opened the crate and I bounded out, shaking myself off and ready to have fun. She led me outside to a patch of grass to do my business, and the combination of scents floating on the cold air told me we were now close to home. I wagged with happiness.

A man gave us a car ride. Gloria sat up next to him and CJ sat with me. I wanted to sit in CJ's lap, I was so glad to be with her again, but when I tried she laughed and pushed me away.

When we got home, Trent was there and so was Rocky! I bounded out of the car and ran to my brother and he sniffed me up and down, no doubt smelling all the dogs and people I'd met since I'd seen him last. Then we wrestled and played in the snow, but I was still feeling insecure and didn't let Rocky pull me more than a few feet away from CJ's feet as she sat on the steps with Trent.

"It was . . . an adventure, that's for sure," CJ said. "I have to say, next time I go to California I want to stay in a place with a shower. The Ford didn't have one."

"What happened to the Ford?"

"God, Gloria made me sell it. Supposedly, I had too much independence—that's the new theory, that I ran off because of independence. Also, she wants me to see a shrink. She's convinced that anyone who wouldn't want to live with her has to be crazy."

"How was it? Having her show up, I mean."

"You want to know what? It was pure, unadulterated Gloria. She comes to this women's shelter and she's saying, 'Thank God, thank God,' and she tells the staff thank you for taking care of her 'little girl.' I think maybe she thought they were going to give her an award or something. Mother of the Year. And then when we get in the car she asks me if I want to go on a tour with her to see celebrities' houses."

Rocky had tried several times to get me to chase him around the yard and now gave up, rolling on his back and baring his throat for me to chew. CJ reached out and petted me. It felt so good to be home.

"So then she gives me this lecture and tells me she's already arranged for a broker to sell the car, which is in Impound, I guess. And then we go out to eat at the Ivy, which is this restaurant where you're supposed to be able to see all these movie stars. She tells me she's disappointed in me and that she loved *her* mother, which is this thing she always says, that her mother was worse and yet Gloria still loved her, so that makes me, I don't know, weak or something. So I'm trying to talk to her about it, about why I ran away, I mean, and she interrupts me to ask if I want to try her wine because in California the wine is as good as in France. In a restaurant, she wants to give a minor wine. And then we pick up Molly and fly first class and she flirts with the flight attendant the whole way—she thinks that because he kept asking if she wanted more wine he must have had a crush on her, though he was like twenty-five years old and obviously not into women, if you know what I mean."

"What about Molly? I mean, what happens now?"

"Well, that's the question, isn't it. I told her if anything ever happens to Molly again I'm going to write a book about how I was forced to run away because my mother was a dog abuser and I'm going to self-publish it and go on a national book tour. That gave her something to think about."

Rocky and I had both stopped wrestling when we heard my name. Now he jumped up and tried to climb on my back.

"Rocky, stop that," Trent said. Rocky dropped off of me and went over to Trent for reassurance.

"Let's walk," CJ said, standing up. She and Trent snapped leashes onto our collars and then we went to the side gate and down the street. It felt so great to be going for a walk!

"Oh, and then she tells me how helpful Shane was,

that he was the one who said I was in LA. This is after I told her what a creep he is! She takes his calls and chats with him and probably does her laugh and everything."

"I tried to find you, you know. I mean, on the Internet, I was looking at postings, anything with your name on it."

"I should have called. I'm sorry. I just . . . It wasn't the best time for me, and when things are bad, I can't make myself communicate."

"I found something, though, while I was looking," Trent said.

"What?"

"Actually, it's more like what I didn't find. I just noticed that on the real estate office site where your mom has an office? Her picture is there, but there are no property listings for her."

"Is it her glamour shot? I hate that."

"Yeah, I think so. It's really fuzzy, out of focus."

"She's pretty sure that someone's going to see that picture and sign her to a record deal."

"You can go back three years on that site and find sales. Your mom's name isn't on any of them."

"What does that mean?"

"I guess it means that in the past three years your mother hasn't sold or listed a house."

"You're kidding."

"No. Check it yourself."

"I had no idea. She's never said anything about it."

Rocky went rigid and saw it the same time I did: a squirrel had bounded into the street and was now frozen, staring at us, probably paralyzed with fear. Our paws digging into the snow, the two of us strained at our leashes, the squirrel darting over to a tree and scrambling up it. CJ and Trent led us over to the tree. Rocky put his paws on the tree and barked, a joyous noise that let the squirrel know we could have caught him if we'd really tried.

"Hi!" a woman called from behind us. I lifted my nose and could smell that I had met her before, though I wasn't sure where.

"Sheryl, hi," CJ said. "This is my friend Trent."

The woman bent and held out her hand for Rocky and me to sniff. She had a glove on that smelled delicious, but I knew better than to try to take it in my mouth. "Hi, Trent. Hi, Molly."

"We met at the Christmas party," Trent said.

"Yes, of course," Sheryl said.

They stood talking for a little bit. Rocky and I kept glancing around for squirrels, but then some uneasiness came over my girl and I snapped my attention back to her. "Um," CJ said. She and Trent looked at each other. "Sheryl, at the party, when Molly signaled . . . We never heard. I mean . . . "

The woman nodded. "Of course. Well, there was . . . a lump. But it was so small, and I was so busy, I would have kept putting it off if it hadn't been for Molly."

I wagged.

"We caught it in plenty of time, my doctor says. So . . . " The woman gave a light laugh. "I called and told your mother about it all; didn't she say anything?"

"No, she didn't mention it. But I've been . . . traveling."

The woman leaned over and kissed me. I wagged

and Rocky stuck his head in the way. "Thank you, Molly," the woman said. "You saved my life."

When we got back to the house, Trent and Rocky left and CJ and I went inside. There was a room I never went into because it was where Gloria liked to sit and look at papers, and this was where we went now. There were no food and no toys, so I had no idea why we'd bother with the place. CJ pulled open drawers and looked at papers, while I curled up in a ball and contemplated a nap.

"Oh no," CJ said quietly. I heard the word "no," but it didn't seem that I was a bad dog.

CJ suddenly stood up and went down the hallway. She felt angry and she was stomping her feet. "Gloria!" she shouted.

"I'm back here!"

We went to Gloria's room. She was sitting in a chair in front of a television.

"What are these?" CJ asked loudly, rattling the papers. Gloria stared, her eyes narrowed, and then sighed.

"Oh. Those."

"Is our house in foreclosure?"

"I don't know. It's too confusing."

"But . . . It says we're six months behind. Six months! Is that true?"

"That can't be right. Has it been that long?"

"Gloria. It says we're in foreclosure proceedings. If we don't do something, we're going to lose the house!"

"Ted said he could loan me some money," Gloria said.

"Who's Ted?"

"Ted Petersen. You'd like him. He looks like a male model."

"Gloria! There are all kind of bills in your desk that aren't even open."

"You've been *snooping in my desk*?"

"We're behind in our house payments and you don't think I have a right to know about it?"

"That office is my private place, Clarity."

The anger was slowly leaving my girl. She dropped into a chair, the papers falling to the floor. I sniffed at them.

"Well, okay," CJ said. "I think we're going to have to tap into Dad's trust."

Gloria didn't say anything. She was looking at the television.

"Gloria, are you listening? You always said there's a provision in there that if we really need the money for something, like if I needed surgery or whatever, we can withdraw funds. I'd say losing the house counts."

"Why do you think we're behind in the first place?"

"Sorry?"

"There wasn't enough in there."

CJ was very still, and I could hear her heartbeat. I nuzzled her hand in concern, but she ignored me. "What are you saying? Are you saying you took the money? Dad's money? My money? *You took my money?*"

"It never was *your* money, Clarity. It was the trust your father set up so that you could live. All the money I spent was for you. How do you think I paid for your food, for the house? How about our trips, the cruise?"

"The cruise? You invaded the trust so we could go on a cruise ship?"

"Someday you'll be a mother yourself. Then you'll understand."

"What about your stuff, Gloria? What about your cars, your clothes?"

"Well, obviously I had to have clothes."

CJ jumped to her feet. The rage in her made her whole body rigid, and I cowered from it. "I hate you! I hate you! You are the most evil person in the world!" she screamed.

Sobbing, she fled down the hallway, and I was right on her heels. She scooped up some things from the kitchen counter as we went out the door and she went to Gloria's car and opened the door. I jumped in— front seat!

CJ was still sobbing as we drove down her street. I looked out the window but did not see the squirrel Rocky and I had chased earlier. CJ's hand was to her ear, holding her phone.

"Trent? Oh my God, Gloria spent all my money. My money, Dad's trust, it's gone! She said she took it out for me, but that's a lie, it's a *lie,* she went on vacations and she bought herself stuff, and it was all my money. Oh, Trent, that was my college fund; that was my . . . Oh God." The grief in CJ was overwhelming. I whimpered, putting my head in her lap.

"No, what? . . . No, I left. I'm driving. . . . What? No, I didn't steal her car. It's not *hers*; she bought it with my money!" CJ shouted.

She was quiet for a moment. She wiped her eyes. "I know. Can I come over? I've got Molly."

I thumped my tail.

"Wait," CJ said. She was quiet, her body still, and then a new emotion boiled up in her: fear. "Trent, it's Shane. He's right behind me."

CJ twisted in her seat, then faced the front. I felt a heaviness that I knew meant the car was changing speed. "No, I'm sure. He's following me! I'll call you back!"

CJ tossed her phone onto my seat and it bounced and fell to the floor in front of me. I looked at it but elected not to climb down to sniff it. "Hang on, Molly," CJ said. I had trouble holding myself steady. I heard a car honk. The car turned and I fell against the door. We stopped suddenly and then were driving again. Another turn came.

CJ took a deep breath. "Okay. Okay, I think he's gone, Molly," she said. She leaned over to pick up her phone, grunting, and then something slammed me so hard I lost track of everything. I heard CJ scream and a shock of pain went through my body and I couldn't see. I felt us falling.

It took me a long moment to understand what was happening. I was no longer in the front seat. I was lying on the inside roof of the car and CJ was above me in her seat. "Oh God, Molly, are you okay?"

I could taste blood in my mouth and was not able to wag my tail or move my legs. CJ unbuckled herself and slid out of her seat. "Molly!" she screamed. "Oh God, Molly, please, I can't live without you, please, Molly, please!"

I felt her terror and her sadness and wanted to comfort her, but all I could do was look at her. She cradled my head in her hands. Her hands felt so good on my fur. "I love you, Molly. Oh, Molly, I'm so sorry, oh, Molly, oh, Molly," she said.

I couldn't see her anymore, and her voice sounded distant. "Molly!" she called again.

I knew what was happening. I could feel the darkness rising all around me, and, as I did so, I remembered being with Hannah, on the last day I was alive as Buddy. How, when I slipped away, I found myself thinking of baby Clarity and hoping she would find a dog to take care of her.

With a jolt, I realized something.

I had been that dog.

NINETEEN

Always before, when the warm, gentle waves swept over me and washed away my pain, I let myself drift with the current, floating without direction. Each time I had been reborn before it had been something of a surprise: I always felt as if I had completed my mission, fulfilled my purpose.

Not this time. My girl was in trouble and I needed to get back to her. When the waves came and the sensation of her hands on my fur faded from me, I actively pushed, fighting to make my limbs respond. I wanted to be reborn.

When awareness came and I knew I had returned, it was a relief. I had the sense that I had been asleep for less time than in the past, which was good. Now I just needed to grow large and strong enough to find my way back to CJ and be her dog.

My mother was a light brown color, as were my two siblings—both sisters, both aggressively seeking to feed. When sounds began to emerge from the liquidy fuzz as distinct and identifiable, I could hear barking dogs. Lots of them.

I was back in a place of barking dogs. After a time, the din became so much a part of the background that I stopped hearing it.

While the light was still muddled and my limbs were weak, I could do nothing more than sleep and feed, but I remembered what to do, how to push forward to my mother, and bit back my impatience with how helpless I was.

There were a couple of different women whose voices I could hear occasionally and whose presence I could feel from time to time. My mother's body would tremble as she wagged her tail as these people came; I would feel it as I nursed.

The first time my vision had cleared and I saw one of these people, though, I was shocked. She was a giant, looming far over us. "Such cuties," she said. "Good dog, Zoey."

My mother wagged, but I was staring up at the enormous woman, blinking, trying to focus. When her hand came down to pet my mother, I cringed— the hand was huge, larger than me, larger than my mother's head.

As we got older, I watched my sisters skittering over to say hi to the giant women when they came to the cage. Fearful, I hung back, not even trailing after my mother when she went to be petted. Why weren't my siblings afraid?

When the woman picked me up, her hands enveloping me like a blanket, I growled at her, though her strong fingers held me trapped. "Hello, Max. You a fierce dog? You going to be a watchdog?"

Another giant woman came up to peer at me. I growled at her, too. "I'm thinking the father is a Yorkie, maybe?" she said.

"Sure looks like Chihuahua-Yorkie mix," the woman holding me said. Her name, I would soon learn, was Gail, and of all the people in that loud place, she spent the most time with me.

They called me Max, and my sisters were called Abby and Annie. When I played with my sisters it was always with a sense that what I should really be doing was finding CJ, though always before, when I'd been in a place of barking dogs, she'd found me. What I needed to do, probably, was wait, and she'd come. My girl had always come.

One day Abby, Annie, and I were let out into a small pen with some other dogs. They were all puppies and ran to meet us, too young to know you're not supposed to directly touch noses and jump up on another dog without pause. I disdainfully slid to the side of the one who assaulted me, ignoring his tongue and moving to show him that we should be politely sniffing each other's genitalia first.

There were other dogs in other pens and when I gazed through the chain fence at them I received a shock: they, too, were enormous! Where was this place, where the dogs and people were gigantic monsters? I went to the fence to sniff a white dog and he lowered his head and it was ten times the size of my mother's. We sniffed through the fence and then I backed up, barking, letting him know I wasn't afraid (though of course I was).

"It's okay, Max. Go play," Gail the giantess said to me.

Other than when we were in pens, we were allowed no time to be off leash. I was being led down a hallway full of cages and dogs back to my cage when I spotted a dog who looked a little like Rocky: same eager set to the head, same thin-boned legs. I knew it wasn't Rocky, but the resemblance was so strong it made me pause—though this dog, like so many others in this place, was gigantic.

That's when it occurred to me: it wasn't that the people and the dogs were huge; it was that I was *little*. I was a tiny little dog!

I had met tiny dogs in my life, of course. But I had never before considered that I might be one—I had always been large, because people sometimes need the protection a large dog affords them. CJ certainly did! I remembered being in the car with her, when the man tried to get inside and he hit the window with a stick and I made him go away by snarling at him. Would a tiny little dog be able to accomplish that?

Yes, I decided. When it happened again, I could still snarl, still let the man know that if he opened the door I would bite him. Wrestling with little dogs had taught me they have very sharp teeth. I would just have to convince bad men that I would be willing to sink mine into their hands. That would stop them from trying to get into the car.

Back in my pen, I watched Abby and Annie play and they watched me watch them. Naturally, they were looking to me for leadership, as I was obviously the more experienced dog. Or at least, they should, though when I went to join their frolicking they ganged up on me instead of submitting to my dominance. That was something else: little dogs usually wound up on their backs, pinned down. I would have to work hard to prove that just because I was small I wasn't a dog that others could oppress.

I put my new resolution into action the next time we were penned with other puppies, letting them know that no matter what their size, I was *the* dog to pay attention to. A goofy black and brown canine, all feet and ears, obviously destined to be as big as Rocky someday, thought he'd put me down with his superior weight, but I slipped out from his forelimbs and went after him with snapping teeth and he fell over on his back in docile surrender.

"Be nice, Max," Gail said to me. Yes, my name was Max, and I was a dog to be reckoned with.

Once my sisters and I were no longer nursing, we were taken for a car ride, in cages, to some outdoor pens. Our mother was kept in a separate kennel, which upset Abby and Annie but didn't bother me: I knew what was coming. It was the time when people came and puppies went home with them.

The open pens had no bottom; they sat right on the ground. I wanted to roll in the green grass, luxuriate in the sun, but I was momentarily stunned by the smells and sounds. The roar of noise was constant, not with barking but with the same sort of mechanical rumbles and shrieks that greeted me the day I was tilted left and right inside a plastic crate, the day CJ picked me up from the place of barking dogs by the ocean. And the smells: cars, dogs, people, water, leaves, grass, and, on top of all of it, food—great gusts of food smells swirling around me. Abby and Annie seemed as dazzled as I was by the sheer volume of sensual stimulus—we just stood there, noses to the wind, drinking it in.

Many people came by, peering into the pens and sometimes spending a little time playing with the dogs within. "Look at the puppies!" people would say when they gazed in on my sisters and me. Abby and Annie would race over in loving enthusiasm, but I always shied away. I was waiting for CJ.

Two men were soon kneeling by our cage, poking their fingers through the fencing, and Gail came over to talk to them.

"We think they have Yorkie in them. Their mother is the Chihuahua over there," she said.

Gail opened the gate and Abby and Annie bounded out, the two men laughing in delight. I slunk along the back of the cage, keeping my head low.

That was the last I saw of my sisters. I was glad that the two men, who were obviously good friends, took them as a pair so that Abby and Annie could see each other the way Rocky and I stayed together.

"Don't worry, Max. You'll find a home," Gail said to me.

A few days later we were back in the same place, and on that occasion my mother, plus a few other dogs, went home with people. Three times the door to my pen was opened, and all three times I slunk down to the ground and growled when people tried to pick me up.

"What happened? Was he abused?" a man asked Gail.

"No, he was born in the shelter. I don't know, Max is just . . . anti-social. He doesn't play well with other dogs, either. I think he'd do well with someone who stays at home and doesn't receive a lot of visitors."

"Well, that's not me," the man said with a laugh. He eventually left with a little white dog.

A while later a man joined Gail at the side of the pen. "Anyone interested in Max today?" he asked. I looked up at him beseechingly, but he made no move to open the cage door so that I could get out and find CJ.

" 'Fraid not," Gail replied.

"We have to put him on the list after today."

"I know."

They stood looking at me. With a sigh, I lay down in the grass. Apparently I would have to wait a while longer before I was let out.

"Well, maybe we'll get lucky. Hope so," the man said.

"Me, too," Gail said. She sounded sad and I glanced up at her before resting my nose between my paws.

And then, on that cloudless, warm afternoon, the thunder of cars and machines vibrating the air and the scents of countless dogs and people and foods filling my nostrils, I caught sight of a woman walking down the street, and I leaped to my feet to see her more clearly. There was something about her bearing, the way she walked, her hair and her skin. . . .

The woman was striding briskly next to an enormous dog, not just compared to me but to every other dog I had ever seen. I was reminded of the donkey who lived on the Farm years and years ago—the dog was that big, with a lean body and an enormous head. As the woman drew abreast of me, the wind caught her scent and brought it to me.

It was, of course, CJ.

I yipped, and my bark, frustratingly quiet compared to all the background noise, earned me a quick glance from the giant dog, but CJ didn't even look my way. I watched her in frustration as she went down the street and disappeared.

Why hadn't she stopped to see me?

A few days later I was back out in the pens in the same grassy area and at precisely the same time of day CJ came by again, walking the same dog. I barked and barked, but CJ didn't see me.

"Why are you barking, Max? What do you see?" Gail asked me. I wagged my tail. *Yes, let me out; I* needed to run after CJ!

The same man came over to see Gail, but I was focused on CJ's retreating back.

"How's our Max doing?" he asked.

"Not so well, I'm afraid. He nipped at a little girl this morning."

"You know, even if we were able to adopt him out,

I don't think anyone would be able to handle him," the man said.

"We don't know that. With better socialization than we can give him, he might be fine."

"Still, Gail, you know my position."

"Right."

"If we didn't euthanize, we'd wind up being populated with nothing but unadoptable dogs, and then we couldn't save any more of them."

"He hasn't bitten anyone!"

"You said that he nipped."

"I know, but . . . he really is sweet; I mean, deep down I think he's a really great animal."

I wondered what it meant that CJ had a dog with her. Was he her dog? Every person needed a dog, especially my girl, but why would she need a dog so big? Though it was true there were a lot more people here than any other place we'd ever lived, so perhaps a big dog like that would be more protection, in case several people tried to get in the car at night in the rain. But surely he wouldn't be able to protect my girl the way I would. Only I had known CJ since she was a baby.

"Tell you what," the man said to Gail. "We'll give Max one more adoption fair—when is it, Tuesday? Okay, one more. Maybe we'll get lucky. But he's already past the established time."

"Oh my," Gail said. "Poor Max."

That night I reflected on CJ. She was older than when I'd been Molly and her hair was shorter, but I would still have recognized her. You don't spend hours and hours gazing at a person to forget what they look like, even if they change a little. And though there was a riot of scents wafting all around me in this place, I could still find her smell on the wind.

The sky was cloudy the next time I was taken to the open-air pen. Gail stood on the other side of the fence and leaned in to talk to me. "This is it, Max. Your last day. I'm so sorry, little guy. I have no idea what happened to you that you're so aggressive. I still think you're the greatest, but I can't have dogs in my apartment, not even a small puppy like you. So, so sorry."

I wasn't expecting to see CJ until late in the day, but after only about half an hour I spotted her, carrying two bags and walking alone, without the big dog. I yipped at her and she turned and saw me. She looked me right in the eyes! She seemed to slow for a second, glancing at the cages and people out on the grass, and then, astoundingly, she kept right on walking.

She'd looked me in the eyes! I yelped and then sobbed, scratching at the fence. Gail came over. "Max, what is the matter?"

I kept my focus on CJ, crying as loud as I could, my heartbreak and frustration pouring out of me. I heard the cage door rattle, and then Gail was bent over, snapping a leash onto my collar.

"Here, Max," she said.

I lunged, snapping, my teeth clicking so close to her fingers I could almost taste the skin. With a gasp Gail jerked back, dropping the leash. I bolted out of the open gate and ran after CJ, the leash trailing on the cement behind me.

What joy to finally be running in the open, chasing my girl! What a great day!

I saw her crossing the street, so I dashed out in front of the cars. There was a loud screech and a big truck, high off the ground, came to a halt right over the top of me. I was able to squirt out from underneath the thing without even having to duck. I dodged another car and then I was on the opposite side. CJ was several yards ahead of me, turning up a walk.

I pursued at a dead run. A man opened the door to a tall building and CJ went into it. The drag from the leash was slowing me a little, but I turned the corner and managed to get through the glass door just as it was easing shut.

"Hey!" the man yelled.

I was in a big room with a slick floor. I skittered, looking for CJ, and then saw her. She was standing in what looked like a closet, a light on over her head. Joyously I ran across the floor, my nails ticking.

CJ looked up and saw me. The doors on either side of her started to come together. I leaped, and then I was inside with her. I put my feet up on her legs, sobbing.

I had found her; I had found my girl.

"Oh my God!" CJ said.

Suddenly the leash snapped taut.

"You're caught! Oh God!" CJ shouted. She dropped her bags and they hit the floor with an explosion of sound and food smells. CJ reached for me, but I couldn't go to her. The leash was pulling me backward.

"Oh no!" CJ screamed.

[TWENTY]

CJ threw herself on the floor, her hands reaching
for me and fumbling desperately at my neck as I
slid helplessly back, my collar so tight it choked off
my breathing. She was full of fear and was screaming,
"No! No!"

The leash pulled me relentlessly backward and I
banged up against the wall behind me and then with
a snap my collar came off. It fell to the ground and
there was a loud grinding noise and, with a shudder,
the black lips of the doors opened slightly and the collar disappeared.

"Oh, puppy," CJ cried. She pulled me to her and
I licked her face. It felt so wonderful to be held in
her arms again, to taste her skin and smell her famil-

iar scent. "You could have been killed right in front of me!"

I also smelled dogs and a cat and, of course, the pungent smell of the liquids leaking from the bags she had dropped.

"Okay, good dog, good puppy. Hang on." She laughed. She scooped up her wet bags. "Oh boy," she said sadly.

When the doors opened I followed her down a short carpeted hallway, the smell of a dog getting stronger as CJ stopped in front of a door. She fumbled with it and pushed it open.

"Duke!" she called, nudging the door shut with a hip.

I heard the dog before I saw him: He was the enormous canine I'd seen walking on a leash with CJ. He was a white and gray dog, with blotches of black fur on his chest that were larger in total area than my mother. He stopped still when he saw me, his tail coming straight up in the air.

I marched right up to him, because I was here to take care of CJ. He lowered his head and I growled at him, not giving an inch.

"Play nice," CJ said.

I couldn't even reach up to sniff him properly, though when he tried to sniff at me I clicked my teeth at him in warning.

CJ spent a few minutes in the kitchen while the giant dog and I circled each other uneasily. I could smell a cat and knew one lived here, but didn't see it anywhere. CJ came out, wiping her hands on a towel, and

214 | W. BRUCE CAMERON

scooped me up. "Okay, puppy, let's see if we can figure out where you belong."

I stared down with contempt at the big dog, who was watching forlornly. He might get to go for walks with CJ, but she would never pick him up for a cuddle.

We went back out and got into the same little room where we'd met, and then she carried me down a hall to some glass doors that opened to the outside. The man who had yelled at me was there.

"Hello, Miss Mahoney, is that your dog?" he asked.

"No! But he nearly got hung in the elevator. Um, David? I'm afraid I dropped a bottle of wine saving this little guy and some of it seeped onto the elevator floor."

"I'll see to it immediately."

The man reached a gloved hand toward me and I gave him a warning growl because I couldn't tell if he was trying to touch me or CJ—and nobody was going to touch CJ while I was around. He pulled his fingers back with a jerk. "Spunky," he said.

My name was Max, not Spunky. I ignored him.

CJ carried me down the street and it was with alarm that I registered the smells of the outdoor dog pens. I squirmed in her arms, turning away. "Hi, I think this might be one of your dogs," my girl said as I put my head on her shoulder and licked her ear.

"It's Max!" Gail said from behind me.

"Max," CJ said. "He's such a sweetie. He ran right into the elevator in my building as if he lived there. The leash got caught in the doors and I was afraid he was going to be strangled."

CJ was stroking me and I burrowed my head in the

crook of her neck. I did not want to go back to the place of the barking dogs. I wanted to be right here.

"What a love dog," CJ said.

"No one has ever called Max a love dog," Gail said.

I kissed CJ's face and snuck a look at Gail, wagging my tail a little to let her know I was happy now and she could go back to taking care of other dogs.

"What kind of dog is he?"

"The mother is a Chihuahua. The father, we're thinking Yorkie."

"Max, you're a Chorkie!" CJ smiled down at me. "So, anyway. Where do you want me to put him?"

Gail was watching me; then she looked up at CJ. "Truthfully? I don't want you to put him anywhere."

"Sorry?"

"Do you have a dog?"

"What? No, I can't. I mean, I'm dog-sitting at the moment."

"So you like dogs."

CJ laughed. "Well, I mean sure. Who doesn't like dogs?"

"You'd be surprised."

"Actually, now that you mention it, I have met someone who didn't like dogs." CJ was gently pushing me away from the tight snuggle I had going against her shoulder.

"Max obviously likes you," Gail observed.

"He's really sweet."

"He's scheduled to be euthanized tomorrow morning."

"What?" I felt the shock flash through CJ, the way

her hands tightened on me and she took a small step back.

"Sorry, I know it's . . . I know it sounds brutal. We're not a no-kill shelter."

"That's horrible!"

"Well, sure it is, but we do our best and when we can we foster them out to no-kills. But they're full, we're full, and we have new dogs coming in every day. We normally can place puppies, but Max has never warmed up to anybody and he's overdue. We need the space."

CJ pulled me away and looked at me. Her eyes were moist. "But . . . ," she said.

"There are other dogs who need help. Rescue is like a river; it has to keep flowing. Otherwise even more dogs would die."

"I didn't know that."

"Max has never warmed up to anybody except you. He snapped at me this morning, and I'm the person who's been feeding him. It's as if he picked you, out of all the people in New York. Can you take him? Please? We'll waive the fee."

"I just got a cat two weeks ago."

"Dogs and cats that grow up together usually do fine. You'll be saving his life."

"I can't; I just . . . I'm a dog walker, I mean, I'm an actress, but I've been walking dogs, and they're all big."

"Max can handle himself around big dogs."

"I'm sorry."

"You sure? All he needs is a chance. You, you're his chance."

"I'm so sorry."

"So tomorrow he dies."

"Oh God."

"Look at him," Gail said.

CJ looked at me and I squirmed in pleasure at the attention. She brought me within range and I licked her chin.

"Okay," CJ said. "I can't believe I'm doing this."

After we left the dog cages we went to a place full of the sound of squawking birds and rich with animal smells I'd never scented before and CJ put a collar on me and snapped a leash onto it. My head held high, I walked at her ankles, glad to be back in charge of protecting her.

Soon we were back in the small closet where I'd finally been able to get back to CJ. The wet spill from her bag was gone, but I could still smell the residual scent from the sweet liquid. I strode confidently next to her in the hall, but she scooped me up as she opened the door. "Duke?" she called.

There was a noise like a horse running and the huge dog came dashing up to us. I showed him my teeth. "Duke, Max is going to live with us now," CJ said. She held me out and as the dog, Duke, raised his nose I gave him a warning growl. His ears dropped a little, and he wagged his stiff tail. CJ didn't put me down.

"Sneakers?" she called. She carried me into a bedroom, Duke following us, and there was a young cat lying on the bed. Her eyes widened when she saw me. "Sneakers, this is Max. He's a Chorkie."

CJ dropped me on the bed. I figured I knew how to handle cats—you just have to let them know you won't hurt them as long as they stay in line. I trotted right up to this Sneakers, but before I had a chance to lay a paw on her the cat spat at me and raked me in the face with her tiny sharp claws. They hurt! I scrambled back, too shocked to do anything but yelp, and fell off the bed. Duke lowered his massive head and licked me, his tongue the size of my face.

That was my introduction to these creatures, neither of whom seemed to recognize the significance of my arrival or my importance to CJ.

That night CJ cooked some wonderful things, the smell of meat filling the apartment. Duke followed her around, sticking his head on the counter to see what she was doing. "No, Duke," CJ said, shoving him away. I was reduced to standing on my hind legs and scrabbling at CJ's calves for attention. "Okay, Max, you're a good dog," she said to me.

I was a good dog, and Duke was "no, Duke." That's what I got out of the exchange. Unfortunately, Sneakers was in the bedroom and missed this indication that I was the favored pet.

While she was cooking, CJ also played with her hair and her clothes, though not in a game in which a dog could participate. She put on shoes that smelled like they'd taste good, and after that her footsteps rang with sharp percussion in the kitchen.

Soon there was a noise at the door and CJ picked me up and opened it. "Hi, honey," she said to the man standing there. He was stocky and had no hair on his head and he smelled like something burned and peanuts and a pungent spice of some kind.

"Whoa, what's this?" he said. He stuck his fingers

right in my face and I growled at him, showing my teeth.

"Max!" CJ said. "Come in. It's Max; he's sort of my new dog."

"Wait, sort of?" He edged inside and CJ shut the door.

"He was on death row for tomorrow. I couldn't let them put the little guy down. He's so cuddly."

The man was leaning in too close to CJ. I showed him my teeth again.

"Yeah, cuddly. What's Barry going to say when he gets back and you've got a new dog in his apartment?"

"He's already letting me keep Sneakers. Max isn't really any bigger."

Duke was trying to shove his big stupid head under the man's hand, and the man pushed him away. CJ set me down and I glared at the man—I didn't yet know if he posed any sort of threat and at my size I couldn't afford to let down my guard until I was sure.

"I'm cooking broccoli beef," CJ said. "Want to open the wine, Gregg?"

"Hey, come here," the man said.

CJ and the man held each other very close and then went down the hall. I followed but was too short to get on the bed with them. Duke might have jumped up with ease, but Sneakers streaked out the door when CJ and the man went in and Duke was more interested in following the cat. Sneakers went under the couch. I could have crawled under there after her pretty easily but elected to forgo the opportunity to let the cat slash at me again. Duke, on the other hand, was apparently dumb enough to think he could get under there if he just worked hard enough. Snorting and groaning, he shoved his head under the couch until he actually moved the thing on the rug. I wondered how long Sneakers would tolerate this before she demonstrated to Duke why she had claws.

After a while, CJ and the man came back out. "Well!" CJ said with a laugh. "Good thing I turned off the burners. Hi, Max, did you have fun with Duke?" Duke and I both looked at her, hearing our names and a question. "You want to open that wine?"

The man was standing by the table, his hands in his pockets. CJ came back out of the kitchen, which was still alive with tantalizing smells. "What is it?"

"I can't stay, baby."

"What? You said—"

"I know, but something's come up."

"Something's come up. And what exactly is that, Gregg?"

"Hey. I've never lied to you about my situation."

"Your situation that you said was ending, is that the situation you mean?"

"It's complicated," he said.

"Well, yeah, I guess it is. Why don't you give me an update on the 'situation' as it currently stands? Because I thought that in the process of 'never lying to me' you were pretty clear that the situation was all but over."

CJ was angry. Duke lowered his head, frightened, but I was rigid and alert. The man's name was Gregg and he was making my girl angry.

"I gotta go."

"So this was what, a pit stop? Bootie call?"

"Baby."

"Stop! I'm not a baby!"

Now Gregg was getting angry, too. The situation was spinning out of control. I darted over and snapped at Gregg's pant leg. "Hey!" he shouted. He swung his foot, narrowly missing me.

"No!" CJ yelled. She reached down and picked me up. "Don't you ever try to kick my dog."

"Dog tried to bite me," Gregg said.

"He's just protective. He was raised in a shelter."

"Well, you need to train him or something."

"Okay, let's completely change the subject, then, and talk about the dog."

"I don't know what you want!" Gregg shouted. "I'm late to a thing." He strode rapidly to the door and yanked it open, turning on the threshold. "This isn't easy for me, either. You could at least show some appreciation for that fact."

"It certainly is one of the more appreciable facts, I'll give you that."

"I don't need this," the man said. He shut the door forcefully.

CJ sat down on the couch and buried her head in her hands. I couldn't get up on the couch to comfort her. Duke came over and rested his gigantic head in her lap, as if that were any help.

She sobbed as she took her shoes off and threw them on the floor. They were, I decided, bad shoes.

After a few minutes, CJ went into the kitchen and brought out two pans and set them on the table and ate right out of the pans. She ate and ate and ate, while Duke watched attentively.

I felt pretty sure I knew what was going to happen next. And it did—within half an hour, she was in the bathroom, vomiting. She shut the door on me, so I sat on the floor, whimpering, wishing I could help her with her pain. It was my purpose to take care of CJ, and at that moment I felt that I was not doing a good job.

TWENTY-ONE

The next day we all went for a walk except Sneakers. I've seen cats outside and they don't walk with people; they mostly just walk with themselves. Nearly always when a dog walks he walks next to a person. This is just one of many ways that dogs are better pets than cats.

Duke and I were on leashes. I was feeling more kindly disposed toward him than when we first regarded each other, because he had never been anything but submissive—when we played, he would fall to his back and let me climb on his neck and chew on his face. But walking with him was constantly irritating. He pulled left and right at the end of his leash, distracted by one smell or another, yanking CJ off balance and getting in my way. "Duke . . . Duke . . . ," CJ would say. She never once had to say, "Max . . . Max . . . ," because I trotted by her feet like a good dog. Occasionally I barked, though, because otherwise I wasn't sure people could see me—they tended to stare at Duke, probably astounded that he was so bad at walking.

I was glad that my girl had found herself another dog after I, as Molly, left her, but clearly now that we were reunited I was going to be in charge, because Duke just didn't know what he was doing.

Everywhere there were food smells and garbage cans and papers to sniff, but I had to work my little legs so hard to keep up that these delights passed by too quickly for me to enjoy them. We mounted some brick stairs and CJ knocked on the door. It opened and the smell of people and a dog and food came wafting out. A woman was on the other side of the door. "Oh," she said, "is it that time already?"

I could sense an uneasiness in CJ. "Um, yeah, I'm right on time," CJ said.

I could smell a strange dog's scent on the flowerpot next to me and I squatted to mark over it. "My plants!" the woman cried.

"Oh!" CJ reached down and picked me up. "I'm sorry; he's just a puppy."

CJ was upset and it was the woman's fault. When the woman leaned forward to peer at me, I growled at her and she jerked back. "He's all bark and no bite," CJ said.

"I'll get Pepper," the woman said. She left us standing on the doorstep for a few moments and then returned with a rust-colored female dog, much bigger than me but still way smaller than Duke, on a leash that the woman handed to CJ. The dog sniffed me and I growled at her to let her know I was there to protect CJ.

The rust-colored dog was named Pepper, I soon gathered, and as we walked we stopped at more places and soon had a brown female dog named Sally and a hairy, stocky male dog named Beevis, all on leashes in a most unnatural dog family.

This wasn't like being with Rocky or being with Annie and Abby; this was a mix of dogs who were very tense with each other, held too closely together by the leashes that kept us from straying. For the most part we all tried to ignore each other, though Duke tried to play with Sally a little even though we were going for a walk.

More strange than the unnatural nature of the dog pack was CJ's obsession with collecting our poops. On the Farm I'd taken to doing my business in the surrounding woods, and as Molly I generally used a corner of the backyard—a man came on a regular basis to run machines and clean up after me. Occasionally, CJ had picked up after me, usually when we were on someone else's property, but never had it been like her behavior now. CJ methodically scooped up after all the dogs in our pack and even kept Duke's deposits, which were huge. She would carry them with her for a time in little bags and then would leave them in containers on the street, which was even more baffling—why go through all the work of picking them up and carrying them if she wasn't going to keep them?

There are some things people do that dogs just will never understand. Most of the time I assumed that humans, with their complex lives, were serving some greater purpose, but in this instance I wasn't so sure.

Though I was the dog in charge, I tried to be civil to all the other canines, but Beevis did not like me and I did not like Beevis. When he sniffed me his fur went up and he thrust his chest at me. He was bigger than I, but not by a lot—if it weren't for me he would have been the smallest dog there. CJ pulled on his leash so that his face was brought aggressively toward mine, so I snapped at him and he bit the air next to my ear.

"Stop it! Max! Beevis!"

CJ was angry. I wagged my tail at her, hoping she understood none of it was my fault.

CJ took us to a dog park. What a great place! It felt so good to be off leash that I headed off at a flat run, and Duke and Sally followed, though I could turn more quickly than they could and soon was running alone. Other dogs were in the park with their owners, some chasing balls, others wrestling, and a white dog with floppy ears joyfully joined the chase with Duke and Sally—it was so fun to race around with the dogs in pursuit!

I saw Beevis slinking down low and then he launched himself at me. I dodged and he ran after me, growling. I turned a tight circle, but he cut me off. It looked as if I would have no choice but to snap at him, except that Duke galloped up and sort of crashed into the both of us. With Duke towering over him, Beevis was less hostile. I dashed over to CJ, who was sitting on a bench, tried to jump up next to her, but fell short.

Laughing, she picked me up, and I proudly sat in her lap, watching the dogs, smelling the exotic smells, feeling her hands, loving all of it.

When we left the dog park, we retraced our route, dropping off the dogs we'd picked up along the way until it was just Duke and myself, back at CJ's place. I was exhausted, so after a quick snack I fell asleep at CJ's feet.

Over the course of that summer, Beevis and I learned to ignore each other, though he still growled at me when I ran. He couldn't keep up with me, but he was pretty good at cutting me off, so I'd be in the middle of a joyous gallop with a whole pack and then he'd charge into the middle of us to challenge me and the whole procession of running dogs would pull up into a halt and mill around. I couldn't tell if everyone found it as irritating as I did.

At home, I took on the responsibility of guiding Duke toward more polite behavior. He didn't understand that my food bowl was off-limits, so I was forced to nip at him a few times before realization dawned in his eyes. He never really ate my dinner or even all of his own meal most of the time, but I didn't like that huge nose descending from its height and sniffing where I ate. He was also lazy: when someone knocked, Duke didn't think to bark until I did, even though we were the only protection CJ had in the world. I therefore had to be extravigilant and would bark at the slightest sound coming from the direction of the hallway.

I knew we were supposed to bark because CJ was always angry when someone knocked. "Hey! Stop!

Quiet! Enough!" she would yell. I didn't understand the words, but the meaning was clear: she was upset with the knocking and we should keep barking.

When Duke barked, Sneakers usually darted across the floor and scampered under the bed. Otherwise, the cat was much less fearful as the days wore on and, after several incidents of close sniffing, even began to play with me. We'd wrestle and it wasn't exactly the same as wrestling with a dog, because Sneakers would wrap her legs around me, but it was easier than trying to play with Duke, who was ridiculously large and had to crawl on the floor so I could pin him.

The only time there was peace between Sneakers and Duke was when CJ would run a machine on the floor that made a loud noise. It terrified Duke and Sneakers cowered from it as well, though I wasn't worried because I'd encountered similar machines in my time. After CJ put the machine away she would cuddle with us—Duke, Sneakers, and me pressed up against her on the couch, recovering from the trauma of it all.

I knew I was the favorite pet, though, and CJ proved it one evening by snapping a leash onto my collar and walking with me and only me outside in the warm, humid air. Duke followed us to the door, but CJ told him he was a good dog and to stay and then it was just the two of us.

I was now so accustomed to the roar of noise outside that I scarcely noticed it, though I still found the tantalizing odors compelling. The leaves were starting to drop off of some of the trees and swish along the sidewalk, propelled by cooling breezes. We walked several blocks as the night fell, and there were a lot of people out, plus many dogs, so I kept my guard up.

Finally we went up to some doors. CJ fiddled with something on the wall and said, "It's CJ!" and then there was a buzzing noise and we went into the building and my girl carried me up a few flights of stairs. A door opened at the end of a hall and a man stepped out.

"Hi!" he called.

When we got closer, I smelled who it was: Trent!

I was astounded, because I had never thought we'd ever see him again. But humans can arrange for whatever they want to happen, which was how, for example, CJ always managed to find me when she needed me.

Trent and CJ hugged while I stood on my hind legs and reached up to him. Then he laughed and reached down and picked me up.

"Careful . . . ," CJ warned.

"Who is this?" he asked, laughing delightedly as I licked his face. I was so happy to see him! I squirmed in his arms, wanting to press in more closely.

"That's Max. I can't believe how he's acting. He's never like this. He doesn't like most people."

"He's such a sweetie. Kind of dog is he?"

"A Chorkie, half Chihuahua, half Yorkie. That's the best guess, anyway. Wow, I love what you've done with the place!"

Trent laughed and set me down. He lived in the best house ever: there was not a single piece of furniture anywhere. I could race around and around unimpeded.

"I've got stuff on order," Trent said. "Open some wine? God, it is so great to see you!"

I explored the house while he and CJ sat and talked. There were two other rooms, equally empty. I found myself sniffing for Rocky, but there was no sign of him. My brother must no longer be alive. I wondered why Trent didn't have a new dog; didn't people need dogs?

"So how's the new job?" CJ asked.

"It's a great firm. I already was doing some work cofinancing with them when I was in San Francisco, so it's a natural fit. How about you? How's the acting?"

"I've been in a couple of workshops. I love it. There's something about being onstage, having everyone listen to me, laugh at my lines, applauding . . . it's the greatest."

"How odd that Gloria's child would want to perform so that people would pay attention to her," Trent said. "Who could have predicted something like that?"

"And how interesting that an investment banker wants to give me free psychotherapy."

Trent laughed. The sound was exactly the same as I remembered. "You're right. I'm sorry. I've been in therapy myself—if you live in California, it's mandatory. It helped, though, with some stuff."

"I'm sorry about Rocky."

At the sound of my brother's name, I paused, looking at them for a moment before I resumed exploring.

"Yeah. Rocky. Such a good dog. Stomach torsion— vet says it happens a lot with bigger dogs."

I caught sadness coming off of Trent and raced across the floor and sailed into his lap. Trent caught me and kissed my head. "So how did you come to get Max?"

"My place is right down from where they had this dog adoption in Central Park."

"Wait, you live by the park? Your acting must be going *very* well."

"Well, no. I mean yes, I live in a fabulous place, but I'm house- and pet-sitting for this guy Barry. He manages some boxer dude who is training for a fight in Africa."

"This puppy is the cutest little guy in the world," Trent said.

"I know, isn't he? He sure likes *you*."

"Hey, let's order food. Just looking at you is making me hungry."

"What's that supposed to mean?" CJ said sharply. I jumped out of Trent's lap and went over to her.

"You're so thin, CJ."

"I'm an actress, *hello*."

"Yeah, but . . . "

"Leave this alone, Trent."

He sighed. "We used to confide in each other," he said after a moment.

"I've got things under control. That's all you need to know."

"You only let me get so close, and no closer, CJ."

"More therapy talk?"

"Come on. I miss you. I miss our conversations."

"Me, too," CJ said softly. "But there are some things I don't want to talk about with anybody."

They were quiet for a minute. I put my feet on CJ's

knees, and she lifted me up and kissed my nose. I wagged.

After more talking, a man came and brought bags of food. I loved the generous people who sometimes arrived with warm, delicious-smelling meals and handed them over and then left so that people could eat and feed their dogs! We all sat on the floor together and CJ and Trent ate from the bags and gave me a tiny piece of chicken that I ate and a vegetable that I spat out.

"What's her name?" CJ asked at one point.

"Liesl."

"Wait, Liesl? You're dating one of the Von Trapps?" CJ laughed.

"She's German. I mean, she lives in Tribeca, but she came over from Europe when she was nine."

"Tribeca. Huh. So you've been coming to New York and not calling me?"

"A little," Trent admitted.

"That's it. Max, attack. Go for the throat."

I heard my name but didn't understand what I was supposed to do. CJ was gesturing toward Trent, so I padded over to him and he bent down and I licked his face, and they both laughed.

When we left, Trent and CJ stood at the door and hugged for a long time, and the love flowed between them. I realized right then that what would be best for CJ was if we left Sneakers and Duke behind and came to live here in the fun place with no furniture, where she and Trent could love each other. CJ needed a mate, the way Ethan had needed Hannah, and Trent needed a dog.

If the other two pets had to come, though, we'd

need to at least get a couch so Sneakers had something to hide under.

"I'm so, so glad to see you," Trent said.

"Me, too."

"Okay, we'll do this all the time, now that I'm moving here. I promise."

"Really? Sit on the floor and have dinner?"

"Maybe the four of us can get together. Liesl and Gregg, I mean."

"Sure," CJ said.

Trent pulled back, looking at her. "What?"

"It's nothing. It's . . . Gregg's not . . . His family situation isn't fully resolved yet."

"Are you kidding me?" Trent said loudly.

"Stop it."

"You can't seriously be saying—"

CJ put a hand on his mouth. "Don't. This was so nice. Please. Please? I know you care about me, Trent. But I can't stand your judgment."

"I have *never* judged you, CJ."

"Well, that's what it feels like."

"Okay," Trent said. "Okay."

CJ was a little sad, then. The two of us walked out of the place and back home.

TWENTY-TWO

We were all in the dog park as usual. Duke and Sally were over sniffing a big white dog whose name was Bring Me the Ball Tony. Bring Me the Ball Tony was more interested in trying to climb on Sally's back than in paying attention to his owner. I was trying to engage a male dog my size who looked very much like my mother, with the same face and coloring, and I finally managed to persuade him to give chase, so naturally Beevis came running up, growling, his lips back and his ears stiff. My playmate was instantly cowed and shrank away from the aggression, but I turned and snapped at Beevis to let him know he was pushing me too far. Instead of backing away, Beevis came straight at me.

I heard CJ yelling, "No!" but Beevis went up on his rear legs and I followed and his teeth slashed at me, trying to wound me. I bit back and caught a fold of skin in my mouth and then my girl was there, using her legs to push us apart. "No!" she yelled again. She scooped me up and I kept snarling and snapping as Beevis tried to reach me. CJ turned, using her body to block him. "Stop it, Beevis! No, Max, no!"

Then Duke came charging up, reacting to the distress in CJ's voice. He clearly didn't understand what was going on, but his appearance made Beevis back off.

"Oh, Max, your ear," CJ said. I could feel her anxious despair and kept my focus on Beevis, who was circling around uneasily. When I smelled the blood it wasn't immediately clear it was mine, but I felt the sting when CJ put her hand on my ear. She pulled some paper out of her bag and pressed it against the side of my head.

CJ carried me as we walked all of the dogs home. At Sally's house we had to wait a little bit before her person arrived. "I'm so sorry, there was a dog fight. Is it okay to drop Sally back off a little early?" CJ asked.

At Beevis's house, CJ told the man who answered the door, "I'm sorry, but I won't be able to walk Beevis anymore. He fights with the other dogs."

"He does not," the man said. "Not unless the other dog starts it."

I felt CJ getting angry, and even though my ear was sore, I gave the man a growl. Beevis, for his part, was happy to be home and wagged, going inside without a backward glance.

When we got home CJ let Duke in but then left with me in her arms, still pressing her hand to my ear. We went to a Vet—I knew that's what he was because he put me on a metal table and petted me and I could smell a lot of dogs on his clothes. There was a sting in my ear and then he tugged on it a little bit. CJ watched the whole time.

"It's not bad at all. You did the right thing by keeping pressure on it, though. They can bleed a lot," the Vet said.

"Oh, Max. Why do you have to growl at everybody?" CJ asked.

"You want us to go ahead and neuter him, long as you're here?"

"Um, yeah, I guess. Does that mean that Max will have to spend the night?"

"Sure, but you can pick him up in the morning."

"Okay. All right, Max, you're going to stay here for the night."

I heard my name and heard the slight sadness and thumped my tail.

CJ left, which I did not like at all, but the Vet petted me and I fell into a sleep so deep I lost all track of time. When I awoke, it was morning and I was in a cage, wearing a stupid, stiff collar that surrounded my face and funneled all noises and smells directly into my senses. *Again,* was all I thought to myself. I had long given up trying to understand why people liked to put their dogs in such ridiculous situations.

CJ arrived and the Vet let me out of the cage and handed me to her. I was tired and just wanted to fall asleep in my girl's arms. As we left we stopped by the front door to talk to a lady, who smelled like lemons. She said something to CJ.

"What? I . . . I don't have that much," CJ said. She was upset, so I growled at the lemon lady.

"We take credit cards."

"I don't have that much room on my card. Can I give you forty now, and the rest when I get paid?"

"We expect payment at the time of service."

There was a sadness inside CJ, fighting to get out. I licked her face. "It's all I have on me right now," CJ whispered.

Whatever was making her unhappy was obviously Beevis's fault.

She handed over some papers and the lemon lady handed some papers back and then we left the sad Vet's office. I wanted to get down and squirmed, but CJ held me tight.

Both Duke and Sneakers wanted to smell my stupid collar and to put their noses on my ear, which I could feel had something stuck to it. I growled a little at Duke, but Sneakers purred at me, so I let her sniff. It was very strange having her cat face inside the small space formed by the stupid collar.

For a few days, I wasn't allowed to go for a walk with Duke, which made me unhappy. Sneakers, though, was delighted, and would come out from under the bed to play with me and when I lay in the sun would curl up next to me, purring. I liked sleeping with Sneakers but felt like a bad dog who had to wear a stupid collar and Stay instead of going for a walk.

One morning CJ took off my collar, washed my ear, and then, when she put Duke on the leash, she snapped one on me, too. I was going for a walk! We went and picked up all the usual dogs, except neither Sally nor Beevis was there anymore. I didn't miss Beevis, but Duke seemed sad without Sally.

Some days CJ wouldn't get out of bed to walk dogs, so Duke and I would wake her up. Then she still wouldn't walk all the dogs, though she would take both Duke and myself out. Those were my favorite days and I wished they could all be like that. On one such day, CJ used sharp-smelling chemicals on the floors and furniture and ran the machine on the floor that made Duke bark and Sneakers hide. When CJ was finished and put the machine away, Duke tore around the living room as if he'd just been let out of his crate.

I had no choice but to give chase. Excited, Duke bowed down to me, enticing me to wrestle. I climbed on top of him and we played for a while, and then the front door opened. I barked, so Duke barked, too. A man came inside, shouting "Duke!" followed by two other men who put suitcases on the floor and then left. I ran up to the stranger, snarling, while Duke wagged his tail and sniffed at the man's hands.

"Max!" CJ called. She picked me up just as I was thinking about grabbing the man's pants in my teeth, since he was ignoring me and just petting Duke, who was welcoming him even though the man had walked into CJ's place without permission. Duke just didn't understand the whole concept of protection—it was a good thing I was there.

"Welcome home, Barry."

"Hi, CJ. Hey, Duke, you miss me? Miss me, boy?"

He knelt down and hugged Duke, who wagged but then came over to smell CJ, perpetually jealous that she would pick me up to cuddle but never him.

"He doesn't seem like he missed me at all," the man said. He smelled like oils and fruits. When he looked me in the eye, I growled.

"You've been gone a long time," CJ said. "Six months seems like forever to a dog."

"Okay, but I could have put him in a kennel. I paid for a person to stay with him in this house."

"He doesn't know that, Barry."

"Who's this? I thought you said a kitten."

"Right, this is Max. It's a long story. Max, be nice."

Though I was suspicious of the man, CJ seemed okay with him, so when she dropped me to the floor I went back to wrestling with Duke.

"So, did your guy win?" CJ asked.

"What?"

"Your guy. The boxing thing."

Duke rolled onto his back and I seized a wad of throat and shook it gently.

"You really are an airhead, aren't you," the man said.

"What?"

"No, he didn't win."

"Oh. I'm really sorry, Barry. Is that why you're back two months early?"

"Yeah, well, when your fighter loses you don't go on a worldwide press tour, do you? What the . . . What's Duke doing?"

"Duke?" CJ repeated. Duke froze at his name, his legs splayed up in the air, his tongue lolling out, my teeth gently pulling on his skin. "They're just playing."

"Duke! Cut it out!" the man shouted angrily. Duke scrambled to his feet, knocking me aside, and went to CJ with his ears down. I lay on the floor where I'd fallen, panting.

"What's wrong, Barry?"

"You've turned my dog into a wimp."

"What? No, they play really well together."

"I don't want him 'playing' like that with some little rat dog."

"Max is not a rat dog, Barry."

Barry, I decided, was the man's name.

"Okay, well . . . I don't remember giving you permission to have a dog and I sure don't appreciate Duke's behavior. I hired you because you said you had lots of experience. So, fine. I'm back. If you could just go back to your place, let me unwind and get to know my dog again."

CJ was quiet for a moment. I stared at her, feeling her sadness and hurt. "But . . . I don't have a place, Barry."

"What?"

"You said eight to ten months. There was no sense me keeping an apartment if I was going to be here eight months."

"So, what, you're going to stay with me?" Barry asked.

"No! I mean, I'll sleep on the couch and look for a place tomorrow."

"Wait, no. Forget it. I'm . . . I'm stressed. I worked a year on this and he was knocked out in the second round. You can stay here; I'm just dumping my African stuff and heading over to Samantha's anyway.

We're going to go to Hawaii. So you can take two weeks to find a place. That okay? I'll get someone else to take care of Duke for when I'm back in town."

"So I'm fired?"

"It's for the best."

"Well, sure, I can see that."

"Okay, no need for sarcasm. I paid you pretty well and you got a free place out of it and if I'm not happy I'm the customer."

"All of that is true," CJ said.

A little later Barry left. "Bye, Duke," Barry said over his shoulder. Duke thumped his tail at his name, but I could tell he was as relieved as I was to have Barry gone so that CJ wasn't tense anymore. My girl seemed a little sad, though.

The next day, after we went walking with the usual dogs, CJ left Duke and me alone in the house and was gone for a long time. I wrestled with him for a while but became irritated with him because his head was so large and strong it kept knocking me over.

I was asleep when I heard a low, loud moan coming from the bedroom. I went to investigate and found Duke in a high state of agitation, his stiff tail whipping the air, his head under the bed. He was panting with excitement, and the moaning was coming from Sneakers, who was plainly terrified. Duke was so powerful he was managing to lift the entire bed as he drove to jam himself under there to get at Sneakers.

I went right up to Duke and barked at him sternly. He was quivering, too thrilled at how close he was getting to poor Sneakers, who was pressed back against the wall, her ears flat against her head. Duke ignored my barking, so I lunged at him, clicking my teeth.

That got his attention. He retreated, the bed coming down with a thump. I snapped and snarled at him until he was all the way out of the room, then trotted back to check on Sneakers.

I was small enough to crawl under there if I wanted, but I decided to leave Sneakers alone. She was still frightened, and from what I had seen of cat behavior, when they were scared they tended to use their claws.

CJ left us by ourselves every day, and every day Duke treated her departure as a signal that it was time to start harassing poor Sneakers. It got so that the second the door shut Sneakers would dart from wherever she was napping to her hiding place under the bed—if Duke saw her shoot past, he would gallop after her in dumb pursuit, crashing into walls as he tried to take the corner too fast. I'd be running, too, and when I got to the bed I would dive under it and then turn and face Duke's quivering, wet nose, my teeth exposed and a growl in my throat. Duke would moan in frustration and sometimes would even bark, the noise deafening in the small space, but I knew I couldn't back down, and eventually he'd lose interest and go back to the living room to take a nap.

Then one day the pattern changed. We went for our usual walk, but when we returned CJ brought over a crate and opened the door in it and carefully placed Sneakers inside. The crate reminded me of the one I had sat in as Molly, the one that tipped back and forth before winding up in the loud place with all the cars. Sneakers wasn't happy and didn't come over when I pushed my nose up to sniff at her. Then Duke came over, snorting loudly, and Sneakers backed away into the far recesses of the crate.

"Duke," CJ said warningly, and Duke went over to her to see if she was going to give him a treat.

CJ picked up the crate with Sneakers in it and left us alone. This was absolutely baffling: where was she taking Sneakers that we weren't going along as well? We didn't know what to do, so we lay on the floor and gnawed chew toys.

When my girl came back, Sneakers was no longer with her.

Where was Sneakers?

[TWENTY-THREE]

For two days, CJ would take us on a dog walk and
then would leave us alone with no Sneakers. Duke
and I made the best of it—in fact, without a cat in the
home, some of the tension left our relationship and
we were able to wrestle more freely and for so long
that sometimes we'd wind up falling asleep on top of
each other. Well, I was on top, anyway. If Duke had
been on top, I sincerely doubt I would have been doing any sleeping.

On the third day, when we returned from our
walk, a woman was waiting for us outside the door.
Duke, of course, wagged and thrust his big head at
her, while I retreated to CJ's feet and waited rigidly to
see if there was any threat.

CJ called the woman Marcia. After we'd been inside for half an hour, Marcia carefully extended her hand to me and I sniffed it after CJ said, "Gentle, Max," to me in very soothing tones. The hand smelled like chocolate and dogs and some sweet things I couldn't identify.

Duke and I chewed lazily on each other while CJ and Marcia talked. "Okay, I think that's everything," CJ finally said, standing up. Duke and I bounded to our respective feet. Walk?

"So Duke, I guess this is good-bye. Marcia will be taking care of you now," CJ said. A sudden sadness broke inside her and I went to her and put my paws on her leg as she bent over on the couch, taking Duke's head in her hands. I could tell that he knew she was sad by the way his ears dropped and his tail wagged and then drooped. I wondered if he knew what was going on, because I didn't.

"I'm going to miss you, big guy," CJ whispered. I tried to climb up into her lap but couldn't quite make it.

"Oh God, I feel awful," Marcia said.

"Don't. Barry has the right; it's his dog."

"Yeah, but, I mean, Duke thinks he's *your* dog. You can tell. It's not fair to cut off all contact between the two of you."

"Oh, Duke, I'm so sorry," CJ said. Her voice carried a lot of grief.

"Maybe I could call you and we could meet somewhere," Marcia offered.

CJ shook her head. "I don't want to get *you* in

trouble. Barry will fire you in a second. Believe me, I have firsthand experience."

Duke mournfully put his head in CJ's lap, sharing her mysterious sadness. I envied him his height: all I could do was scrabble fruitlessly at her legs, hoping to be noticed.

"Okay." CJ sighed. "Nice meeting you, Marcia. Come on, Max." CJ reached down and scooped me up, and now I was above Duke, looking down at him. CJ snapped a leash onto my collar but not onto Duke's, and all of us went to the door.

"Bye," CJ said quietly. She opened the door and Duke lunged to follow her outside, dragging Marcia with him as he struggled with her grip on his collar. CJ, still holding me, blocked Duke. "No, Duke. You stay. I'm sorry."

They managed to get the door shut. CJ dropped me to the floor and I shook myself, ready for whatever we were doing. Inside our home, Duke gave the door a workout, his paws making it rattle loudly in the frame.

As we went down the hall, I heard Duke's sad, heartbroken barking and wondered again what was going on. Why wasn't Duke coming with us? He wanted to go!

My girl was crying and I kept looking up at her in concern, but she didn't say anything more to me. We took a very long walk, first on the loud, smelly streets and then up a whole lot of stairs. CJ rattled a doorknob and then it swung open, and I instantly smelled Sneakers.

"Welcome home, Max," CJ said.

We were in a small kitchen, with a bowl of Sneakers' food on the floor that I went over to sniff. The kitchen also had a bed in it, which was where I found Sneakers. She was lying on a pillow and stood, arching her back, when she saw me.

Sneakers had her own house! I didn't understand it but thought maybe it had something to do with the way Duke was always harassing her when CJ would leave the three of us alone. Perhaps to protect Sneakers CJ found this new house at the top of all the stairs, a place where the cat would be safe. Now I was being shown that this was where Sneakers lived, and soon we'd be going back home to Duke, who would smell Sneakers on me—I wondered what he would conclude from that! Would he figure out that CJ and I had been to Sneakers' house?

People do whatever they want, but as far as I was concerned, cats already ate better food than dogs, so to give one a house seemed unfairly indulgent.

Sneakers purred and circled around me, rubbing against me, and we played a little. She seemed awfully glad to see me there without Duke. I could smell another person's hands on her, a strong, flowery scent that reminded me a little of Gloria.

We didn't go home that night—CJ slept in the small bed and I did, too, curled up at her feet. Sneakers prowled around a little in the house and then leaped nimbly up to try to snuggle with me, but it was too uncomfortable for both of us and when CJ mumbled and moved her legs Sneakers jumped back to the floor and didn't try to come up again that night.

What she did do, though, was sit at the front door and meow a little the next morning, and CJ said,

"Okay, you want to go see Mrs. Minnick? Let's see if she's home," and then we went out into the hallway and knocked on the door next to us. The woman who opened the door carried the strong scents I'd smelled on Sneakers, so I knew she and Sneakers had been spending time together. In fact, Sneakers walked right in as if she lived there.

"Oh, hello, Sneakers," Mrs. Minnick said, smacking her lips in an odd way as she spoke. I held myself stiffly but didn't growl, because the woman was clearly feeble and not a threat.

From that point on, Sneakers seemed to regard every opening of the door as an opportunity to dash over and wait to be let in to see Mrs. Minnick. I didn't know what the attraction was, but clearly Sneakers liked it there. I didn't have any opinion about Mrs. Minnick at all, other than the fact that her mouth made strange clicking noises when she talked.

CJ and I still took dog walks, but now we had to go a long way to pick up the first one, who was named Katie, and missing from the usual pack were Sally and Duke and Beevis.

I didn't miss Beevis at all.

One day it rained on the way to get Katie and I was so cold I was shivering. "Oh, Max, I'm so sorry," CJ told me. She held me in her arms until I was warm, and the next time the wind was cool she slipped a blanket on me that I could wear. "You like your sweater, Max? You look so handsome in your sweater!" I loved the feel of the tight sweater on all sides of me and it had the added benefit of keeping me warm. I was proud to wear it because I felt it showed that CJ loved me more than she loved Sneakers, who didn't even rate a collar. "You look so cute in your sweater, Max! You're my sweater better dog," CJ crooned to me. I wagged, loving to be in the center of her world.

When CJ removed the sweater it made a ripping sound, every single time. I came to associate that sound with the end of a walk and the start of a nap.

I didn't know why we never went back home, and I didn't know why Duke didn't walk with us anymore. I knew Sneakers probably didn't miss Duke, but I found that I did. As irritating as he could be sometimes, he was big and goofy and fun to play with. He let me be in charge and followed my lead, and I could feel people's wariness when CJ was protected by both of us. He had been part of our family.

This was, I reflected, how people ran the world. One day they would decide to live somewhere else and to stop playing with certain dogs.

Sometimes CJ would sit on the only piece of furniture she had besides the bed, a lone stool, and toss a small ball around in the kitchen and it would bounce and I would chase it, my nails scrabbling on the slick floor. "Oh, Max, I am so sorry this place is so tiny," she said to me. I loved the game and, now that I was used to it, I loved the new home better than the old place, because it meant that I could be closer to CJ.

We were playing with the ball when it sailed up onto the bed and I leaped right up after it! I was a little surprised, because I'd never managed to get up there before, and I know Sneakers was startled because she jumped to her feet, her eyes large and her tail puffy.

"Max!" CJ said, laughing in delight.

When CJ put on the nice-smelling shoes and spent a lot of time playing with her hair I knew that Gregg was coming over, and sure enough, there was soon a knock on the door and I ran to it, barking, while Sneakers fled. I could smell Gregg on the other side, so I kept barking. CJ picked me up.

"Max, be nice," she said, opening the door. Gregg came in and touched his face to CJ's while she held me away from him. I growled.

"Friendly as ever, I see," he said.

"Max, you be gentle. Gentle, Max." I had figured out that "gentle" meant "don't bite," but I kept my cold glare on Gregg to let him know not to try anything.

"Nice place," Gregg said, looking around. CJ put me down and I went over to sniff his pant legs, which smelled like wet leaves.

"Yes, let me take you on the grand tour. Stay close to me so you don't get lost," CJ said with a laugh. "This is the kitchen dining room great room."

"So I have a surprise."

"Really? What?"

"We're going away. Upstate. Three days."

"You're kidding!" CJ clapped her hands together and I looked at her curiously. "When?"

"Now."

"Sorry?"

"Now, let's leave now. I don't have to be anywhere for the next couple of days."

"What about . . . "

Gregg waved his hand. "There's some kind of deal with some property; she had to leave town."

CJ stood very still, looking at him. "That's actually

not what I meant. What I meant is that I can't exactly leave right *now*, Gregg. Not, like, this instant."

"Why not?"

"I have clients. I'd have to find coverage. I can't just take off."

"Your clients are dogs," Gregg said. I could hear some anger in his voice and I gave him a threatening stare, which he ignored.

"They rely on me. If I'm not there, I have to find someone else to cover for me."

"Geez!" Gregg looked around. "There's no place to even sit down to talk about this."

"Well, sure, I mean, we could sit on the bed," CJ said.

"Okay, that's a good idea," Gregg said.

Gregg and CJ went to the bed to hug. Sneakers jumped down and I jumped up, licking CJ in the face.

"Max!" she sputtered, laughing.

Gregg was not laughing. "Uh . . . ," he said.

"Come on, Max," CJ said, picking me up. She carried me to the bathroom and Sneakers followed, snaking in and around CJ's ankles. "Stay," CJ said.

She shut the door and Sneakers and I regarded each other unhappily.

Stay?

Sneakers came over to me and sniffed me, seeking comfort, then went over to the door and sat there expectantly, as if I could open it for her. I scratched at the bathroom door a few times, whimpering, then gave up and curled myself into a ball on the floor, waiting.

Some time later, CJ opened the door. I raced around the kitchen, thrilled to be out. This was so much fun!

CJ was barefoot, but she put the nice-smelling shoes back on, hopping on one foot as she did so. I put my feet on her legs and she smiled down at me. "Hi, Max. Good dog."

I wagged at being a good dog.

"So, okay," Gregg said. "If you can't, you can't. I get it."

"I'm sorry, I just need more warning. Even just a day or two. There's a guy I met at the park, he's a dog walker, I bet you he could sub for me, but I don't know how to get in touch with him."

"This kind of thing, there is no warning."

"Well . . . but sometime soon, that will no longer matter, right? I mean, you said just a few more months."

Greg looked around. "Man, this place is tiny even for New York, you know?"

"Gregg? You did say just a few more months. Right? *Right?*"

Gregg ran his hand through his hair. "I gotta be honest, CJ. This just isn't working for me."

"What?"

"I mean . . . " Gregg looked around the kitchen. "This isn't very convenient."

"Oh. Right. Because most of all, I'm a convenience." CJ sounded angry.

"You know what? There's that abusive tone you always use with me," Gregg said.

"Abusive? Seriously?"

"You know what I mean."

"No, actually, I don't. What are you trying to say?"

"See, it's just that you've gone from being understanding to now you have all these demands. I had this great trip planned for us and you all of a sudden can't go. And you've known all along what I have to deal with at home. I just . . . I've been thinking about it, and . . . "

"Oh my God, Gregg, you're doing this *now*? Like you couldn't have said something *before*? Or wouldn't that have been 'convenient' for you."

"You're the one that brought it up. I was happy to go on a trip and everything, but you had to start pushing."

"Pushing. Wow."

"I think maybe we need a break for a while, see how we feel."

"How I feel is that you're the biggest mistake I've ever made in my life."

"Okay, that's it; I'm not taking any more abuse from you."

"Get out of here, Gregg!"

"You know what? None of this is my fault!" Gregg shouted.

I now understood that Gregg was making CJ hurt and angry and I lunged at him, snarling, aiming for his ankles. He danced out of the way and then CJ scooped me up.

"Dog tries that again I'm kicking him into the next century," Gregg said. He was angry, too. I struggled to get down to bite him, but CJ held me tight.

"Leave. Now. Don't come back," CJ snapped.

"Small chance of that," Gregg spat.

Once Gregg left, CJ sat at her table and cried. I whimpered and she picked me up and I tried to lick her face, but she forced me to lie in her lap.

"I am so stupid, so stupid," she said, over and over again. I didn't understand anything she was saying, but the feeling flowing off of her was as if she felt like a bad dog. She took off her shoes and after a while got up and got some ice cream out of the freezer to eat.

After that I didn't see those shoes again for a long time. We walked with dogs most days and often went to a park, where I would search everywhere for the scent of Duke. I never once smelled him, though there was plenty of evidence of many, many dogs. Sneakers divided her time between our house and Mrs. Minnick's, which was fine because it meant that I got to spend more time with it being just CJ and myself. The days became cooler and I pretty much wore the tight sweater every time we went outside.

When the shoes finally came out I prepared myself for another encounter with Gregg, but I was pleasantly surprised when, upon charging the door after I heard a knock, I smelled the person on the other side. Trent!

"Hi, stranger!" CJ called as she opened the door. A blast of flower smell hit me—Trent held blooms in his arms. They hugged each other. Over the scent of flowers, Trent's hands smelled faintly of soap and something buttery when he bent down to see me. I wagged, wriggling under his friendly hands.

"I just can't believe how Max behaves around you," CJ said as she ushered him in. She set the flowers down—the whole house instantly filled with the odors.

"You know, I like this place a lot better than the last one," he said.

"Oh stop. Can you believe that they told me it had

a stove? I said to the lady, hello, a stove has more than one burner, that's a hot plate."

Trent sat on the counter, which I didn't like because it meant I couldn't reach him. "Rent's got to be a little less here than the penthouse, I imagine."

"Well, yeah, but you know New York. It's still not cheap. And the dog walking's not been going very well—turns out when you lose a famous client you lose a couple unfamous ones, too."

"Are you doing all right, though?"

"Yes, fine."

Trent looked at her.

"What is it?" CJ asked.

"You look really thin, CJ."

"Come on, Trent. Please."

They were silent for a long moment.

"Well, hey, I have news," Trent finally said.

"They put you in charge of the world's financial system?"

"Well, sure, but that was last week. No, it's, um, Liesl."

"What?"

"I'm going to propose to her this weekend."

I felt a shock run through CJ. She sat down on the stool. I went over to her, concerned. "Wow," she finally said. "That's . . . "

"Yeah, I know. Things were a little rough between us there, I think I told you about that, but lately, I don't know. It just seems right, you know? We've been together for a year and a half. It's like a conversation we've never had, right there in front of us, so I thought, time to talk about it. Want to see the ring?"

"Sure," CJ said softly.

Trent reached into his pocket and pulled out a toy and handed it to CJ. She didn't hold it down to me to sniff, so I figured it couldn't be much fun.

"What is it, CJ?"

"This just seems, I don't know. Fast, or something. Like, we're so young. Married."

"Fast?"

"No, forget it. The ring's beautiful."

Shortly after that, CJ and Trent left. When she came back she smelled deliciously of meat, but she was alone. I was disappointed because I was hoping Trent would stay to play, just as he had always done when he had Rocky. I wondered if the lack of a dog was what was keeping Trent from coming over as often as he once did. Not for the first time, I thought that Trent really needed a dog.

CJ seemed sad. She lay on her bed and dropped her shoes on the floor, and then I could hear her crying up there. Sneakers jumped on the bed, but I couldn't imagine a cat being as much comfort as a person's dog. When you were sad, you needed your dog. I backed up, then ran at the bed and leaped up. CJ reached for me and held me tightly.

"My life is nothing," she said. There was real grief in her words, though I didn't know what she was saying or even if she was talking to me or Sneakers.

After a time, my girl fell asleep, even though she was still dressed in the same clothes she'd worn when she'd left with Trent. I jumped down and paced the bedroom, distressed at how sad she was.

Probably because I was upset and trying to figure

out what was going on, I made a connection that hadn't occurred to me before: every time CJ put on the nice-smelling shoes, she was sad. They might have a delicious scent, but they were sad, sad shoes.

I knew what I needed to do.

TWENTY-FOUR

I thought if I chewed the sad shoes my girl wouldn't be sad anymore, but when she woke up and saw the pieces scattered across the floor she was not happy.

"Oh no!" she screamed. "Bad Max! Bad Max!"

I was a bad dog. I should not have chewed the shoes.

I went to her with my head down and my ears back, nervously licking my lips. CJ dropped to her knees and sobbed, burying her face in her hands. Sneakers came to the end of the bed to watch us. I anxiously put my paws on my girl's legs, but that didn't help at first, not until she gathered me up in her arms and clutched me to her. Then the sadness flowed from her as she cried.

"I am alone in the world, Max," CJ said to me. I didn't wag, because the way she said my name was so full of grief.

CJ eventually threw the shoe pieces away. From that morning forward, it seemed as if she moved more slowly, a vague sadness in her moods and motions. We still went for walks with a few other dogs nearly every day, but CJ didn't light up with happiness when she saw them, and when the first snow fell she sat and watched Katie and me tearing around the dog park without laughing once.

I wished Trent would come over—CJ was always happy when Trent was around. But he didn't and my girl never said Trent's name into her phone.

Instead, I heard "Gloria." CJ was sitting on her stool, talking. She had her phone by her face.

"How have you been, Gloria?" she said. I had been playing with Sneakers in the bedroom, but now I trotted into the kitchen, curious. Gloria wasn't there, though—CJ was just talking, saying, "Uh-huh. . . . Uh-huh. . . . Huh.

"Hawaii? That sounds really nice," CJ said, while I yawned and circled on my pillow, getting comfortable. Sneakers came padding over and leaped up on a counter and pretended not to care that I was there.

"Uh-huh. That's nice," CJ said. "Well, listen, Gloria, I have to ask you . . . I'm wondering if I could borrow some money. Just . . . I'm falling behind a little. I'm looking for a job, and also trying to find more dog-walking clients, but it's not happening. . . . Uh-huh. Well, sure, I understand; that must have been expensive. . . . Right, I get it, you couldn't very well go with old, *stale* luggage. No, I'm not, I'm just listening to what you are saying. . . . Okay, I was just asking, Gloria; I don't want this to get into some big discussion."

Sneakers finally lost patience and jumped down, coming over to me and purring at me. When I didn't budge, she curled up against me on my pillow. I sighed.

With a loud bang CJ set her phone down. She was clearly angry at it, but I knew from the shoe episode that this didn't imply she wanted me to do something about it. In my opinion, though, phones were not good toys. She went to the refrigerator and opened it and stood there looking inside for a long time, then looked at me. "Let's go for a walk instead, Max," she said.

It was bitterly cold outside, but I didn't complain. Eventually CJ scooped me up, though, holding me as we walked, and with my feet no longer on the wet ground I became cozy and warm.

A light knock on the door many evenings later alerted me and I barked loudly. CJ had been in bed most of the day, just lying there, and much of the time I had been with her. She roused herself, though, while I stood with my nose at the crack in the door. I was wagging at the scent: Trent!

"Who is it, Max? Hello?" my girl called.

"CJ, it's me."

"Oh." CJ looked around, running her hand through her hair, then opened the door.

"Hi, Trent."

"My God, I've been worried about you. Why's your phone shut off?"

"Oh. Um, just a . . . a thing. I need to talk to them."

"Can I come in?"

"Sure."

Trent stepped inside, stomping his feet to get the snow off of them. His coat was wet; he hung it on the hook where my leash was draped. I pranced at his feet, and finally he knelt down, accepting my kisses.

"Hi, Max, how have you been, boy?" Trent said, laughing. Then he stood, looking at CJ. "Hey," he said softly. "You okay?"

"Sure."

"You look . . . Have you been sick?"

"No," CJ said. "I was just taking a nap."

"You never responded to my messages. From before, I mean, when the phone was still working. Are you mad at me?"

"No. I'm sorry, Trent, I know it's hard for you to believe, but I've been a little busy and maybe haven't been able to get back to everyone on a timely basis."

Trent was quiet for a minute. "I'm sorry."

"No, it's okay."

"Look, want to go get something to eat?"

I could feel CJ getting a little angry. She folded her arms. "Because?" I went over to her and sat at her feet in case she needed me.

"Um, I don't know, because it's dinnertime?"

"So you came over here to feed me? Why don't I just chirp and you can puke into my mouth?"

"No. CJ, what are you doing? I came over to see how you were."

"To check up on me. See if I'm getting all my meals."

"That's not what I said."

"Well, I can't. I have a date."

Trent blinked. "Oh."

"I have to get ready."

"Okay. Look, I'm sorry if—"

"You don't have to apologize. I'm sorry that I got angry. But you should go."

Trent nodded. He reached for his coat, taking it off the hook, the leash underneath swaying tantalizingly. I glanced at CJ, but it didn't look as if she was planning to take a walk. Trent shrugged on the coat, then looked at CJ. "I miss you."

"I've just been so busy."

"Do you miss me, too?"

CJ looked away. "Of course."

A sadness rose up within Trent then. "Well, how do I get in touch with you?"

"When I get my phone back up I'll call you."

"Let's grab . . . coffee, or something."

"Sure," CJ said.

They hugged then. CJ was sad, too; it swirled around both of them. I didn't understand why they were both feeling so bad, but sometimes there are things going on between people that dogs are not supposed to comprehend.

Trent left and Sneakers came out from under the bed. I wished she hadn't hidden—there was no reason to hide from Trent; he was good.

A few days later CJ and I were coming back from walking with the dogs and there was a woman standing in front of our door with a piece of paper. CJ was panting a little from coming up the stairs. I barked at the stranger.

"Lydia!" CJ said. She stooped and picked me up, and I stopped barking.

"I was just posting notice," the woman said.

"Notice," CJ repeated.

The woman sighed. "You're just so far behind, honey. Can you pay anything toward rent today?"

"Today? No, I'm . . . I get paid on Friday; I could maybe pay most of a payment then?"

My girl felt afraid. I growled at the woman, because I could only conclude that she was the source of CJ's agitation. "Shush, Max," CJ said, folding a hand over my nose. I growled through the hand.

"Friday you'll be down another payment; that's why I'm here. I'm sorry, CJ, but I'm going to have to ask you to either catch up or go. I have rent and bills myself."

"No, I get it. Okay, I get it," CJ said. She wiped her eyes.

"Do you have family? People you can turn to?"

CJ held me more tightly and I stopped baring my teeth at the woman. I could sense that CJ needed my comfort more than my protection.

"No. My dad died in a plane crash when I was little."

"I'm so sorry to hear it."

"I'll move out. Thank you for your, for all of your patience. I promise I will pay you the money I owe you. I'm looking for a better job."

"Just take care of yourself, dear. You look as if you haven't eaten in a week."

The woman left. CJ went into her apartment, carrying the piece of paper that the woman had handed her. CJ sat on her bed and when I whimpered she picked me up and set me down beside her and I climbed into her lap. She felt full of sadness and fear.

"I've become my mother," she whispered.

A little while later, CJ stood up and started gathering her clothes and putting them into a suitcase. She fed me some cheese and gave me Sneakers' food when Sneakers turned up her nose at it. Normally I would have been delighted with these wonderful treats, but there was something odd about the way CJ gave them to me, with a cold, detached gloom, that took some of the joy out of it.

CJ pulled out Sneakers' crate and put all of Sneakers' toys in it and also the cat's bed. Sneakers watched all this without expression, while I paced around at CJ's feet, feeling anxious. I felt better, though, when CJ clicked my leash onto my collar, picked up Sneakers and the crate, and went next door to Mrs. Minnick's house. "Hi, Mrs. Minnick," CJ said.

Mrs. Minnick held out her hands and took Sneakers, who was purring. "Hi, CJ," she said.

"I have this huge favor to ask of you. I'm . . . I have to move. And where I'm going won't take pets. So, I was wondering if you would watch Sneakers for a while? For maybe, always? She's so happy here."

Mrs. Minnick's face broke into a huge smile. "Are you sure?" She held Sneakers out at arm's length. "Sneakers?"

Sneakers stopped purring, because she did not like the way she was being held. I put a paw on CJ's leg, because I was impatient to get going on our walk.

Mrs. Minnick stepped back and CJ set the crate inside the door.

"All of her things are in there. Also a few cans of food, but she hasn't been eating much lately."

"Well, I've been feeding her over here."

"I figured. Okay. Again, thanks so much." CJ took a step forward, closer to Mrs. Minnick, who was holding and stroking the cat. "Sneakers. You are a good cat," CJ said, pushing her face into the cat's fur. Sneakers rubbed her head against CJ, purring. "Okay," CJ whispered.

I whined anxiously at the grief pouring out of my girl.

Mrs. Minnick was watching CJ. "Are you sure you're fine?"

"Oh yes. Sneakers, you are my favorite kitty; you be good."

"You'll come visit?" Mrs. Minnick asked uncertainly.

"Of course. Soon as I'm settled in the new place, I'll come by. Okay? I have to go now. Bye-bye, Sneakers. I love you. Good-bye."

The cat hopped out of Mrs. Minnick's arms and trotted into the woman's home. Sneakers was mostly a good cat, but she was making CJ sad and I didn't like that.

After leaving Sneakers with Mrs. Minnick we went for a very strange walk. First I did my business in the snow, and then CJ picked me up and carried me and we walked and walked. I loved the way the warmth of her kept me snug and safe. CJ seemed really tired and sad, though, and I wondered where we could possibly be going.

Finally she stopped and let me down on the ground. I sniffed at the snow, not recognizing any of the scents. CJ knelt on both knees, leaning down to me. "Max."

I licked her face and it brought the sadness back, which didn't make much sense to me. Usually when I licked her it made her happy.

"You have been such a good, good dog. Okay? You have been the most wonderful dog a girl in the city could ever want. You protected me and took care of me. I love you, Max. Okay? No matter what happens, don't ever forget how much I love you, because it's true." CJ was wiping her face, the tears flowing onto her hands. The sadness in her was so awful it made me afraid.

After a minute she stood, taking a breath. "Okay," she said. She carried me a little farther and then some of the scents were familiar, and I knew we were going to see Trent. I felt a sense of relief—Trent would help CJ. Whatever was going on was beyond a dog's understanding, but he would know what to do.

Trent opened his door. "God, what's happened?" he asked. "Come in."

"I can't," CJ said, standing in the hallway. "I've got to go. I need to go to the airport." She set me down and I ran to Trent, leaping up and wagging. He reached down and patted my head, but he was looking at CJ.

"The airport?"

"It's Gloria, she's really sick, and I need to be there."

"I'll go with you," Trent said.

"No, no, what I need, can you watch Max? Please? You're the only other person in the whole world that he likes."

"Sure," Trent said slowly. "Max? You want to hang here for a few days?"

"I need to go," my girl said. She did not seem any happier here with Trent.

"Want me to ride to the airport with you?"

"No, that's okay."

"You seem really upset, CJ."

CJ took a deep, shuddering breath. "No, I'm okay. I guess I have some unreconciled . . . some stuff about Gloria. It doesn't matter. I need to go."

"What time's your flight?"

"Trent, *please,* I can manage, okay? Just let me go."

"Okay," Trent said softly. "Say good-bye to CJ, Max."

"We already . . . " CJ shook her head. "Okay, right. Bye, Max." She dropped to one knee. "I love you. I'll see you soon, okay? Bye, Max." CJ stood. "Bye, Trent."

They came together in a fierce hug. When they pulled apart, I could feel Trent being a little afraid. I looked around but didn't see any threat. "CJ?" he asked her in a small voice.

She shook her head, not meeting his eyes. "I have to go," CJ said. She turned and I made to follow, but my leash pulled me up short. I barked at her, but CJ didn't look back. She went straight to the little room with the double doors, and when they opened she stepped inside and turned and then, in one frozen moment, she finally looked at me. She met my eyes, then looked and gave a smile and a little wave to Trent.

Even from there, I could see her tears, reflected in the harsh overhead lights of the little room. I barked again. Then the doors shut.

Trent picked me up and looked at me. "What's really going on, huh, Max?" he whispered. "I don't like this. I don't like it at all."

[TWENTY-FIVE]

Now things were entirely different. I was staying in Trent's house, which was bigger than where I lived with CJ. I still took dog walks, though—a woman named Annie came over every day with a happy fat yellow dog named Harvey and let herself into Trent's house and took me with her. It was strange to me that her name was Annie, because my sisters at the place of the barking dogs had been Abby and Annie. I concluded that some people loved dogs so much they called themselves by dog names. Annie smelled like a lot of different cats and dogs, which seemed to confirm my theory. The first day she came over I rushed toward her, barking fiercely so that she'd know that I wasn't intimidated by her Harvey, but Trent was

there and snatched me up off the floor and then Annie reached for me and grabbed me out of Trent's
arms and I didn't know what to do about that. Normally when I was snarling people didn't hug me to
their chests. She cooed to me and rocked me and I felt
myself letting down my guard completely. CJ wasn't
there and didn't need my protection, so maybe it was
okay if I let Annie take certain liberties.

Annie and Harvey and I walked with other dogs,
but Annie did it wrong—we didn't stop to get Katie
on the way, though we did stop for a dog named Zen,
who was big but with very short legs and heavy ears
that almost touched the ground. He looked very much
like Barney, the dog who lived with Jennifer when
Rocky and I were puppies. When I snarled at Zen he
collapsed and rolled on his back and passively let
me sniff him all over. I wouldn't be getting any trouble
from him. Less cooperative was a tall dog with curly
hair named Jazzy. Jazzy didn't want to play with me.

Trent only came home at night, usually carrying a
bag of food that he would eat silently, standing in the
kitchen. He seemed very tired and sad. He would hold
his hands out to me and I smelled a lot of different
things, but never once did I smell my girl.

"Oh, Max, you miss her, don't you," Trent said
softly to me. I wagged to show that I had heard my
name and that I liked it when he stroked the top of
my head.

I was very fond of Trent and was sorry he didn't
have a dog, but I needed to be with CJ. I didn't understand where she was and why she had left me here.
Sometimes I would dream that she was there next to

me, but when I opened my eyes I was always in Trent's home, always alone.

Did CJ go back to live with Sneakers? Was that why she had been so sad? I had felt the same sort of sadness in Hannah when, as Buddy, I'd been taken to the Vet for the last time. It was a *good-bye* kind of sad. CJ, though, needed me in her life, which was why she kept coming for me every time I was a puppy. Nothing would ever change that, so whatever was keeping me apart from her, I knew it had to be temporary.

One afternoon when Annie and Harvey brought me back to Trent's house, Trent was sitting in the living room. "Oh, hi!" Annie said. "Is this the day?"

"Yes," Trent said.

Harvey sat on the threshold, waiting to be told it was okay to be let in. He was one of those dogs who were always looking to their people for permission for things. I could be that kind of dog, but CJ never asked it of me. "Okay, Harvey," Annie said. Harvey came in and went over to see if I'd left any food for him in my bowl. I never did, but he checked every time, just in case.

Annie stooped and held her arms out to me, and I sheepishly went to her and let myself be cuddled, while Harvey stuck his big friendly nose in her face and got cuddled, too. "You have a good day today, Max."

When Annie left, Harvey went with her without a backward glance.

"Look what I have for you here, Max," Trent said. It was like a crate, only the sides were soft. Trent seemed really excited to show it to me. I sniffed it carefully. When I was Molly, the crate had been much bigger—but then again, so had I.

Thinking of being Molly and the disorienting trip I once took in a crate made me wonder if we were going to see CJ. When Trent told me to get into the soft crate, I went without complaint, though I could barely see out of a small mesh covering one end. It was a little disconcerting when he picked the whole thing up, so different from when people gathered me in their arms and lifted me off the ground.

We took a car ride, both Trent and I sitting in the backseat. I was frustrated that he didn't let me out of the soft crate so I could look out the window and bark at any dogs I might see. The car was warm, though, which was nice compared to the windy, wet, cold air that flowed into the soft crate when Trent and I left his building.

We went into another building and I was disappointed because it wasn't loud—it was quiet, hushed, even, though I could smell many people and chemicals. I couldn't see much of what was happening, and the way Trent moved the soft crate while he walked with it made me a little dizzy.

Then we entered a small room and he set the crate down. "Hey," he said softly. I heard a rustle.

"Hi," someone said in a weak, cracking voice.

"Brought someone to see you," Trent said. He fumbled with the soft material of the crate and I licked his fingers through the mesh, eager to be let out. Finally he reached in and grabbed me. He hoisted me up in the air and I saw a woman lying in a bed.

"Max!" the woman said, and that's when I realized

it was CJ. Her smell was odd—sour and covered with chemicals—but I recognized her. I struggled to get out of Trent's arms, but he held me tight.

"You need to be gentle, Max. Gentle," Trent said. He carefully handed me to CJ, who reached for me with her warm, wonderful hands. I burrowed into her, moaning and crying a little—I couldn't help it, I was so glad to see my girl.

"Okay, easy, Max. Okay? Easy," Trent said.

"He's okay. You missed me, didn't you, Max. Yes, baby," she said. I wondered why her voice was so thin and raspy—it didn't sound much like her at all. There was a plastic leash hanging on her arm, and the room echoed with a beeping noise that was very unpleasant.

"How are you feeling today?" Trent asked.

"Throat still hurts from the tube, but I'm getting a little better. Still nauseated," CJ said.

I wanted to sniff her up and down to explore all the strange new scents clinging to her, but her hands had a tension in them as they held me, willing me to be still. I did what she wanted.

"I know you think you look like crap, but compared to when you were in ICU, it's like you're ready to run a marathon. Your color is back in your cheeks," Trent said. "Your eyes are clear."

"I'm sure I look fabulous," CJ muttered.

A woman stepped into the room and I gave her a low growl to let her know CJ had her protection with her.

"No, Max!" CJ said.

"Max, no," Trent said. He came over and put his hands on me as well, so that I was pretty effectively pinned as the woman gave CJ something odorless to eat and a small cup of water to drink. It was actually very nice to have both of them holding me, and I remained still.

"What's his name?" the woman asked.

"Max," Trent and CJ said together. I wagged.

"He's not supposed to be in here. Dogs are never allowed."

Trent took a step in her direction. "He's such a small dog and he doesn't bark or anything. Couldn't he visit for just a minute?"

"I love dogs. I'm not going to tell anyone, but if you get caught, don't you dare say I knew about it," the woman replied.

When the woman left, Trent and CJ said, "Good dog," at the same time, and I wagged.

I could feel a lot of dark emotions in my girl, sadness and hopelessness intermingled, and nuzzling her couldn't seem to lift her mood. She also was tired—exhausted, even—and soon her hand was no longer holding me but just resting, held there by gravity.

I was confused. Why was CJ in this room? Even more perplexing and upsetting was the fact that Trent soon called me and pulled me away from CJ by my leash.

"We'll come back in a few days, Max," Trent said. I heard my name but didn't understand.

"Good boy, Max. You go with Trent. No, don't bring him back; I don't want to get in trouble with the entire medical establishment," CJ said. I wagged at being a good boy.

"I'll be back tomorrow. Sleep tonight, okay? And

call me anytime if you can't sleep; I'm happy to talk," Trent said.

"You don't have to come here every day, Trent."

"I know that."

We went back to Trent's house. Over the next several days Annie still came to take me for walks with Harvey and Jazzy and Zen, but now, when Trent returned home in the evening, I could faintly pick out CJ's scent on his hands among all the other odd smells.

We went back to the little room a day or two later and CJ was still taking a nap in the same bed. She smelled a little better, though, and was sitting up when Trent let me out of the soft crate.

"Max!" she called happily. I bounded into her arms and she hugged me. There was no longer a leash on her arm and the beeping noise had stopped. "Close the door, Trent; I don't want Max getting in trouble."

While CJ and Trent talked, I curled up in a ball under her arm, staking claim to the spot on the bed so that if Trent left he wouldn't try to take me with him. I was dozing off when I heard the door open and a woman say, "Oh my God!" from the doorway. I instantly recognized the voice.

Gloria.

She swept into the room, carrying flowers that she pushed at Trent as she went to CJ's bedside. Gloria smelled of those flowers, plus so many other sweet scents it made my eyes water.

"You look awful," Gloria said.

"Nice to see you, too, Gloria."

"Are they feeding you? What is this place?"

"This is a hospital," CJ said. "You remember Trent."

"Hello, Miss Mahoney," Trent said.

"Well, of course I know it's a hospital; that's not what I meant. Hello, Trent." Gloria pushed her face at Trent and then turned back to CJ. "I have never been so worried in my life. The shock of it nearly killed me!"

"Sorry about that," CJ said.

"Honey, you think I haven't had bad times, myself? Yet I have always found the strength to go on. You're only a failure if you see yourself as a failure; I've told you that. For this to happen . . . I nearly fainted. I came the second I heard."

"Well, ten days," Trent said.

Gloria looked at him. "Sorry?"

"I called you ten days ago. So it wasn't exactly the second you heard."

"Well . . . there was no point for me to come while she was in a coma," Gloria said with a frown.

"Of course," Trent said.

"She does have a point," CJ said. She and Trent grinned at each other.

"I can't stand hospitals. Absolutely hate them," Gloria said.

"You are unique in that," CJ said. "Most people love them." This time Trent laughed.

"So, Trent. Do you suppose a mother could talk to her daughter?" Gloria asked coldly.

"Sure." Trent pushed himself off the wall.

"Take your dog, too," Gloria told him. I looked at CJ when I heard the word "dog."

"It's my dog. His name is Max," CJ said.

"Call me if you need anything," Trent said as he walked out the door.

Gloria went over and sat in the lone chair. "Well, this place is certainly depressing. So is Trent back in the picture?"

"No. Trent was never 'in the picture,' Gloria. He's my best friend."

"All right, call it whatever. His mother, who naturally couldn't wait to phone me the second she heard my daughter had taken pills with anti-freeze, says that he's a vice president of his bank. Don't believe him when he acts like that's a big deal—at banks, they hand out titles to everybody; it's how they avoid paying them a decent salary."

"He's an investment banker and he *is* very successful," CJ responded testily.

"Speaking of investments, I have pretty important news."

"Do tell."

"Carl is going to propose."

"Carl."

"I told you about Carl. He made a fortune selling coin thingies, what you put a quarter in for machines like dryers at the Laundromat. He has a home in Florida with a sixty-four-foot sailboat! He also has an apartment in Vancouver and owns part of a hotel in Vail where we can go whenever we want. Vail! I've always wanted to go to Vail but have never met the right person. They say Vail is like Aspen only without all the locals to ruin it."

"So you're getting married?"

"Yes. He's going to propose next month; we're going to the Caribbean. That's where he proposed to both his wives. So, you know, two and two together. Want to see his picture?"

"Sure."

I looked up, yawning, as Gloria handed over something. CJ squealed with laughter. "This is Carl? Is he a Civil War veteran?"

"I'm sure I don't know what you mean."

"He's like a thousand years old."

"He is not; he's very distinguished. I'll ask you not to be rude. He's going to be your stepfather."

"Oh lord. How many times have I heard that? What about the one who paid off the mortgage, who you made me call 'Dad'?"

"Most men are unreliable. Carl's different."

"Because he's ancient?"

"No, because he is still friends with his ex-wives. That says something."

"Sure does." CJ put her hand on my head and I became drowsy with the warm feeling of pure love. Soon I was asleep. I woke up, though, when I heard and felt anger in CJ.

"What do you mean you won't discuss it?" CJ asked Gloria.

"That family was horrible to me. We won't have anything to do with them."

"But that's not fair to me. I'm related to them by blood. I want to know them, who I come from."

"I raised you all by myself without help."

I felt a rising sense of sadness in CJ, but she was still angry. "I remember so little from when my dad took me there when I was a kid. I remember . . . I remember there was a horse. And my aunts, and grandma. It's all I have, just fragments from when I was like six years old."

"That's how it should be."

"You don't get to decide that!"

"Now listen." Gloria stood up and she was angry, too. "You are no longer in high school and I won't have you behaving like a spoiled child. You're going to be living under my roof, with my rules. Understand?"

"No, she won't," Trent said quietly from the doorway.

They both turned to look at him as he came in.

"This is not your concern, Trent," Gloria said.

"It is my concern. CJ doesn't need this right now. She's supposed to avoid stress. And she's not going home with you. Her acting career is here."

"Oh . . . I don't think I'm ever going to be an actress," CJ said.

"Exactly," Gloria said.

"Then you'll be *something*. You can do whatever you want. You're not helpless, CJ. You get to decide *you* have the power," Trent said emphatically.

"What are you talking about?" Gloria asked coldly.

"You believe me, don't you, CJ?" Trent demanded.

"I . . . I can't stay, Trent. I can't afford—"

"I have more than enough room at my place—you can move into the spare bedroom until you're back on your feet."

"What about Liesl?"

"Oh. Liesl." He laughed. "We broke up again. I think this one's going to stick, because I'm not begging her to take me back. I realized finally that what she likes is the drama of breaking up and getting back and breaking up. . . . It's like an addiction."

"When did this happen?"

"The night before you . . . dropped off Max."

I wagged.

"I feel awful you've been dealing with that and I never asked," CJ said.

"It's okay; you've been a little distracted," Trent said with a wry grin.

"Can we please get back to the subject?" Gloria demanded.

"Meaning, what *you* want to talk about?" CJ responded.

"No, that's not what I mean at all. I mean that we're leaving Wednesday. Arrangements have already been made," Gloria said firmly.

"You need to be with someone who believes in you. Me, I believe in you. I've always believed in you," Trent said.

I could feel Gloria's anger getting worse. "No one is going to accuse me of not 'believing in my daughter.' I supported this whole ridiculous move to New York, didn't I?"

"*Supported* it!" CJ replied.

"You're not good for her, Gloria. She needs to heal. You're the last person who could help her with that," Trent said.

"I am her *mother*," Gloria said icily.

"Well, yes, you gave birth to her, that much is true. But she's a grown-up. Once a child grows up, your work is done."

"CJ?" Gloria said. I looked at Gloria, who was staring at CJ, and then at Trent, who was looking at Gloria, and then finally at CJ, who was looking back and forth between them. Gloria put her hands on her hips.

"You've never thanked me. All the sacrifices I've made," she said bitterly. She turned to stalk out, pausing in the doorway to glare at her daughter. "I'll be back tomorrow, and we're leaving the day after, as scheduled. There's nothing more to be said." She glared at Trent. "By *anybody.*"

I wagged because Gloria was leaving. I always felt a little less stressed with her gone.

When Trent and I went back to his home that night, I wondered if this was the new routine: we'd sleep at his place, then go to CJ's new room with the slick floors. CJ seemed to prefer to live in smaller and smaller places.

Trent tossed a rubber toy for me that bounced crazily across the kitchen, and I chased it and brought it back to him and he laughed and told me I was a good dog.

Later, as he was bending over to scoop some delicious wet food on top of the dry food in my dish, I caught a metallic, unmistakable odor on his breath. I was surprised, but I did what I was trained to do a long time ago.

I signaled.

TWENTY-SIX

A few days after the visit from Gloria, CJ came to live at Trent's place. She put her things in a different room from Trent's and some of her clothes still had Sneakers' smell on them. The new living arrangements seemed to fatigue her, as she spent an awful lot of time in her bed and was sad and weak and in pain for most of it. I tried to cheer her up by delivering her chew toys, which Trent kept bringing home in little bags, but other than holding them slackly in her hand for me to tug on, CJ wasn't interested much in playing.

Trent would come home at least once during the day to let me out. "It's no problem; I'm right around the corner."

"Maybe tomorrow I'll feel up to taking Max for a walk," CJ said.

"Take your time," Trent said.

They liked to play a game where Trent would sit by her and wrap her arm in a sweater like mine and then squeeze a little ball. I would hear an odd hiss, and CJ and Trent would hold still. "Good, BP is still good," Trent would usually say. When it came off, her sweater made the same ripping sound as mine.

I was not allowed to play with that ball because it was apparently Trent's favorite.

It was Trent who fed me, and I learned that to earn a meal I had to signal when I smelled the odd metallic odor on his breath, which was most times.

"Aren't you going to pray, Max?" he would ask me sometimes. I would signal, and then he would say, "Good boy, Max," and reward me with dinner.

"Max prays before he eats dinner," Trent told CJ. I was scampering around the room, burning energy, but I froze when I heard my name mentioned with the word "dinner." I'd already eaten but would not have objected if Trent wanted to give me a treat.

"What do you mean?" CJ asked, laughing.

"I swear. He bows his head down and clasps his hands together, like he's saying grace. It's really cute."

"I've never seen him do that," CJ said.

"Pray, Max!" Trent called to me. I could tell I was supposed to be doing something, so I sat and barked. They both laughed, but they didn't give me a treat, so apparently I had done it wrong.

When CJ finally got up out of bed to go to the couch, she went very, very slowly, pushing a thing that looked a little like a chair in front of her that she held on to very tightly. The chair-thing had tennis balls on it, yet she didn't throw them for me to chase. I scampered around at her feet, delighted to see her up, but she was breathing loudly and didn't seem happy.

Trent, though, was very pleased when he walked in the door. "You made it to the couch!" he greeted her, smiling.

"Yeah, only took me an hour."

"That's really great, CJ."

"Sure it is." CJ looked away with a sigh. I jumped up on the couch and nuzzled her hand to help her feel better.

Every day after that CJ would get out of that bed to move around the apartment, always pushing the thing with tennis balls. Then one day we started taking walks outside. The snow was melting the first time we did this, so the car tires were making loud ripping noises on the pavement and everywhere I could hear dripping and splashing. We only went a few feet down the sidewalk, the tennis balls on CJ's chair-thing getting wet. A few days later, it had snowed again and we only went a few steps before we turned around. The day after that, the sun was out and it was warm and the snow was melting and under it I could smell new grass.

Our house had an outside room called a balcony. Trent put a box lined with rough carpet out there and called me to it. "This is where you can go to the bathroom, okay, Max? It's your own special porta-potty."

The rough carpet was softer than the cement floor of the balcony. I loved to lie on it when it was breezy and open my nose to the intoxicating mix of smells from the loud streets below. Sometimes I'd smell Mrs.

Warren, the lady who often came out onto the balcony next to ours. "Hello, Max," she would say to me, and I'd wag.

"You're not supposed to lie in it, Max," Trent told me when he came out to see me there. CJ laughed with delight. I didn't know what was going on but resolved that if it made my girl so happy I'd lie on the rough carpet as often as possible.

As the days turned warmer, CJ would take her chair-thing and walk farther and farther, always going very slowly. On none of these walks did we stop to pick up Katie or any other dogs.

I became familiar with our route and looked forward to stopping at a bed of nose-level flowers along the way. There was some male dog I had never before met who had always marked the plants, and I sniffed very carefully before raising my leg in the same area.

"Max loves to stop here and smell the flowers," CJ told Trent one time when they were both walking me.

"Good dog, Max. Stop and smell the roses," Trent said. I heard that I was a good dog but was much more focused on the scent of that other dog.

Some days were better than others for CJ. On one of her bad days she was lying in bed when I heard fumbling at the front door, so I raced up to it, barking. When it opened, I was astounded to smell who was with Trent.

Duke!

Duke bounded into the room, full of manic energy. I raised up on my back legs and took his head in my front paws and licked at his lips, truly glad to see him. His big tongue came out and slapped against my face over and over and he was moaning and shaking, so happy was he to be with me. He dropped onto his back so I could climb on him, and we wrestled and squirmed joyously together.

"Come on back, guys," Trent said. We went to CJ's room and she sat up in bed.

"Duke!" she called out.

Duke was so excited to see her that he jumped right up on her bed. CJ gasped with pain. "Hey!" Trent yelled.

The lamp next to CJ fell to the floor and there was a flash and then the room was darker. Duke, panting, leaped around, crashing into things, then launched himself back on the bed. "Get off, Duke!" CJ said, and she was angry.

Snarling, I bit at Duke's heels, and he shrank to the floor, his ears back.

What my girl needed, I realized at that moment, was calm and stillness. When Duke jumped on her it hurt her and his boisterous behavior made her and Trent mad.

To be a good dog in this house meant being less loud and active. CJ needed quiet.

With Duke finally more under control, CJ pulled his head to her and scratched his ears. "Okay, Trent, how did you pull *this* off?" she asked.

"Not hard to track Barry down. I just called him at his office and explained what I wanted. He wasn't going to say no," Trent said.

CJ stopped scratching Duke and looked at Trent. "You mean, he wasn't going to say no to *you*."

"Right. Well . . ."

"Oh, Duke, I am so, so happy to see you," CJ crooned.

I jumped up on the bed but did so nimbly and crept up to where Duke was getting all the love. I knew CJ would want me there, too. I was the most important dog in the situation.

After Duke left, CJ and Trent had dinner at the table instead of back in her bedroom. I liked it better when she ate in bed because she often would hand me little morsels, but they seemed happier sitting with just their legs within reach of my nose, for some reason. I sat patiently under the table, on patrol for falling food.

"Maybe dialysis wouldn't be that bad," Trent said.

"Oh God, Trent."

"I'm just saying, if it has to happen, we'll deal with it."

"If it happens to me, *we* will deal with it?" CJ said sharply.

For a few moments there was nothing but the sound of their forks on their plates.

"I'm sorry," CJ said softly. "I do appreciate everything you're doing for me. God, that was so Gloria of me."

"No, you've been through a lot, you're in pain, and dialysis is scary. It makes sense for you to get pissed for me to suggest it would somehow be my experience, too. But what I really meant is that I'll support you every way I can, no matter what it takes. That's all."

"Thank you, Trent. I don't deserve a friend like you," CJ replied.

When they were done eating, Trent put food in my bowl. I loved the plinking sound of dinner landing in my metal bowl, and danced circles waiting for him to put it down.

"Now watch. Pray, Max, pray."

Trent held the food away from me, but he was leaning over and I caught the smell on his breath. I knew what he wanted, and signaled.

"See?" Trent said, laughing delightedly.

"That's so weird. I've never seen him do that before," CJ said.

"He's saying grace," Trent said.

As the weather grew warmer, CJ and I would venture farther and farther on our walks. She eventually stopped pushing her tennis ball chair-thing out in front of her but would lean on a hooked stick a little as we slowly made our way down the sidewalk. I had learned to be very patient and would walk next to her at the pace she wanted to go—protecting her now meant making sure she didn't fall over or feel pain from walking too fast. Sometimes Trent would come home in the middle of the day and walk with us, and he, too, adopted a slow gait.

It had been so long since I had been on a car ride, I had pretty much written off the idea that I would ever get to be a front-seat dog again, though there were always plenty of cars in the streets. So I was surprised when I was put in a crate, one with hard sides and a lot more room to move around in than the soft one, and carried out of the building by Trent. He put me on the backseat of a big car.

"Buckle the crate in," CJ said. "It's safer with the seat belt on."

I yipped a little when the car drove off with Trent at the wheel. Had they forgotten I was here?

"Oh, Max, I know, but we're right up front. You're safer in the back," CJ said.

I hadn't heard anything I understood, but I could feel the love in CJ's voice. I pondered my reaction. I wanted to keep barking until they let me out of the crate, but I remembered the time when, as Molly, I left the ocean with CJ and I took the long noisy ride with a dog barking the whole way—nobody let him out of *his* crate, and his barking was irritating to me. I didn't want to irritate CJ—not upsetting her was how I took care of her now. So I settled down with a long, forlorn sigh.

"First time I've ever left New York in August. I was always so envious of everybody—the heat was murderous," CJ said.

It was a long car ride.

"You're not going to tell me where we're going? Not even now?" CJ said after a while.

"You'll figure it out," Trent replied. "Until then I want it to be as much of a surprise as possible."

It was very hot outside every time we stopped, but we spent the night in a place so cold I slept under the blankets with CJ. Trent had a different room, but it smelled pretty much the same as ours.

As I fell asleep, I thought of the last really, really long car ride I'd taken, where we wound up going to the ocean. Was that where we were headed now?

We had been driving a long time the second day and CJ slept a lot of the time, but when she woke up she suddenly became very excited.

"Oh my God! Are we going where I think we are?" she asked.

"Yeah," Trent said.

"How did you find it?"

"It wasn't hard to do. Public records. Ethan and Hannah Montgomery. So I called and said you wanted to visit."

In my crate I wagged a little at hearing the names Ethan and Hannah spoken in the same sentence.

"Wasn't hard to do *for you*. How come you know how to do all this stuff? I was always so much smarter than you," CJ said.

"Oh right, you were smarter? I can't even reply to that; it's frying my memory circuits."

They both laughed.

"Do they know we're coming?" CJ asked.

"Oh yes. They're pretty excited."

"Oh my God, I can't wait. This is amazing!"

I fell asleep, made drowsy by the steady droning of the car noises.

When I woke up, the scent wafting through the car made me dizzy. I knew where we were, and when the car stopped I cried, eager to get out. "Okay, Max," Trent said. Warm evening air flowed over me as Trent opened my crate door and held my leash. I bounded into the grass.

Ultimately I shouldn't have been surprised: eventually everyone returned to the Farm.

Several people poured out of the house and ran down to see me and also CJ.

"Aunt Rachel?" CJ asked uncertainly.

"Look at you!" the woman shouted, hugging CJ as the others milled around.

There were three women and two men and one little girl. I recognized the scents of all but the little girl.

"I'm your aunt Cindy," another woman said. She bent down to offer her hand to sniff, but Trent pulled me back, my collar going tight as he yanked the leash.

"Uh, that's Max; he's not real friendly," Trent said.

I was wagging, so happy to see everyone and to be back home. Were we going to live here now? That would be fine by me.

"He seems nice," Cindy said. I strained forward and managed to lick her hand and Trent laughed. Pretty soon Cindy picked me up and I was nose-to-nose with everyone in the family.

"Let's go inside," Cindy said. She handed the leash to the little girl, whose name was Gracie.

It was such a pleasure to mount the wooden steps, even though it did take more of an effort than when I was a bigger dog. Proud that I knew my way, I forced myself through the door first, feeling the leash go slack as Gracie dropped it.

There was a woman sitting in a chair in the living room. She was old, but I'd know her scent anywhere. I bounded right across the room and into her lap. It was Hannah, Ethan's mate.

"My goodness." She laughed as I squirmed and licked at her face.

292 | W. BRUCE CAMERON

"Max!" Trent called. He sounded stern, so I hustled off Hannah's lap and ran over to see what sort of trouble I'd gotten into. He snagged my leash.

"Grandma?" CJ said.

Hannah stood up slowly and CJ walked to her and they hugged for a long time. They were both crying, but the love and happiness between them swept through and touched everyone who was watching.

TWENTY-SEVEN

We did not stay on the Farm to live, but we spent more than a week there. I loved racing around with my nose down, tracking all the familiar scents. There were ducks in the pond, a whole family as always, but though I stood and watched them for a while, I didn't bother to chase them. Not only was there never any profit in that, but the two largest ones were as big as I was. It was the first time in a long while that I thought about how small a dog I was as Max. It did not seem right that a dog should be the same size as a duck.

There were strong horse smells in the barn but no horse to be found, which I considered fortunate. If CJ had wandered in there I would have faced down that horse again, but the prospect of doing so as Max, and not Buddy, made me more than a little afraid.

CJ spent much of her time walking and talking with Hannah, who moved at the same slow speed as my girl. I stayed by their side, proud to be protecting both of them. "I never gave up hope," Hannah said. "I knew that this day would come, Clarity. CJ, I mean, I'm sorry."

"That's okay," CJ said. "I like it when you call me that."

"I could barely contain myself from screaming like a teenager when your boyfriend telephoned."

"Oh, Trent? No, he's not my boyfriend."

"He's not?"

"No. We've been best friends forever, but never like as a couple."

"Interesting," Hannah said.

"What? Why are you looking at me like that?"

"Nothing. I'm just happy you're here, that's all."

One afternoon it rained and the roar on the roof was as loud as the cars I could hear from my special carpet on the balcony, only without the honking. The windows were open and the wet, earthy smells came flooding into the room. I lay lazily at CJ's feet as she and Hannah sat and ate cookies without giving me one.

"I feel guilty that I didn't try harder," Hannah told CJ.

"No, Grandma, no. If Gloria sent you that lawyer letter . . . "

"It wasn't just that. Your mother moved so many times after Henry . . . after the plane crash. And life has a way of getting so busy you don't notice how quickly time is passing. Still, I should have done something, maybe hired my own lawyer."

"Are you kidding? I know Gloria. I grew up with her. If she said she'd sue you, she meant it."

My girl went to Hannah and they hugged. I sighed, smelling the cookie crumbs still on the plate. Sometimes people will set a plate down for a dog to lick, but most of the time they forget.

"I have something for you, though," Hannah said. "See that box on the shelf, the one with the pink flowers? Look inside."

CJ crossed the room and I sprang to my feet, but she merely picked up a box and brought it back. It didn't smell very interesting.

CJ held the box in her lap. "What are these?" she asked. Whatever was inside smelled like papers.

"Birthday cards. Every year I bought you a card and wrote you what had happened since your previous birthday. Marriages, births . . . they're all in there. I didn't realize when I started how many cards I'd wind up writing. At one point I had to find a bigger box. No one expects to live into her nineties." Hannah chuckled.

CJ was playing with the papers in the box, completely oblivious to the obvious connection between the cookie crumbs and her deserving dog, Max.

"Oh, Grandma, this is the most wonderful gift I've ever received."

At dinner I would lie under the table and Rachel and Cindy and other people would sit with CJ and talk and laugh and everyone was very happy. So I was surprised the day when Trent began moving suitcases out of the house and into the car, because I knew it meant that despite how happy CJ was, we were leaving.

Humans do that: though it might be more fun at the Farm, or a dog park, they will decide to leave and then that's it; they leave. It's the job of the dog to go with them once he's marked the area with his scent.

I was in my crate in the car. My girl had completely forgotten I was a front-seat dog. "It's like Grandma gave me all the memories of my life, the life I missed. All my memories in a box," CJ said as we drove. She was crying and I whimpered, wanting to comfort her even though I couldn't see her.

"It's okay, Max," CJ told me. I wagged at my name. "I'm not crying because I'm sad. It's just, I'm so happy to have seen them, and yet to know I missed so much, and that I could have missed so much more . . . "

"It's overwhelming," Trent said quietly.

"God, yes." She sighed.

I curled up in a ball. Clearly, whatever was going on, they were not going to invite me out to be a part of it.

After driving for many hours, I sat up in my cage, because for the second time on the car ride the smells were familiar. Eventually the car stopped and I waited patiently in my crate to be let out, but CJ and Trent just sat in their seats.

"Okay?" Trent said.

"I don't know. I don't know if I want to see her."

"Okay."

"No," CJ said. "I mean, whenever I see her I just

wind up feeling bad about myself. Is that terrible? She's my mother."

"You get to feel however you feel."

"I don't think I can do it."

"Okay then," Trent said.

Well, I'd had as much of this as I could stand. I yipped in frustration.

"Be a good dog, Max," CJ said. I wagged at being a good dog.

"So, you're sure? You want us to leave?" Trent asked.

"Yes. No! No, I should go in; I mean, we're right here," CJ said. "You wait, okay? I'll run up and see which kind of mood she's in."

"Sure. Max and I will sit tight."

I wagged. The car door opened and I could hear CJ getting out. I waited expectantly when the door shut, but she didn't come around to let me out.

"It's okay, Max," Trent said. I whimpered. Where was my girl? Trent leaned over and stuck his fingers through the bars and I licked them.

The door opened and the car rocked as CJ jumped back in. I wagged, hoping she would let me out and pet me to celebrate her return, but she just shut her door. "You won't believe this."

"What?"

"She moved. The woman who answered the door has lived there for a year, and she bought it from some old man."

"You're kidding. I thought that boyfriend of hers, the one whose father was a senator, paid off the mortgage so she'd always have a home," Trent said.

"That's right, but she apparently sold it anyway."

"Well . . . you want to call her? Her cell phone is probably the same."

"No, you know what? I'm going to take this as a sign. It's like the joke where your parents move and don't tell you their forwarding address—well, that's what Gloria has done to me. Let's just go."

We started driving again. With a sigh, I settled down.

"Do you want to drive past your old place?" CJ asked.

"No, that's okay. This trip was for you. I have a lot of good memories about that house, but after my parents retired and sold it—I'd rather keep it as it was in my memory than see all the changes, you know?"

We drove for a long time without anyone making any sounds. I was sleepy, but I woke up when I heard CJ's voice, because there was a little bit of fear in it.

"Trent?"

"Yeah?"

"That's true, isn't it. This trip was all for me. Everything you've done since I went into the hospital has been for me."

"No, I had fun, too."

"The whole thing. Tracking down my relatives. Making the detour so I could see Gloria even though we both knew that at the last minute I'd probably turn chicken."

I cocked my head. Chicken?

"Ever since we were kids growing up, you've been there for me. You know that? You're my rock."

I turned around in my box and lay down.

"But that's not why I love you, Trent. I love you because you're the best man in the world."

Trent was quiet for a moment. "I love you, too, CJ," he said. Then I felt the car turn and slow to a stop. I stood up in my crate and shook myself.

"I think maybe I need to stop driving for a minute," Trent said.

I waited patiently to be let out, but all I could hear was rustling around in the front seat, plus what sounded like eating noises. Could they be having chicken? I didn't smell any, but the thought made me agitated anyway. I finally barked.

CJ laughed. "Max! We forgot all about you."

I wagged.

As it would turn out, that was not the last time we saw Hannah and her whole family. Not long after we returned home, I was taken to a big room full of people sitting in rows of chairs, as if we were going to play the game that Andi had taught me when I was Molly. Trent held me tightly, but I squirmed out of his arms when I smelled Cindy and Rachel and Hannah. Rachel laughed and scooped me up and held me to Hannah and I licked her face. I was careful and gentle in my behavior, though, not at all like Duke would have been, because Hannah seemed frail and there was always someone holding her by the arm. Trent's sister, Carolina, and his mother and father were there, too, which was a surprise to me because I never smelled them on Trent and so had assumed they were no longer alive.

I was so happy to see all of them! CJ was happy, too,

as happy as I could ever remember her being. There was so much joy and love in the air, flowing through the people in the chairs and between CJ and Trent, that I couldn't help but bark. CJ picked me up and cuddled me. "Shhh, Max," she whispered, kissing my nose.

I wore something soft on my back and walked with CJ between the people to where Trent was standing, and I sat there with them while they talked and then they kissed and everyone in the room yelled and I barked again.

It was such a wonderful day. Every table was draped with cloth so that there were little rooms under each one, rooms with people's legs and morsels of meat and fish. Flowers and plants everywhere made the whole place smell as wonderful as a dog park. I played with laughing children who chased me, and when Trent picked me up to take me outside to do my business I couldn't wait to get back in.

CJ wore large folds of cloth so that there was a little room under there, too, though no food—just her legs. When I crawled under there my girl always giggled and reached in to pull me out. "Oh, Max, are you having fun?" CJ asked me after one such incident. She scooped me up and kissed me on the top of my head.

"He's been running around like a maniac the whole time," Trent said. "He'll sleep like a log tonight."

"Well . . . that's good," CJ said, and they both laughed.

"It's a perfect day. I love you, CJ."

"I love you, too, Trent."

"You're the most beautiful bride in the history of weddings."

"You're not so bad yourself. I can't believe I get to be married to you."

"For as long as you want. Forever. You're my wife forever."

They kissed, which they had been doing a lot, lately. I wagged.

"I got a message from Gloria," CJ said finally, setting me down.

"Oh? Did she unleash the curse of the seven demons upon us and our lands?"

CJ laughed. "No, actually, for her it was pretty nice. She said she was sorry she had to boycott the wedding, but she knew I'd understand why."

"I *don't* understand," Trent replied.

"It's okay. She told me she was proud of me and that you're a good catch and to have a wonderful wedding even though she's not here. She also said her biggest regret was that she'd always thought she'd sing at my wedding."

"Well, that's not my biggest regret," Trent said.

By the end of the day I was so full and so exhausted it was all I could do to wag my tail as people bent to kiss me and talk to me. I was held up to Hannah and I kissed her face, licking something sweet off her lips, my heart full of love for her.

"Good-bye, Max, you are such a sweet doggy," Hannah said to me. "Such a good, good dog."

I loved hearing those words come from Hannah's mouth.

That winter CJ was able to take longer, quicker walks. Trent would still play with his rubber ball every day, sitting next to her and making hissing noises with it. How it never once occurred to him to throw it for me I will never understand.

"BP good," Trent would usually say. In this instance "good" had nothing to do with "dog." "You take your amino acids?"

"I'm so sick of this low-protein diet. I want a hamburger with a steak on top of it," CJ told him.

We didn't have Happy Thanksgiving that year, though one day it *smelled* like it throughout the whole building. Trent and CJ left me alone for several hours and when they came home the wonderful scents of Happy Thanksgiving were all over their clothes and hands. I sniffed them suspiciously. Could people even have Happy Thanksgiving without a dog? Seemed unlikely.

We did have Merry Christmas, though. Trent built a thing in the living room that smelled like my outside carpet and hung cat toys from it. When we tore open packages, mine had a delicious chew toy in it.

After Merry Christmas CJ started leaving me alone most of the day several days a week, but she never smelled like any of the other dogs, so I knew she wasn't walking them without me.

"How were your classes today?" Trent would often ask on these days. She seemed happy to have left me alone, which made no sense. In my opinion, being without a dog should just make people sad.

I could tell, though, that sometimes she was feeling

very weak and tired. "Look how puffy my face is!" she wailed to Trent.

"Maybe we should talk to the doctor about increasing your diuretics."

"I spend all my time in the bathroom as it is," she replied bitterly. I nuzzled her hand, but she didn't take as much pleasure in the contact as I did. I so wanted her to feel the happiness that I felt whenever we touched each other, but people are more complicated creatures than dogs. We always love them joyfully, but sometimes they're mad at us, like when I chewed the sad shoes.

One day my girl was very sad and when Trent came home she was sitting in the living room, looking out the window, with me in her lap. "What's wrong?" he asked.

She started crying again. "It's my kidneys," she told him. "They said it's just too dangerous for us to have children."

Trent put his arms around her and they hugged. I pushed my nose in between them so that they both petted me. Trent was sad, too. "We could adopt. We adopted Max, didn't we? Look how well that turned out."

I wagged at my name, but CJ pushed him away.

"You can't fix everything, Trent! I screwed up. This is the price we all have to pay because of it, okay? I don't need you telling me everything is okay." CJ stood up, dumping me on the floor, and stomped away. I trotted right at her heels, but when she got to the end of the hall she shut the door in my face. After a minute I turned and went back to Trent and jumped into his lap, because I needed comfort from *him*.

Sometimes people were angry at each other and it would have nothing to do with shoes. It was beyond a dog's comprehension, but the love between my girl and her mate, Trent, I did understand. They spent many days holding each other on the couch and in bed and often sat with their heads nearly touching.

"You are the love of my life, CJ," Trent would often say.

"I love you, too, Trent," CJ would reply. The adoration between the two of them at moments like these made me wiggle with delight.

As much as I liked wearing my sweater, I was happiest when the air turned hot and moist. That year, though, CJ would sit on the balcony with blankets on and I could tell she was cold by the way she hugged me to her. I could feel her fading, losing strength, becoming more and more tired.

The woman named Mrs. Warren often came out onto her balcony next to ours to play with plants. "Hi, Mrs. Warren," CJ would say.

"How are you feeling today, CJ, any better?" Mrs. Warren would reply.

"A little," CJ usually told her.

I never saw Mrs. Warren anywhere but on her balcony, though I sometimes smelled her in the hallway. She did not have a dog.

"Look at my wrists; they're all swollen," CJ told Trent when he came home one afternoon.

"Honey, have you been out here in the sun all day?" he asked.

"I'm freezing."

"You didn't go to class?"

"What? What day is it?"

"Oh, CJ. I'm worried about you. Let me check your BP."

Trent got his special ball out and I watched him alertly as he squeezed it, thinking maybe this time he'd let me have a turn with it.

"I think it's probably time to talk about . . . about a more permanent treatment regimen."

"I don't want to do dialysis, Trent!"

"Honey, you're the center of my universe. I'd die if anything happened to you. Please, CJ, let's go to the doctor. *Please.*"

CJ went to bed early that night. Trent didn't give me the command to pray when he fed me, but the odor on his breath was so strong I did it anyway. "Good dog," Trent said in the way people will praise dogs without really even looking at them.

The next morning, just after Trent left, CJ fell down in the kitchen. One minute she was making a second trip from the balcony to the kitchen to fill a can of water and the next she toppled to the floor. I felt the crash through the pads in my feet and when I ran to her and licked her face she was unresponsive.

I whimpered, then barked. She didn't move. Her breath smelled sickly and sour as she shallowly in-haled and exhaled.

I was frantic. I ran to the front door but could hear no one on the other side. I barked. Then I ran out on the balcony.

Mrs. Warren was kneeling, playing with her plants. I barked at her.

"Hello, Max!" she called to me.

I thought of my girl lying in the kitchen, unconscious and sick. I needed to communicate what was happening to Mrs. Warren. I pushed forward until my face was sticking out between the bars and I barked at her with such high urgency that a clear note of hysteria rang in my voice like a bell.

Mrs. Warren knelt there looking at me. I barked and barked and barked.

"What is it, Max?"

Hearing my name as a question, I turned and ran back into the apartment, so Mrs. Warren would know the problem was in there. Then I ran back out onto the balcony and barked some more.

Mrs. Warren stood up. "CJ?" she called tentatively, leaning out to try to see into our home.

I kept barking. "Shush, Max," Mrs. Warren said. "Trent? CJ?"

I kept barking. Then Mrs. Warren shook her head, went to her door, opened it, and stepped inside. When she slid her door shut I was so dumbfounded I stopped barking.

What was she doing?

Whimpering, I dashed back in to my girl. Her breathing was getting weaker.

TWENTY-EIGHT

Though it was hopeless, I went to the door and desperately scratched at it. My nails carved a groove in the wood, but that was all. I was crying my fear, my voice shrill and brittle. Then I heard a noise on the other side, the sound of footfalls. I barked and put my nose to the crack at the bottom of the door and smelled Mrs. Warren and a man named Harry, who often carried tools with him in the hallway.

The door opened a crack. "Hello?" Harry called.

"CJ? Trent?" Mrs. Warren said. They cautiously pushed into the room. I headed toward the kitchen, looking over my shoulder to make sure they were following.

"Oh my God," Mrs. Warren said.

A few minutes later some men came and put CJ on a bed and took her away. Mrs. Warren picked me up while this was happening, petting me and telling me I was a good dog, but my heart was pounding and I was sick with a frantic fear. Then she put me down and she and Harry and everyone left and I was alone in the place.

I fretfully paced back and forth, anxious and worried. The light faded and it was night and still CJ wasn't home. I remembered her lying with her cheek pressed to the floor of the kitchen and the thought made me whimper.

When the door finally opened it was Trent. CJ was not with him.

"Oh, Max, I'm so sorry," he said.

He took me for a walk and it was a relief to be able to lift my leg on some shrubbery. "We have to be there for CJ, now, Max. She isn't going to like dialysis, but she has no choice. We have to do it. This could have been much, much worse."

When CJ came home a few days later she was very tired and went right to bed. I curled up next to her, relieved and yet apprehensive about how sad and frustrated she seemed.

From that point forward, CJ and I would take a trip every few days in the back of a car that would pick us up out in front of our building. At first, Trent always went with us. We'd go to a room and lie there quietly while some people fussed over my girl. She always felt weak and ill when she arrived and was exhausted and sad when she got up off the couch, but I realized it was not the fault of the people who were bending over her, not even when they hurt her arm. I didn't growl at them as I might have before.

The day after we went to this place was usually a good day for CJ. She felt stronger and happier.

"They say it will probably be years before I get a kidney," CJ said one night. "There are just so few of them available."

"Well, I was wondering what to buy you for your birthday," Trent replied with a laugh. "I've got one just your size right here."

"Don't even think about it. I'm not taking yours or any other living person's. I put myself in this position, Trent."

"I only need one. The other one's a spare; I hardly ever even use it."

"Funny guy. No. I'll get one from a cadaver eventually. There are some people who have gone twenty years on dialysis. It will happen when it happens."

That winter CJ walked in the door one day with a plastic crate. I was astonished when she opened the door and out walked Sneakers! I rushed up to the cat, frankly excited to see her, and she arched her back and drew her ears back and hissed at me, so I skittered to a stop. What was wrong with Sneakers?

She spent the day sniffing around the apartment, while I followed her, trying to interest her in a little game of tug-on-a-toy. She would have nothing to do with me.

"How are Mrs. Minnick's kids doing?" Trent asked at dinner.

"I think they're feeling guilty. They hardly ever visited her, and then one day she was gone," CJ said.

I watched Sneakers leap silently onto a counter and regard the kitchen disdainfully from her perch.

"What? What is it?" Trent said.

"I'm just thinking about Gloria. Is that how I'm going to feel? One day she'll be gone and I'll regret I didn't make more of an effort?"

"Want to go see her? Invite her to come out?"

"Truthfully? I have no idea."

"Just let me know."

"You're the best husband in the world, Trent. I'm so lucky."

"I'm the lucky one, CJ. My whole life, I only really wanted one girl, and now she's my wife."

CJ stood and I leaped to my feet, though all she did was jump on Trent's chair with him, pressing her face to his. They started to lean, falling sideways.

"Okay, be brave now," CJ said as they slid off the chair and landed on the floor, laughing. Then they wrestled for a while. I looked over at Sneakers, who didn't seem to care about anything at all, but what I felt between Trent and my girl was a love both powerful and complete.

Sneakers eventually became more affectionate. She might be walking through the room and then, without warning, would pad over to me and rub her head against my face, or lick my ears while I lay curled on the floor. But she never wanted to play any wrestling games like we used to. I couldn't help but feel that the time she had spent without a dog in her life had been bad for her.

CJ and Trent spent cool evenings wrapped in a blanket together on the balcony and cold nights lying together on the couch. Sometimes CJ would put on nice-smelling shoes and they'd leave in the evening, but when they returned they were always happy—though even if she'd been sad I doubted I would have done anything to her shoes.

We took walks down the streets and in the park. Sometimes CJ would fall asleep on a blanket on the grass and Trent would lie with her, watching her, a smile on his face.

When we spent the day in the park I was always famished and wanted to eat as soon as we got home. I was dancing around impatiently in the kitchen on one such day, watching Trent make my dinner, when there was a slight change in the routine.

"Going to take forever to finish my degree and then, when I think of my master's, it's like I'm going to be in my thirties. That used to seem so old!"

CJ held my bowl up in the air. "Okay, Max. Pray," she said.

I tensed. I wanted dinner, but the command only made sense in the context of the odor that sometimes lingered on Trent's breath.

"He always does it for me," Trent remarked. "Max? Pray!"

CJ had my dinner and I was starving. I went over to Trent and, as he was leaning down, caught the scent. I signaled.

"Good dog!" Trent praised. CJ put my bowl down and I raced over to eat. I was conscious of her standing over me, her hands on her hips.

"What is it?" Trent asked CJ.

"Max never prays for me. Just you."

"So?"

I was bolting down my food. "I want to try something when he's finished," CJ said. I focused on my eating. When I was done I licked the bowl. "Okay, call him."

"Max! Come!" Trent said. I obediently went over to him and sat. There had been a time when he would call me and always give me a treat when I responded, but sadly, those days had passed for some reason.

"Now, lean down close to him, like you're putting the food bowl on the floor," CJ said.

"What are we doing?"

"Just do it. Please."

Trent bent down to me. The odor was particularly strong today.

"Pray!" CJ called.

I obediently signaled.

"Oh God. Is that possible?" I snapped my head up and focused on CJ. A jolt of fear had come off her, and now she had her hand to her mouth. I went to her, nuzzling her, not sure what the threat was.

"CJ, what's wrong? Why do you look like that?" Trent asked.

"There's something I want you to do for me," CJ replied.

"What? What is it?"

"I want you to go to the doctor."

"What? Why?"

"Please, Trent!" CJ replied, her voice breaking. "You have to do this for me!"

Over the next year, Trent became very sick. Many times he would vomit in the bathroom, and it would remind me of how CJ used to throw up on a regular basis, which she did not do anymore. CJ seemed just as upset when Trent vomited as when she used to do it herself, and I always whimpered anxiously for both of them.

Trent's mother and father came to visit several times, and his sister, Carolina, and a man and some children from the wedding showed up as well, from which I concluded that Carolina now had a family. These visits were odd, though, not at all like when everyone gathered at the Farm, in that only the children seemed happy and ready to laugh and pay attention to a good dog.

All of the hair on Trent's head came off and I could make him laugh by licking his scalp while he lay in bed. CJ would laugh, too, but there was always an underlying sad desperation in her, a constant anxious worrying.

"I don't want this to be my last Christmas with my husband," she said that winter.

"It won't be, honey; I promise," Trent replied.

I had learned from watching Duke's rambunctious conduct with CJ how *not* to behave around a sick person, so I concentrated on being calm and comforting, which Trent and CJ both seemed to appreciate very much. It had been my job to keep threats at bay and I had done that, and now it was my job to try to keep the sadness away, and that required a different set of behaviors.

I still went with CJ a few times a week to lie on the couch and let people fuss over her. They all knew me and loved me and petted me and told me that I was a good dog, and I knew it was because I would lie quietly and not jump around the room. When we left the place with the couch it always seemed to me that my girl wasn't nearly as sick as she had been when we first started going, but I was just a dog and could have been wrong.

One night CJ and Trent were cuddled on the couch together and I was burrowed in snug between them. Sneakers was across the room, watching us expressionlessly. I never knew what cats were thinking, or even if they were thinking.

"I just want you to know, I've got plenty of insurance and investments. You'll be okay," Trent said.

"But we're not doing that. You're going to get better. You are getting better," CJ said. She felt angry.

"Yes, but just in case, I want you to know it."

"It doesn't matter. It's not happening," CJ insisted.

There were a few times when Trent would be gone for days at a time and CJ would mostly be missing as well, though she always came home to walk me and feed me and always smelled like Trent, so I knew the two of them had been someplace together.

One day it was just the two of us, CJ and me, sitting in the grass on a warm summer day. I'd run around as much as I'd wanted and was now content to sit in my girl's lap. She stroked my head.

"You are such a good dog," she told me. Her fingers scratched the itchy part along my spine and I groaned in pleasure. "I know what you were doing, Max. You weren't saying grace, were you? You were trying to tell us about Trent, trying to say you could smell his cancer. We just didn't understand at first. Did

Molly tell you that? Does she talk to you, Max? Is that how you knew? Is she an angel dog, watching over us? Are you an angel dog, too?"

I liked hearing the name Molly spoken by CJ. I wagged.

"We got it in time, Max. Because of you they got it and it hasn't come back. You saved my husband. I don't know how, but if you talk to Molly, would you tell her thank you for me?"

I was pretty disappointed when Trent's hair grew back on his head, because my licking his scalp always made him laugh. But things change: CJ's hair, for example, was longer than it had ever been, a glorious tent that would fall over me when she bent over. And when Trent bent over I could no longer detect that metallic odor. When he said "Pray" to me now I looked at him in frustrated confusion. What did he want? I was even more confused when, after I sat and stared at him for a long moment after the Pray command, he and CJ both laughed and clapped and said, "Good dog!" and fed me a treat—though I had done *nothing*.

It cannot be a dog's purpose to understand what people want because it is impossible.

The summer after Trent's hair grew back some men came and took everything from our home. CJ spoke to them and led them through the house, so I knew it was okay, but I still barked at them out of habit. CJ put me in my crate when I barked and also put Sneakers in the cat crate, which I felt was a bit of an overreaction on CJ's part.

Sneakers and I went for a long car ride in the backseat of a car, still in our crates.

At the end of the car ride the same men were there, this time carrying all of our things into a new house. What fun to explore the unfamiliar rooms! Sneakers sniffed around suspiciously, but I was rampant with joy, racing from place to place.

"This is where we live now, Max," Trent said. "You don't have to live in an apartment anymore."

Since he was talking to me, I ran over and put my paws on his legs and he lifted me up in the air. I looked smugly down at Sneakers, who was pretending not to care. Trent was a good man. He loved CJ and me and I loved him. That night, as I dozed off, curled against my girl with Trent sleeping on the other side of the bed, I thought about how devoted Rocky had been to Trent. You can usually tell that a man is good if he has a dog who loves him.

We didn't ever go back home again. We were in a small house with stairs and, most delightfully, a grassy lawn in the back. Sneakers was unimpressed with the yard, but I loved it out there. It was quieter and there were fewer food scents, but I could hear the musical sound of barking dogs and smell the plants and the rain.

Trent left most days right after breakfast, but CJ stayed home to be with me. There was a little room she liked to sit in with a desk and a couch and soft chairs and a bed for me to lie in. Friends would come over and sit in a different room, one that had a door to the outside, and then CJ and I would go down the hall to bring the friends into CJ's favorite room to talk. I learned never to bark at any of these people, though I always knew when they were waiting in the other room and would go to the door wagging my tail.

"Good boy, Max," CJ would say.

Sometimes the people would be sad and I learned that if I jumped up into their laps a little of the sadness would go away as they petted me and cried. I loved that my girl had so many friends who came to visit.

I was happy. A year went by, and then another. CJ was always a little sick, but gradually she seemed to be improving, getting stronger.

We had lived in the new house for a long time when my legs began bothering me in the winter. They were stiff and sore when I woke up in the morning, slowing me down. Our walks outside became as halting and short as they had been when CJ was very sick and pushed a chair in front of her.

Sneakers was slowing down, too. The two of us often napped on the couch at opposite ends, getting up in the middle of the day to switch places.

"You okay, Max? Poor dog. Is the medicine doing you any good?" CJ would ask me. I could hear the concern in her voice and I would wag at my name. My purpose now was to be with my girl when she went to lie on the couch every few days, and to snuggle with her and take as many naps as possible. That's what she needed.

I did my best to hide my pain from her and Trent. I could feel her sharp concern whenever she could tell that my joints were flaring with a sensation very much like when Beevis tore into my ear and made it bleed.

I no longer tore around in the backyard, barking

with sheer joy. I was too tired. I still felt the joy; I just kept quiet about it.

Sometimes I would be lying in the sun when CJ would call me and I would lift my head, but my legs wouldn't seem to want to move. CJ would come and pick me up and hold me in her lap and I would feel her sadness, so I'd struggle against the weakness that was enfeebling me and manage to lift my head and lick her face.

"Are you having a good day, Max? Are you in much pain?" she asked me after a particularly bad spell, when I was barely able to move for several minutes. "I think maybe it's time. I've been dreading this moment, but tomorrow, I'll take you to see the Vet. You won't have to suffer anymore, Max. I promise."

I sighed. It felt good to be held by CJ. Her hands as they stroked me seemed to smooth away the pain. Trent came out and I felt him right there, too, his hand petting me.

"How's he doing?" Trent asked.

"Not good at all. I came out and I thought he was gone."

"Such a good boy," Trent murmured, stroking me. "You're the best dog, Max. You took care of CJ your whole life. Now it will be my job. You can let go any time you need to. I won't let you down. Okay? You did a good job, Max."

"Oh, Max," CJ whispered. She sounded so, so sad.

Just then, I felt a familiar sensation rising up within me, a warm and gentle blackness. Something was happening inside me, something swift and surprising.

The searing agony in my joints began to withdraw. "Max?" CJ said. Her voice sounded far away.

I was unable to move, or to see them anymore. My last thought, as I felt the rising waters float me away, was that I was glad CJ and Trent still had Sneakers to take care of them.

Sneakers was a good cat.

TWENTY-NINE

I was vaguely conscious of sleeping for a long time, of awakening from a long, long nap. Eventually I opened my eyes, but everything was milky and dark.

When my vision cleared enough for me to be able to focus on my mother and my siblings, I saw that we were all colored with splotches of brown, white, and black and all had short fur.

I could not hear CJ's voice, nor could I smell her. There were other people, though, many of them, often wearing long, flowing clothes and also small blankets on their heads.

We were in a tiny room with a few rugs on the floor and light coming in from a window up close to the ceiling. My siblings—two girls and three boys—were involved in continual play, wrestling and, as we got older, merrily chasing each other. I tried to ignore them to concentrate on sitting in front of the door to watch for CJ, but the fun was just too infectious.

For the first time it occurred to me to wonder if any of them had experienced other lives and had people they, too, needed to find, but they sure didn't act like it. I was the only puppy who seemed to have any concerns at all beyond playing, playing, playing.

The people who came to see us were all women. I soon learned to identify their smells and discern that though their garments were all the same, there were six separate people, all of them older than CJ but younger than Hannah. The women delighted in us, coming in to laugh as the puppies jumped on them and tugged on their long robes. They picked me up and kissed me, but one of them in particular paid more attention to me than the other women did. "This is the one," she would say. "See how calm he is?"

"There's no such thing as a calm beagle," one woman responded to this.

"Oh, Margaret, a puppy isn't going to work out," said another. "I know they're cute, but they're too full of energy. We should get another mature dog like Oscar was."

The woman holding me was, I soon realized after hearing her name a number of times, called Margaret.

"You weren't here when we got Oscar, Jane," Margaret said. "We had several false starts, and when we finally found Oscar he was with us such a short time before he passed. I think training a puppy from the start will give us many years."

"But not a beagle," the first woman said. "A beagle

is too hyper. That's why I didn't want to foster a pregnant beagle in the first place."

I wondered which one of the women was named Beagle.

I could tell from the heaviness in my bones and muscles that I was destined to be a bigger dog than I had been as Max. I felt a sense of relief that I wouldn't need to devote so much energy to proving to dogs and people that inside I was a big dog who could protect my girl. When the woman set me down I went over and jumped on one of my sisters—I was already larger than she was, and I enjoyed being able to dominate her with my size rather than my attitude.

Soon after we had started eating mushy food out of a communal bowl, we were led outside into a grassy area that was fenced in. It was spring and the air was warm and fragrant with flowers and new grass. I could smell that we were in a humid climate with rains frequent enough to support many species of trees and bushes. My siblings thought the yard was pretty much the most wonderful place imaginable and reacted every morning to being let out into it by racing around in circles. I thought it was silly but generally joined in the fray because it was fun.

I wondered when CJ would come get me. That had to be why I was a puppy again. Our fates were inextricably linked, so if I was reborn it must be that my girl still needed me.

One day a family entered the yard—two little girls and a man and a woman—led by one of the six women who took care of us. I knew what their presence meant. The puppies all ran over to play with them, but I hung back, though when one of the little girls picked me up I couldn't resist kissing her giggling face.

"This one, Daddy. This is the one I want for my birthday," the little girl said. She carried me over to her father.

"Actually, one of the nuns has already spoken for that one," the woman said. "He's going to have a job. We hope, anyway."

The little girl dropped me to the ground. I gazed up at her, wagging. She was older than when CJ was called Clarity but younger than when Rocky and I were taken home by Trent and CJ—I had never known my girl at this particular age. When the little girl scooped up one of my brothers, I was oddly disappointed. I would have enjoyed playing with her some more.

In rapid succession, my siblings went home with other people, until soon I was the only dog left to be with my mother, who was named Sadie. The two of us, my mother and I, were out in the yard taking a nap when several of the women came out to see us. I picked up a small rubber bone and carried it over to the women, hoping one of them would want it and would chase me.

"You've been such a good dog, Sadie, such a good mother," Margaret said.

I tossed the rubber bone and pounced on it so they would call me a good dog, too.

"You're going to love your new home," another woman said.

A third woman picked me up and held me nose-to-nose with my mother. We sniffed each other, a bit disconcerted by the awkward and unnatural situation.

"Say bye-bye to your puppy, Sadie!"

The woman snapped a leash onto Sadie's collar and led her away. Margaret held me so I couldn't follow my mother—clearly, something was going on.

"I'm going to call you Toby, okay? Toby, you're a good dog, Toby. Toby." Margaret crooned to me. "Your name is Toby."

It occurred to me that my name must be Toby. I was stunned—Toby had been my very first name, long, long ago. Margaret obviously knew that.

Humans know everything, not just how to take car rides or where to find bacon but also when dogs are good or bad and where dogs should sleep and what toys they should play with. Still, I was astounded to hear Margaret call me Toby. I'd always marked every new life with a new name.

What did it mean that I was Toby again? Did it mean it was all starting over, that I would next be named Bailey?

Sadie did not come back, and gradually I came to understand that this place full of women draped in blankets was my new home—a home like none I'd ever been in. For the most part, I lived in the fenced-in area, though at night I was brought in and put in the room where I had been born. I wasn't lonely, though—throughout the day women would come out to see me, often tossing a rubber ball or pulling on a toy with me. I soon learned to recognize most of them by smell, even though their hands all were cloaked in similar scents.

What was bewildering was that unlike any other life, there was no single person for me to take care of.

More women than I could ever count would play with me and talk to me and feed me. It was as if I was the dog for everyone there.

Margaret taught me a new command: "Be Still." At first she would hold me down and say, "Be Still," and I thought she wanted to wrestle, but she kept saying, "No, no, Be Still." I had no idea what she was saying, but I knew that "no" meant I was doing something wrong. I tried licking her and squirming and every other trick I could think of, but none of them pleased her. Finally I gave up in frustration. "Good dog!" she said, giving me a treat even though I hadn't done anything.

This went on for several days until finally it dawned on me that "Be Still" meant "just lie there." Once I made that connection, I could lie down and not move for as long as she wanted, though I could scarcely contain my impatience—why did we have to wait so long for me to get a treat?

Then Margaret took me places I'd never been before inside the building. I saw women sitting and women standing and women eating—this last group seemed the most interesting to me, but we spent no time with them before moving on. Margaret wanted me to "Be Still" while sitting in people's laps. I didn't care much for the whole operation, but I cooperated.

"See how good he is? Good dog, Toby. Good dog."

One woman went to a couch to lie down and I was placed on a blanket next to her and given the command. The woman was giggling and I was dying to kiss her face, but I did as I was told and got a treat out of it. I was still lying there motionless, holding out for another morsel, when several women gathered around me.

"All right, Margaret, I'm convinced. You can take him to work with you and see how he does," said one of the women.

Margaret reached down and picked me up. "He'll be fine, Sister."

"No, he won't. He'll upset everyone and chew on everything," another woman warned.

The next morning Margaret put a collar on me and led me on a leash out to her car. "You're so good, Toby," she said to me.

We took a car ride and I was a front-seat dog! I wasn't tall enough to stick my nose out the window yet, though.

Margaret took me to a place very much like where I'd gone with CJ to sit with her on the couch. I could smell many people and could tell some of them were sick. It was quiet, and the floor was soft.

Margaret carried me around and people petted me and hugged me, or, in the case of a few of them, they lay unmoving in their beds and gazed at me. "Be Still," Margaret commanded. I concentrated on not moving, because I'd learned this was what was required when people were ill. I did not signal when I caught the strong, familiar scent coming off of a couple of them— the smell that had been on Trent's breath for so long. I'd learned that the command to signal under such circumstances was "Pray," and no one instructed me to do that.

Margaret soon put me down on the ground outside in a yard that was walled in on all sides. I had a lot of energy pent up inside me and ran around for a while, and then Margaret gave me a rope with a rubber ball on the end of it and I shook it and dragged it around, wishing I had another dog with me to join in the fun. I could see, on the other side of the windows, people watching me, so I made sure I put on a show with that rope.

Then Margaret took me back inside the building and introduced me to a cage. "Okay, Toby, and this is your home." A new pillow was on the floor of the cage, and when Margaret squatted and patted it I dutifully went over and sat on it.

"This is your bed, Toby. Okay?" Margaret said.

I didn't know if I was supposed to stay on the pillow, but I was tired and took a nap. I woke up when I heard Margaret speaking. "Hi, would you page Sister Cecilia for me, please? . . . Thanks."

I gazed drowsily at her. She smiled at me when I yawned, a phone to her face.

"Cecilia? . . . It's Margaret. I'm still at the hospice with Toby. . . . No, even better than that. They love him. This afternoon some of the guests even sat and watched him play out in the courtyard. No barks, not even once. . . . I really do, yes. . . . Thank you, Cecilia. . . . No, of course, but I don't think that's going to happen. He's a very special dog."

I heard the word "dog" and wagged my tail a couple of times before easing back into sleep.

Over the next several days I adjusted to my new life. Margaret came and went, but not every day, and I soon learned the names of Fran and Patsy and Mona—three other women who liked to take me around for visits with people who were lying in beds. Patsy smelled strongly of cinnamon and faintly of dog, and none of them wore the flowing clothing that Margaret wore. They'd tell me to Be Still, so I'd lie there with the person. It reminded me a little of when CJ's friends would come to visit and cry and I would lie on the couch with them. Sometimes the people wanted to play with me and sometimes they petted me and often they just wanted to nap, but nearly always I could feel their joy coming through.

"You're an old soul, Toby," Fran said to me. "An old soul in a young dog's body."

I wagged, hearing the praising tones in her words. People are like that; they can talk and talk without ever saying "good dog," but that's what they mean.

Other than those visits, I had the run of the place. Everyone called out to me, some of them sitting in chairs that moved when Fran or one of the others stood behind them and pushed. The people loved me and hugged me and snuck me treats.

One place I loved was the kitchen, where a man named Eddie was always cooking. He would tell me to sit and then give me a wonderful treat, even though Sit was the easiest of tricks for a dog.

"You and I are the only men in this place," Eddie would say to me. "We got to stick together, right, Toby?"

Always before I had been with just one person and had devoted my life to loving that person. At first that person was Ethan—so sure was I that loving him was the reason I was a dog that when I started taking care of baby Clarity it was only because I knew Ethan would want me to. Gradually, though, I came to love CJ just as much, and began to understand that it wasn't disloyal to Ethan to do so. Dogs can love more than one person.

At this place, though, I had no particular person at all—my purpose seemed to be to love each one of them. It made them happy.

I was a dog who loved many people—it's what made me a good dog.

My name might be Toby, but I had come a long, long way since the first time that was what people called me. I knew many more things now, things I had learned along my life's journey. I understood, for example, why I was being told to "Be Still." Many of the people lying in bed had pains in them that I could sense, and if I climbed on them to play I might hurt them. I only had to step on one man's stomach one time to learn my lesson—his sharp cry rang in my ears for days, making me feel awful. I was not Duke, a rambunctious dog who couldn't control himself. I was Toby. I could Be Still.

When I was wandering around on my own and not being taken places by Mona, Fran, or Patsy, I would go see the man I had stepped on. His name was Bob, and I wanted him to know I was sorry. As was the case in most rooms, he had a chair pulled up next to his bed, and by leaping first onto this I was able to land on his blankets without hurting him. Bob was asleep every time I went to visit him.

One afternoon Bob was alone in his bed and I could

feel him easing away from this life. The warm waters were rising up around Bob, washing away his pains. I lay quietly next to him, being with him as best I could. It seemed to me that if my purpose was to provide comfort to people who were ailing, it was even more important that I be with them when they were breathing their final breaths.

Fran found me lying there. She checked on Bob and covered his head with his blanket. "Good dog, Toby," she whispered.

From that point forward, whenever I knew someone's time was close I would go into their room and lie on their bed with them to provide comfort and company as they left this life. Sometimes their families were gathered around and sometimes they were alone, though usually one of the many people who spent their days in the building helping the sick was sitting there quietly.

Occasionally family members would feel fear and anger when they saw me.

"I don't want the death dog near my mother!" a man shouted once. I heard the word "dog" and felt the sharp lash of his fury and left the room, not sure what I had done wrong.

Most of the time, though, my presence was welcomed by everyone. Having no single person as my master meant that I was given a lot of cuddles. Sometimes people would be grieving as they hugged me and I could feel their sadness lose its grip a little while I was in their arms.

What I missed was other dogs. I loved all the attention from the people, but I missed the sensation of another dog's throat in my mouth. I found myself dreaming about Rocky and Duke and all the dogs in the dog park, which was why I involuntarily barked in surprise when Fran led me out into the yard and there was another dog there!

He was a compact, stocky, strong little guy named Chaucer. He carried the scent of Patsy's cinnamon on his fur. We immediately began wrestling, as if we'd known each other for years.

"This is what Toby needed," Fran said to Patsy with a laugh. "Eddie says he's seemed almost depressed."

"It's a treat for Chaucer, too," Patsy said.

Chaucer and I both looked up. Treat?

After that day, Chaucer came to visit a lot, and though I had Be Still to do, I always found time to wrestle with him.

Other dogs sometimes came with families to be in the rooms with the beds, but they were always anxious and rarely wanted to play, even if they were let out in the yard.

A few years went by like this. I was a good dog who had done many things and could be comfortable in my new role as the dog who belonged to no one and yet to everyone.

When it was Happy Thanksgiving there were always lots of people and lots of smells and lots of treats for a deserving dog. When it was Merry Christmas time the women who wore blankets on their heads came to play with me and give me treats and to sit around the big indoor tree. There were cat toys on the tree, as always, but no cats to play with them.

I felt content. I had a purpose—not as specific as taking care of CJ, but I still felt important.

And then one afternoon I jerked out of my nap, my head cocked. "I need my shoes!" a woman called from one of the rooms.

I instantly recognized her voice.

Gloria.

[THIRTY]

I scampered down the corridor, nearly knocking over Fran as I barreled into the room. Gloria was in the bed, her strong perfumes filling the air, but I ignored her and focused on the thin woman standing next to her. It was my CJ, watching me in amusement.

I completely broke protocol, abandoning the reserved composure I always adopted in people's rooms, and instead leaped up on my girl, my paws reaching for her.

"Wow!" she said.

I sobbed, my tail low and beating the floor, spinning in circles and jumping. She reached out and put her hands around my face and I closed my eyes and groaned with the pleasure of feeling her touching me.

CJ had come for me at last. Elation went through me in a shiver. I was back with my girl!

"Toby! Get down," Fran said.

"It's okay." CJ dropped to her knees, her joints firing off snapping sounds as she bent them. "What a good doggy."

Her hair was short now and did not drape me as it once did. I licked her face. She smelled of sweet things, and of Gloria. CJ was, I realized, frail and weak, her hands trembling a little as they touched me. This meant I needed to contain myself, which seemed scarcely possible. I wanted to bark and run around the room and knock things over.

"Toby is our therapy dog," Fran explained. "He lives here. He comforts our guests—they really love having him around."

"Well, not Gloria," CJ said with a laugh. She gazed fondly into my eyes. "Toby, you're a therapeagle!"

I wagged. Her voice had a slight quaver to it and sounded strained, but I loved hearing it all the same.

"Clarity stole my money," Gloria declared. "I want to go home. Call Jeffrey." CJ sighed but kept stroking my head. Gloria, I realized, was still as unhappy as ever. She was also really old; I could tell by her smells. I had been around a lot of really old people lately.

Patsy came in, smelling like cinnamon and Chaucer as usual. "Good morning, Gloria, how are you?" Patsy asked.

"Nothing," Gloria said. She slumped in her bed. "Nothing."

Patsy stayed with Gloria while CJ and Fran went into a little room with a small table. "Why, Toby, are you coming, too?" Fran laughed when I darted in the door before it closed.

"Such a nice dog," CJ said. I wagged.

"He certainly seems to have taken a shine to you."

CJ sat in a chair, and I picked up a quick flash of pain as she did so. Concerned, I pressed my head to her knees. Her hand came down and absently petted me, a light tremor in the fingers. I closed my eyes. I had missed her so, so much, but now that she was here it was as if she had never left.

"Gloria has good days and bad days. This is a pretty good day. Most of the time she's not really lucid," CJ said.

I wagged. Even hearing Gloria's name spoken by CJ gave me pleasure.

"Alzheimer's can be so cruel, its progression so inconsistent," Fran replied.

"That thing about the money drives me crazy. She tells everyone I stole her fortune and her house. The truth is I've been supporting her the past fifteen years—and of course whatever I sent her, it was never enough."

"In my experience there nearly always will be unresolved issues in situations like this."

"I know. And I should be better able to cope with it all. I'm also a psychologist."

"Yes, I saw that from your file. Do you want to talk about how that affects your relationship with your mother?"

CJ took a deep, reflective breath. "I guess. The light went on for me in grad school—Gloria's a narcissist, so she never really questions her own behavior or thinks she's ever done anything to apologize for. So no, there will never be any closure with her—there wasn't a chance at that even when she was fully functional. But a lot of children have narcissistic injuries, so having her for a parent has really helped me with my work."

"Which is in high schools?" Fran asked.

"Sometimes. My specialty is working with eating disorders, which are nearly always most acute in adolescent girls. I'm semi-retired, though."

I realized at that moment that there was a ball under one of Fran's cabinets. I went over and stuck my nose under there, inhaling deeply. It had Chaucer's scent painted on it. What was Chaucer doing with a ball in here?

"I also read that you've been on dialysis for more than twenty-two years? I hope you don't mind my asking, but it would seem you'd be a good candidate for a transplant. Was that never a consideration?"

"I guess I don't mind answering that," CJ said, "though I'm not sure what these questions have to do with Gloria."

I dug at the ball with my paws, touching it but otherwise failing to dislodge it.

"Hospice isn't just about the guest. It's about the needs of the whole family. The better we know you, the better we can serve you," Fran said.

"All right, sure. I did have a transplant, actually— the twenty-two years is cumulative. I received a kidney from a cadaver donor when I was in my thirties. It gave me more than two decades before it began to fail. They call it chronic rejection, and there's really nothing that can be done about it. I restarted dialysis seventeen years ago."

"What about another transplant?"

CJ sighed. "In the end, there are just so few organs available. I couldn't see taking one when there were others more deserving who were waiting in line."

"More deserving?"

"I destroyed my kidneys in a suicide attempt when I was twenty-five years old. There are children who are born with conditions that, through no fault of their own, require transplant. I'd already taken one. I wasn't going to use up another."

"I see."

CJ laughed. "The way you just said that brought back about fifty hours of psychoanalysis. Believe me, I've thought this all out."

I leaned into CJ's leg, hoping she'd get the ball for me.

"Thank you for even discussing it, then," Fran said. "It just helps to know."

"Oh, my mother would have mentioned it to you. She delights in telling everybody I drank anti-freeze. I've had her in assisted care for the past three years—she had all the people there convinced I was the spawn of the devil. . . . "

I yawned in agitation. Did no one else care about the ball?

"What is it? Why did you just pause?" Fran asked after a moment.

"I was just thinking that maybe she *won't* tell you. She's been more and more unresponsive, and, of course, she's pretty much stopped eating. I guess part of me is having trouble adjusting to the idea that this is truly the end."

"It's hard," Fran said, "to lose someone who has been so important in your life."

"I didn't think it would be," CJ said very quietly.

"You've experienced loss before."

"Oh, yes."

I sat up, watching my girl, the ball forgotten. She reached for a fluffy piece of paper and pressed it to her eyes. "My husband, Trent, died last fall."

They sat quietly. My girl reached down to me and I licked her hand. "That's how I came to be exposed to hospice. Trent passed peacefully, surrounded by people who cared about him."

There was another long, sad pause. I liked hearing Trent's name, but there was no scent of him clinging to CJ. It was similar to when, as Max, I realized Rocky's smells were no longer all over Trent. I knew what it meant when a smell faded away, whether it was man or dog.

It was good to be with CJ, but I was sad to think I would never see Trent again.

"Does Gloria's disease stir up feelings about your husband?" Fran asked gently.

"Not really. This is so different. Besides, I *always* have feelings about Trent. He was the friend I could always turn to who never asked for anything for himself. I think for a long time I modeled my understanding of love based on my relationship with my mother. When I finally shook that off, Trent was waiting for me, and we had the most wonderful life together. I couldn't have children, so it was just the two of us, but he made every day seem special. He liked to surprise me with trips—and planning a getaway when your wife needs dialysis takes some doing. But that was Trent, the most capable man I've ever met. He could do whatever he decided to do. Through everything that happened—and it was no picnic, with my transplant and the immunosuppressants and the trips to the emergency room—he was always my rock. Even now, I can't really believe he's gone."

"He sounds very special," Fran said. "I would have liked to have known him."

From that day forward, my girl would come to visit Gloria and I would greet her at the door and stay by her side until she left. Sometimes CJ pulled treats out of her pocket and fed them to me without me having to do any tricks. "Such a good dog," she would whisper.

Eddie told me I was a good dog, too, and he reinforced the sentiment with meat treats!

"'Dog' is 'God' spelled backward; you know that. That's why you're here, to help the nuns do God's work. So I figure a little stew meat between us boys is the least I can give you," Eddie said. I never knew what he was saying, but his treats were the best I'd ever had!

Just as I had once watched the baby Clarity for Ethan, I now reasoned that it was my job to take care of Gloria for CJ. I spent a lot of time in Gloria's room even when CJ wasn't there with her. I didn't try to jump on Gloria's bed, though, because the one time I tried it her eyes were filled with terror and she screamed at me.

Some people just don't appreciate having a dog around. It's sad to think there are people like that. I knew Gloria was that way—maybe that's why she could never be truly happy.

Fran and CJ became friends and often ate lunch together out in the courtyard. I would lie at their feet and watch for falling crumbs.

Falling crumbs were my specialty.

"I've got a question for you," CJ told Fran at one of these lunches, "but I want you to think about it before answering."

"That's exactly what my husband said to me when he proposed," Fran replied. They both laughed.

I wagged at CJ's laughter. She seemed to have so many sharp pains digging at her from inside; I could sense them from the way she'd start and gasp when she moved, or when she exhaled in a long, loud sigh as she carefully sat down. Any time she laughed, though, the pain seemed to retreat.

"Well, it's not *that* kind of proposal," CJ said. "What I'm thinking is that I'd like to work here at the hospice. In counseling, I mean. I see how hard it is for you and Patsy and Mona to keep up—and I'd volunteer. I really don't need money."

"What about your current practice?"

"I've been winding that down for a long time—I only work as a consultant now as it is. To tell you the truth, I'm finding it harder and harder to relate to teenagers—or maybe it's the other way around. I tell them I identify with what they are going through and I see the skepticism in their eyes—to them, there's little difference between being in your seventies and being a hundred years old."

"We normally discourage any volunteer relationships with the hospice by family members until a year after the guest has passed."

"I know; you said that. That's why I want you to think about it—I believe an exception could be made for me. I know very, very well what it's like to lie in bed and feel horrible—I do it three times a week. And certainly what I'm going through with Gloria gives me tremendous insight into how families feel."

"How is your mother?"

"She's . . . It won't be much longer."

"You've been a good daughter, CJ."

"Yeah, well, maybe under the circumstances. Not sure Gloria will agree, or would ever have agreed. So will you think about it?"

"Of course. I'll talk to the director and to the nuns about it, too. It's really up to them, you know. The rest of us are just employees."

About a week after that, I was sitting at CJ's feet in Gloria's room when I felt a change come over Gloria. I could hear that her breathing was getting lighter and lighter, and then it would stop, and then she'd take a couple of deep breaths. With each cycle, though, the breathing was weaker, the exhalations more gentle.

She was passing.

I jumped up on the chair next to her and looked at her face. Her eyes were closed, her mouth open, her hands clutched across her chest. I glanced back at CJ, who was asleep. I knew she would want to be awake, so I barked, a single, sharp yip that sounded very loud in the silent room.

My girl awoke with a start. "What is it, Toby?" She stood and came over to stand beside me. I lifted my nose and licked her fingers. "Oh," she said. After a moment, she reached down and clutched Gloria's hand in hers. I saw tears falling from her eyes and could feel the sad pain in her. We stood like that for several minutes.

"Good-bye, Mom," CJ finally said. "I love you."

When Gloria took her last breath and faded away, CJ went back to her chair and sat down. I jumped into her lap and curled up and she held me, rocking softly. I did what I could for her, being with her as she grieved.

At the end of that day, I walked with CJ and Fran to the front doors.

"I'll see you at the service," Fran said. They hugged. "Are you sure you're okay to go home alone?"

"I'm okay. To tell you the truth, it's actually a relief to have it over with."

"I know."

CJ looked down at me and I wagged. She knelt, wincing a little as she did so, then gathered me to her.

"You're such an amazing dog, Toby. What you do for everyone, comforting them and guiding them at the end—you're just a miracle, an angel dog."

I wagged—"angel dog" was something like "doo-dle dog," another name that meant I was good and I was loved.

"Thank you so, so much, Toby. You be a good dog. I love you."

CJ stood, smiled at Fran, and walked out into the night.

CJ didn't come back the next day, nor the next. More days went by, until I no longer rushed over to the sliding doors when they gasped open—my girl, it seemed, didn't need me right now.

That was just how things were. I would rather have gone with CJ wherever she was, but my job now was to take care of and love everyone in my building and to be with people as they left this life. And also to Sit for Eddie so that he would feed me chicken.

I knew that if CJ needed me, she could find me, just as she always had done before.

In the meantime, all I could do was wait.

THIRTY-ONE

A nd then one day, when the brown leaves outside scuttled before the wind so loudly I could hear them from everywhere in the building, my girl walked in the door. I was wary as she came up the sidewalk because I wasn't sure it was her—there was an odd hitch to her walk, a limp, and the bulky coat across her shoulders hid her frail thinness. But when the door whooshed open and the blustery wind blew her wonderful scent into my face I scampered across the floor and right up to her. I was careful not to jump up, fearing I might knock her over, but my tail wagged with joy and I closed my eyes when her hand came down to stroke me.

"Hello, Toby, did you miss me?"

Fran walked up and embraced her and CJ put some things on a desk in one of the rooms, and from that day forward we lived life backward from the way we had always lived it before. Now CJ left at night and didn't return until morning, instead of leaving in the morning and not coming back until night. She never took me to the room with the couches, but I could smell that she was still going there on a regular basis.

CJ moved through the building, visiting people in the rooms and talking to them and sometimes hugging them. I was always at her heels, but when she left at night there was often someone who needed me on their bed, so I would lie there with them, and sometimes their family members would hold me.

People were often in pain when they talked to CJ, whether they were lying in bed or standing next to it, but usually after a quiet conversation I could feel their pain lessen a little. Often someone in the family would reach for me, and it was my job to let them hug me for as long and as hard as they needed to, even if it made me uncomfortable.

"Good dog," CJ would say. "Good dog, Toby."

Often Fran or Patsy would be in the room with CJ, and they said the same thing. "Good dog, Toby."

I was glad to be a good dog.

CJ was in pain, too—I could sense it, could see how it slowed her down. Hugging me made her feel a little better, too.

One family was very sad because a woman who was lying in bed was suffering and had a strong metallic tang to her breath. There was a man her age and three children who were the age CJ had been when I was Molly. When one of the children picked me up and put me in bed with the woman I did Be Still.

"Dawn," CJ said to the oldest of these children, a girl taller than CJ and with long, light hair that smelled of flowery soap and whose hands carried with them the strong scent of apples. "Would you join me for a cup of coffee?"

I felt some alarm go through Dawn. She looked at her mother, who was sleeping, unaware of my presence next to her, then up at the man, her father, who nodded. "Go ahead, honey."

I could feel something like guilt stirring in Dawn as she reluctantly left her mother's side. I decided that whatever was happening, CJ needed me more to be with her and Dawn than with the woman in the bed. Moving as carefully as possible, I eased onto the floor and silently padded down the hall after my girl.

"Hey, you want something to eat? A banana, maybe?" CJ asked.

"Sure," the girl said. I soon smelled the pungent, sweet smell of a new fruit mingling with the apples on the girl's hands as they made chewing noises. I lay down at their feet under the table.

"It must be hard to be the oldest. Your sisters look up to you; I can tell," CJ said.

"Yeah."

"Do you want to talk about it?"

"Not really."

"How's your dad doing?"

"He's . . . I don't know. He keeps saying we have to fight. But Mom . . . "

"She's not fighting anymore," CJ said softly after a moment.

"Yeah."

"Must be very stressful."

"Uh-huh."

They sat for a little while.

"What are your comfort foods?" CJ asked.

"Peanut butter," Dawn replied with a wry laugh. "Oh, and you know those lasagnas you can heat up?"

"Eating helps with the stress," CJ said.

Dawn was quiet.

"And then when you've eaten too much?" CJ asked quietly.

A jolt of alarm went through Dawn. She sat up in her chair. "What do you mean?"

"When I was in high school I had this problem. I could always make myself feel better by eating," CJ said. "But with every bite I'd be hating myself because I already felt fat and I knew I was just putting on pounds—I could practically feel my butt getting bigger. So then I got rid of what I ate."

When Dawn spoke I could hear the tremor her heartbeat put in her voice. "How?"

"You know how, Dawn," CJ replied.

Dawn inhaled sharply.

"My eyes had little bits of blood in them all the time. Just like yours," CJ said. "Sometimes my cheeks were as swollen as yours, too."

"I have to go."

"Sit with me for just a bit longer, would you?" CJ asked.

Dawn shuffled her feet. I could tell that she was afraid.

"These aren't my own teeth, you know," CJ continued. "I lost them when I was young, from all the acidity—people my age often have implants, but I had them in college."

"Are you going to tell my dad?" Dawn asked.

"Does your mom know?" CJ replied.

"She . . . I think she does, but she never said anything to me. And now . . . "

"I know. Dawn, there's a program. . . . "

"No!" Dawn said sharply. She pushed her chair back from the table.

"I know how you feel. How awful it is to have this secret, how it can make you hate yourself."

"I want to get back to my mother's room."

They both stood. I eased to my feet, yawning anxiously. CJ was not as tense as Dawn, but strong feelings were running through both of them.

"I'm on your side, Dawn," CJ said. "In the coming days and weeks, any time you feel that urge, that uncontrollable need, I want you to call me. Will you do that?"

"Will you promise not to tell my dad?"

"Only if I know for sure you're not going to hurt yourself, honey."

"Then you're *not* on my side," Dawn blurted. She turned and walked away much more rapidly than my girl could move.

My girl sighed sadly, and I nudged her with my

hand. "Good dog, Toby," she said, but she wasn't really paying attention to me.

I was lying next to Dawn's mother when she died, and they were all very sad and the children clutched me and I did Be Still for them. Fran and Patsy were there, but CJ was not. Often, even if CJ was in the building, I would be with Fran or Patsy because they would need me more.

It was a good way to pass the years. There was no dog door, but whenever I walked up to the door to the small yard it would swish open for me, and the smells out there told me when it was going to snow or rain and when it was summer and when it was fall. Chaucer still came to play on a regular basis, though once he learned Eddie could be counted on for treats we spent almost as much time in the kitchen as we did out in the yard.

"Now Chaucer, you're like me, you work hard, but it's not fancy work. Nobody looks at you and sees anything but a hardworking dog," Eddie said one time. Chaucer whined a little and shuffled his feet, impatient for the treat. "But Toby here, he's a doctor. Neither one of us will ever be smart as Toby."

I wagged at my name. Chaucer licked his lips.

"You both get bacon today, though."

I could hardly contain myself. Bacon!

Sometimes CJ would be gone for a week or two at a time, but she always came back. One day at lunch, shortly after one of her long absences, I could feel that CJ was a little afraid as she talked to Fran, so I sat up alertly.

"We have a new guest coming in. Probably as early as Monday," CJ said.

"Oh?" Fran said.

"Me. I'm the guest."

"*What?*"

"It's almost a blessing, Fran. There are so many things going wrong with me now the doctors almost don't know where to start. And to tell you the truth, I'm tired of it. I'm tired of all the pain and the sleeplessness and the sickness. I'm tired of the forty pills a day. When Gloria died I realized that it meant my obligations were over. I don't owe anybody anything."

"CJ . . ."

CJ shifted in her seat, leaning forward. "This is a decision I reached a long, long time ago, Fran. You won't be able to talk me out of it. At my family reunion I told everyone and said my good-byes. My affairs are in order." CJ gave a little laugh. "This way, I will always and forever be younger than Gloria. That will drive her crazy."

"I think we should talk about this. Maybe you could see someone. . . . "

"I've worked it through with my therapist. Believe me, we've spoken about almost nothing else for the past year and a half."

"I still think—"

"I know what you think, but you're wrong. This isn't suicide; it's acceptance. My doctors say it's only a matter of time before something else happens inside me. They agree with my decision. I'm terrified another stroke might leave me debilitated—after watching Gloria I can't face the idea of something like that happening to my brain. This way, I control what happens, and where and when. Isn't that what hospice is all about? Ensuring that quality of life extends into the dying process?"

"You can't know, though, that you'll have another stroke."

"Fran. I've stopped dialysis."

"Oh God."

"No, you have no idea. The *freedom*. I don't have to go back there ever again. I have had my ups and downs, but it has been a good, long life and I don't regret my decision. Please, try to understand. It feels to me like I've been kept artificially alive, and maybe for a good reason—I've helped a lot of people. But the prognosis is for it all to end badly. I want my leaving to be at a time of my choosing and not artificially extended, with no regard for my quality of life. I don't want to end up a vegetable."

The fear was gone from CJ now. I nuzzled her hand and she stroked me with tenderness.

A few days later, CJ came to the building to live. Right away, though, I could tell that she was feeling more ill than ever before. I jumped up on her bed and remained there with her, sometimes climbing up to be by her head, sometimes curling up in a ball by her feet.

"Good dog, Toby," she always said. Her voice, though, was weaker and weaker. "You're not just a therapeagle; you're an angel dog, just like Max, just like Molly."

I wagged, hearing those names spoken so tenderly. My girl knew who I was, that I had always been with her, taking care of her and guarding against dangers.

Many people came to visit CJ in her room, and CJ was always happy to see them. Some of them I knew, such as Gracie, who had been a little girl when I was Max but was now a grown woman with children of her own. CJ kissed all the children and laughed and the pain inside her receded until it was all but hidden. Another was a woman I recognized from not long ago. Her name was Dawn, the girl with the apple-scented hands, and she sat next to CJ and talked for hours. I left for a while to check to see if Fran or Patsy needed me, but when I came back Dawn was still there.

"People are always asking me what specialty I want, and I just keep telling them that I'm just focused on getting into med school. How do I know what area will appeal to me? I haven't even been accepted yet."

"You will," CJ said. "I know you will."

"You've always believed in me, CJ. You saved my life."

"No, you saved your own life. You know what they say in the program—no one else can do it for you."

"Yeah, I know," Dawn said.

CJ coughed weakly and I jumped up to be next to her. Her hand came down and stroked my back.

"I guess I'd better get going," Dawn finally said.

"I so appreciate you making the trip, Dawn."

They hugged each other and I felt the love flow between them.

"Have a safe flight," CJ said. "And remember, you can always call me."

Dawn nodded, wiping her eyes. She smiled and waved as she left the room, and I snuggled next to my girl, feeling her drop into a deep nap.

One afternoon CJ was feeding me pieces of a ham

and cheese sandwich that Eddie had brought her when she stopped and looked at me. I kept my eye on the sandwich.

"Toby," she said, "listen to me. I know that you're really bonded to me, but I'm going to be leaving you. I could stay, but I've had all the good things this life can offer me and I'm weary of all the bad—especially of what is to come if I try to prolong it. I just want to be with my husband. The only regret I have is leaving my friends, and you're one of those friends, Toby. But I know you are loved and taken care of, and I know that to be loved and to have a job is more important than anything to a dog. You remind me in so many ways of my dog Molly, her gentleness, but also of Max, with his self-assurance. Will you tell my angel dogs I'm coming to be with them soon? And will you be with me in my final moments? I don't want to be afraid—and if you're there, I know I'll be brave. You're my forever friend, Toby."

The love ran strong between us as my girl pulled me close to her.

CJ left one cool, clear spring afternoon. Fran had been sitting with her all day, and I had lain with my head on her chest, her hand loosely stroking my fur. When the hand stopped moving, I looked at Fran, who moved her chair closer and took the now slack hand in hers. Bit by bit CJ let go of life, until, with one final breath, my girl was gone.

"Good dog, Toby," Fran told me. She hugged me and her tears fell on my fur.

I thought about baby Clarity falling off the dock at the Farm. How her eyes had been on me when Gloria picked her up. "Bubby," she'd said. I remembered her coming into the yard with Trent to take me home. I thought about her hugs and kisses, how when I was Max she would hold me to her chest to keep me warm.

I would have to live without her hugs now.

My CJ. She taught me that it was a good thing to love more than just my boy, Ethan, opening my eyes to the fact that I'd actually loved many people in my lives, that loving humans was my ultimate purpose. Her presence in my lives formed the center point of my existence and enabled me to help the people who lay in beds in their rooms to fight off their fears and find ultimate peace and acceptance.

I served those people for many years after CJ left, but never did I let a day go by without remembering her—remembering baby Clarity as she slipped into the horse's kennel, remembering CJ as she held me in the car by the ocean, remembering living with Trent when I was Max.

When a sharp pain made me cry one morning as I did my business, Patsy and Fran and Eddie took me to the Vet, and I knew why they were all going on the car ride. I was nearly blind at that point, but I could still smell the cinnamon and Chaucer on Patsy's hands as she picked me up and carried me, panting, into the Vet's office and laid me on the cool table. Eddie's strong, chicken-scented hands soothed me, and they all whispered in my ear as the quick stab brought with it almost instant relief.

"We love you," they said.

This time as the waves swept over me, they were

not dark but had a frothy luminance dancing on millions of bubbles. I raised my head up and floated toward this brightness, bursting through the water's surface and into the glorious light of sunrise. Gold, the light was gold as it played across the gentle waves, and my vision was suddenly as clear and sharp as a puppy's. A bouquet of wonderful scents met my nose, and my heart leaped when I realized who I was smelling.

"Molly!" I heard someone call.

I whipped my head around and there they were, the people I'd been smelling. Everyone I'd ever loved in my life, standing at the edge of the water, smiling and clapping. I saw Ethan and Hannah and Trent and CJ standing in front, along with Andi and Maya and Jakob and all the others.

"Bailey!" Ethan yelled, waving.

My name was Toby, and Buddy, and Molly and Max and Bailey and Ellie. I was a good dog, and this was my reward. Now I would get to be with the people I loved.

I turned, whimpering with joy, and swam toward those golden shores.

[ACKNOWLEDGMENTS]

This is the part of the book where I have to admit that a lot of people helped contribute to the whole process, and the easiest thing would be to begin at, well, the beginning. In July 2010, yet another book with a dog on the cover joined the burgeoning crowd of books with dogs on their covers—*A Dog's Purpose,* it was called. The first week it was eligible, this novel (my first) leapt onto the bestseller lists, where it remained for nineteen weeks. Now, you can't bribe your way onto those lists, though I'm sure someone has tried. People have to buy the book, and enough people gave *A Dog's Purpose* a chance that it added up to a wonderful run at the bookstore.

And that, you see, led to this, the sequel. No one publishes the sequel to a book that didn't sell, so the best place to start thanking people is with everyone who bought my novel in the first place. Because of you, *A Dog's Journey* found a home with Tom Doherty Associates, an imprint of Macmillan, the same people who did such a great job supporting *A Dog's Purpose.*

At Tom Doherty, I want to thank Kristin Sevick, my editor, who gave me such great advice and wonderful ideas while the novel was still in manuscript that I found my way to exactly the book I wanted to write. I want to thank Linda Quinton, who has been a tireless advocate for my novels and who has shown innovation, wisdom, and (I need to say it) tolerance in dealing with my books and my aspirations. Thanks to Karen Lovell, for her publicity magic and marketing support. Thanks to Kathleen Doherty, for making my books important to school kids, and to Tom Doherty, for being the man behind the curtain.

I wouldn't even have a published novel if it weren't for Scott Miller, my agent at Trident Media. Scott believed in me when we couldn't sell anything to anybody, and I won't forget that, Scott.

Kayla Ibarra has been here at the worldwide headquarters of Cameron Productions, Inc., and without her we wouldn't have been able to respond to reader requests or run the amazing Dog of the Week program at www.adogspurpose.com. That website was designed and implemented by the amazingly talented Hillary Carlip at www.flyhc.com.

Researching this book was easy because my daughter Georgia works in animal rescue at Life is Better Rescue in Colorado, which she owns and runs. You do amazing work and I'm proud of you.

Much of what I know about hospice and end-of-life care I learned from my aunt Lucy, who volunteered for decades at Angela Hospice in Livonia, Michigan. She introduced me to Bob Alexander, and he, Barb Iovan, Mary Ann Joganic, LMSW, Peggy Devos, RN, and Karen Lemon, RN, CHPN, BS, were patient and kind in answering my questions and helping me to understand what it means to have a family member in hospice care. I want to thank them, both for their information and their gentle assistance to Aunt Lucy when she passed away this last summer. Aunt Lucy, you were a second mother to me.

Speaking of hospice, my friend Dannion Brinkley and his Twilight Brigade are on a mission to raise society's consciousness about the needs of the dying and to make sure no one, especially our nation's veterans, dies alone. Thank you, Dannion.

I would urge anyone facing end-of-life choices to read *Final Gifts: Understanding the Special Awareness, Needs, and Communications of the Dying* by Maggie Callanan and Patricia Kelley (Bantam, 1997). It's a wonderful book.

I never write a book about animals without reading Temple Grandin's invaluable *Animals Make Us Human: Creating the Best Life for Animals* (Houghton Mifflin Harcourt, 2009) and *Animals in Translation: Using the Mysteries of Autism to Decode Animal Behavior* (Mariner Books, 2006). Catherine Johnson is the coauthor of both of these works and I regret that I failed to give proper credit in earlier citations of these two wonderful books.

While researching canines I came across a wonderful little gem of a book by Roger Abrantes called *Dog Language: An Encyclopedia of Canine Behaviour* (Wakan Tanka Publishers, 1997). It really helped me decode what was going on in the dog park! I also recommend, and found really helpful, *How Dogs*

Think: What the World Looks Like to Them and Why They Act the Way They Do by Stanley Coren (Free Press, 2005) and *Inside of a Dog: What Dogs See, Smell, and Know* by Alexandra Horowitz (Scribner, 2010).

When it came to understanding eating disorders, I was able to turn to friends of mine who have done battle with such demons and, to respect their privacy, I will not name them here. They know I'm grateful for their insights. I also can recommend *Life Without Ed: How One Woman Declared Independence from Her Eating Disorder and How You Can Too* by Jenni Schaefer and Thom Rutledge (McGraw-Hill, 2003), *Eating in the Light of the Moon: How Women Can Transform Their Relationship with Food Through Myths, Metaphors, and Storytelling* by Anita A. Johnston, Ph.D. (Gurze Books, 2000), and *Unbearable Lightness: A Story of Loss and Gain* by Portia de Rossi (Atria, 2010).

My friend Dina Zaphiris, the "Behavior Savior," has been training dogs to detect cancer, much the way that Andi does during the life of Molly. Thank you, Dina, for your advice, your help, and for being such a good second mother to Tucker.

Of course, that's not it, meaning that a book doesn't come together just because of some research, a great team, and a public willing to read the finished product—my personal support group starts with my parents, Bill and Monsie Cameron, who never told me anything other than if I wanted to be a novelist, I could be a novelist. My sister Julie has turned her medical practice into a bookstore and literally cheers for me with every success, whether minor or major.

I am so blessed to have her in my life. My sister Amy, the schoolteacher, and her friend Judy Robben did an amazing job writing the study guide for *A Dog's Purpose,* and for my other novel, *Emory's Gift*. I'll probably talk them into doing the same for *A Dog's Journey,* as well. She could have been Miss America, but instead decided to just help plain old Bruce.

As could be expected from such a wonderful father as myself, I've got great children and children-in-law. My daughter Georgia's animal rescue wouldn't be possible without Christopher, her husband, who tirelessly and without complaint works at her side. Daughter Chelsea and her husband, James, flew out to be with me on the day *Emory's Gift* was released and even went to Hawaii to celebrate the event. My son, Chase, recruited Charlie Salem and, between the two of them, have done a wonderful job supporting my writing.

Thanks to my Nobel Prize–winning sister-in-law, Maria Hjelm, for running the Northern California campaign, and for giving the world Ethan, Maya, and Jakob. Thanks, Ted, for doing your part in that.

By the time anyone reads this, my newspaper column, which ran for thirteen glorious years, will have folded. It was my decision: after winning (in 2010) the Newspaper Columnist of the Year Award, I decided that my weekly musings, which started with a column called "The Family Meeting" and focused mainly on raising children, had run its course. I'm going out on top of my game and before it becomes possible to write about grandchildren. Bob Bridges has been my copy-editor for nearly every single one of my columns, all of it on a volunteer basis. Thank you, Bob. And thanks to my column editor, Anthony Zurcher, and to Jack Newcombe, and everyone else at Creators, for syndicating my column.

Thanks to Gavin Palone, for his belief and support of my writing and for staking his professional reputation on it.

Thanks, Geoff Jennings, for being tirelessly supportive in word and deed, and to all the independent bookstores that got behind *A Dog's Purpose* and pushed.

Thank you, Deb Mangelsdorf, for your wise advice about dogs and veterinary medicine.

Thanks, Claire LaZebnik, a wonderful writer and great friend, who helps keep me mentally steady when I'm about to fall, or throw myself, off the high wire that is being an author in today's world. (Not that I'm complaining—I *wanted* to be on the high wire!) Thanks to all the LaZebniks, for sharing Claire and everything else with me.

Julie, Norma, Marcia—the Coven. Thank you, I'm still under your spell.

Maxine Lapiduss is a genius.

Toni Marteney, thank you for starting the Bruce Cameron fan club in Hawaii. When are you going to fly me out for a meeting?

Tucker, you're a good dog.

Ted and Evie Michon created one of the most beautiful things I've ever seen: Cathryn Michon.

Cathryn, you know how much of you is in everything I write. Your love gives me purpose, it is a gift, it makes me treasure the journey.

Read on for a preview of

A DOG'S
WAY HOME

Available
from Tom Doherty Associates

A FORGE HARDCOVER

ONE

From the beginning, I was aware of cats.

Cats everywhere.

I couldn't really see them—my eyes were open, but when the cats were nearby I registered nothing except shifting forms in the darkness. I could smell them though, as clearly as I could smell my mother as I took nourishment, or my siblings stirring next to me as I worked my way to find life-giving milk.

I didn't know they were cats, of course—I just knew they were creatures not like me, present in our den but not attempting to nurse alongside me. Later, when I came to see that they were small and fast and lithe, I realized they were not only "not dogs," but were their own distinct kind of animal.

We lived together in a cool, dark home. Dry dirt underneath my nose gave up exotic, old smells. I delighted in inhaling them, filling my nose with rich, flavorful aromas. Above, a ceiling of parched wood dropped dust into the air, the roof pressing down so low that whenever my mother stood up from the packed depression in the earth that served as our bed to leave my siblings and me—squeaking in protest and huddling against each other for reassurance—her upright tail was halfway to the beams. I did not know where my mother went when she departed, I only knew how anxious we were until she returned.

The sole source of light in the den came from a single square hole at the far end. Through this window to the world poured astounding scents of cold and alive and wet, of places and things even more intoxicating than what I could smell in the den. But even though I saw an occasional cat flicker through the hole out into the world or returning from some unknown place, my mother pushed me back whenever I tried to crawl toward the outdoors.

As my legs strengthened and my eyesight sharpened I played with the kittens as I would with my siblings. Often I singled out the same family of cats toward the back recesses of our communal home, where a pair of young kitties were particularly friendly and their mother occasionally licked me. I thought of her as Mother Cat.

After some time spent romping joyfully with the little felines, my own mother would come over and retrieve me, pulling me out of the pile of kittens by the back of my neck. My siblings all sniffed me suspiciously when my mother dropped me next to them. Their responses suggested they did not care for the residual whiff of cat.

This was my fun, wonderful life, and I had no reason to suspect it would ever change.

I was nursing drowsily, hearing the peeping sounds of my brothers and sisters as they did the same, when suddenly my mother lunged to her feet, her movements so unexpected that my legs were lifted off the ground before I dropped from the teat.

I knew instantly something bad was happening.

A panic spread through the den, rippling from cat to cat like a breeze. They stampeded toward the back of the den, the mothers carrying their mewing offspring by the backs of their necks. My siblings and I surged toward our mother, crying for her, frightened because she was frightened.

Strong beams of light swept over us, stinging my eyes. They came from the hole, as did the sounds: "Jesus! There's a million cats in the crawl space!"

I had no sense of what was making these noises, nor why the den was filled with flashing lights. The scent of an entirely new sort of creature wafted toward me from the hole. We were in danger and it was these unseen creatures that were the threat. My mother panted, ducking her head, backing away, and we all did our best to stumble after her, beseeching her with our tiny voices not to leave us.

"Let me see. Oh Christ, look at all of them!"

"Is this going to be a problem?"

"Hell yes it's a problem."

"What do you want to do?"

"We'll have to call the exterminator."

I was able to distinguish a difference between the first set of sounds and the second, a variation of pitch and tone, though I wasn't sure what it meant.

"Can't we just poison them ourselves?"

"You got something on the truck?"

"No, but I can get some."

My mother continued to deny us the comfort of her teats. Her muscles were tense, her ears back, her attention focused on the source of the sounds. I wanted to nurse, to know we were safe.

"Well, but if we do that, we're going to have all these dead cats all over the neighborhood. There's too many. If we were just talking one or two, fine, but this is a whole cat colony."

"You wanted to finish the demo by the end of June. That don't give us a lot of time to get rid of them."

"I know."

"Look, see the bowls? Somebody's actually been feeding the damn things."

The lights dipped, joining together in a burning spot of brightness on the floor just inside the hole.

"Well that's just great. What the hell is wrong with people?"

"You want me to try to find out who it is?"

"Nah. The problem goes away when the cats do. I'll call somebody."

The probing lights flickered around one last time,

and then winked out. I heard dirt moving and distinct, heavy footfalls, so much louder than the quiet steps of the cats. Slowly, the presence of the new creatures faded from the hole, and gradually the kittens resumed their play, happy again. I nursed alongside my siblings, then went to see Mother Cat's kitties. As usual, when the daylight coming through the square hole dimmed, the adult cats streamed out, and during the night I would hear them return and sometimes smell the blood of the small kill they were bringing back to their respective broods.

When Mother hunted, she went no farther than the big bowls of dry food that were set just inside the square hole. I could smell the meal on her breath and it was fish and plants and meats, and I began to wonder what it would taste like.

Whatever had happened to cause the panic was over.

I was playing with Mother Cat's relentless kittens when our world shattered. This time the light wasn't a single shaft, it was a blazing explosion, turning everything bright.

The cats scattered in terror. I froze, unsure what I should do.

"Get the nets ready; when they run they're going to do it all at once!"

A sound from outside of the hole. "We're ready!"

Three large beings wriggled in behind the light. They were the first humans I had ever seen, but I had smelled others, I now realized—I just had not been able to visualize what they looked like. Something deep inside of me sparked a recognition—I felt strangely drawn to them, wanting to run to them as they crawled forward into the den. Yet the alarm crackling in the frenzied cats froze me in place.

"Got one!"

A male cat hissed and screamed.

"Jesus!"

"Watch it, a couple just escaped!"

"Well, hell!" came the response from outside.

I was separated from my mother and tried to sort out her scent from among the cats, and then went limp when I felt the sharp teeth on the nape of my neck. Mother Cat dragged me back, deep into the shadows, to a place where a large crack split the stone wall. She squeezed me through the crack into a small, tight space and set me down with her kittens, curling up with us. The cats were utterly silent, following Mother Cat's lead. I lay with them in the darkness and listened to the humans call to each other.

"There's also a litter of puppies here!"

"Are you kidding me? Hey, get that one!"

"Jesus, they're fast."

"Come on, kitty-kitty, we won't hurt you."

"There's the mother dog."

"Thing is terrified. Watch it don't bite you."

"It's okay. You'll be okay, girl. Come on."

"Gunter didn't say anything about dogs."

"He didn't say there would be so many frigging cats, either."

"Hey, you guys catching them in the nets out there?"

"This is hard as hell to do!" someone shouted from outside.

"Come on, doggie. Damn! Watch it! Here comes the mother dog!"

"Jesus! Okay, we got the dog!" called the outside voice.

"Here puppy, here puppy. They're so little!"

"And easier than the damn cats, that's for sure."

We heard these noises without comprehension as to what they might mean. Some light made its way into our space behind the wall, leaking in through the crack, but the human smells did not come any closer to our hiding place. The mingle of fear and feline on the air gradually faded, as did the sounds.

Eventually, I slept.

When I awoke, my mother was gone. My brothers and sisters were gone. The depression in the earth where we had been born and had laid nursing still smelled of our family, but the empty, vacant sense that overcame me when I sniffed for Mother brought a whimper from me, a sob in my throat I couldn't quiet.

I did not understand what had happened, but the only cats left in the space were Mother Cat and her kittens. Frantic, seeking answers and assurance, I went back to her, crying out my fear. She had brought her kittens out from behind the wall and they were gathered back on the small square of cloth I thought of as their home. Mother Cat examined me carefully with her black nose. Then she curled around me, lying down, and I followed the scent and began to nurse. The sensation on my tongue was new and strange, but the warmth and nurture were what I craved, and I fed gratefully. After a few moments, her kittens joined me.

The next morning, a few of the male cats returned. They approached Mother Cat, who hissed out a warning, and then went to their own area to sleep.

Later, when the light from the hole had been its brightest and had started to dim, I picked up a whiff of another human, a different one. Now that I understood the difference, I realized I had had this scent in my nose before.

"Kitty? Kitty?"

Mother Cat unexpectedly left us on our square of cloth. The odd flash of cold that came with her departure shocked all of us, and we turned to each other for comfort, squirming ourselves into a pile of kittens and dog. I could see her as she approached the hole, but she did not advance all the way out—just stood, faintly illuminated. The male cats were on alert, but they did not follow her to the human.

"Are you the only one left? I don't know what happened, I wasn't around to see, but there are tracks in the dirt, so I know there were trucks. Did they take all the other cats?" The human crawled in through the hole, momentarily blotting out the light. He was male—I could smell this, though I would not learn until later the distinction between man and woman. He seemed slightly larger than the first humans I'd seen.

Again, I was drawn to this special creature, an inexplicable yearning rising up inside me. But the memory of the terror of the day before kept me with my kitten siblings.

"Okay, I see you guys. Hi, how did you get away? And they took your bowls. Nice."

There was a rustling sound and the delicious smell of food wafted onto the air. "Here's a little bit for you. I'll go and get a bowl. Some water, too."

The man backed out, wriggling in the dirt. As soon as he was gone the cats surged forward, feeding ravenously on whatever was spilled on the dirt.

I alerted to the approach of the same person sooner than the cats, as if they were unable to identify his scent as it grew stronger. The males all reacted, though, when he reappeared at the hole, fleeing back to their corner. Only Mother Cat stood fast. A new bowl was shoved forward and there was a meal in it, but Mother Cat made no approach, just stood watching. I could sense her tension and knew she was ready to bolt and run if he tried to capture us like the other humans had.

"Here is some water, too. Do you have kittens? You look like you're nursing. Did they take your babies? Oh, kitty, I am so sorry. They're going to tear down these houses and put up an apartment complex. You and your family can't stay here, okay?"

Eventually the man left, and the adult cats cautiously resumed eating. I sniffed Mother Cat's mouth when she returned, but when I licked her face she turned abruptly away.

Time was marked by the shifting light pouring in from the square hole. More cats came; a few who had been living with us before, and a new female, whose arrival triggered a fight among the males that I watched with intense interest. One pair of combatants lay locked together for so long that the only way I knew they were not asleep was the way their tails flickered, not wagging in happiness but communicating a real distress. When they broke their clinch they stretched out on the ground, noses nearly touching, and made un-catlike sounds at each other. Another fight consisted of one male lying on his side and smacking another one, who was on all four feet. The standing one would tap the sprawling one on the top of the head and the one lying down would respond with a series of rapid clawings.

Why didn't they all get up on their back two legs and attack each other? This behavior, while stressful for all the animals in the den, seemed utterly pointless.

Other than Mother Cat I had no interaction with the adults, who acted as if I did not exist. I tangled with the kittens, wrestling and climbing and chasing all day. Sometimes I would growl at them, irritated with their style of play, which just seemed wrong, somehow. I wanted to climb on their backs and chew on their necks, but they couldn't seem to get the hang of this, going limp when I knocked them over or jumped on top of their tiny frames. Sometimes they wrapped their entire bodies around my snout, or batted at my face with teeny, sharp claws, pouncing on me from all angles.

At night I missed my siblings. I missed my mother. I had made a family, but I understood that the cats were different from me. I had a pack, but it was a pack of kitties, which did not seem right. I felt restless and unhappy and at times I would whimper out my anguish and Mother Cat would lick me and I would feel somewhat better, but things were just not the way they should have been.

Nearly every day, the man came and brought food. Mother Cat punished me with a swift slap on my nose when I tried to approach him, and I learned the rules of the den: we were not to be seen by humans. None of the other felines seemed at all inclined to feel the touch of a person, but for me a growing desire to be held by him made it increasingly difficult to obey the laws of the den.

When Mother Cat stopped nursing us, we had to adjust to eating the meals the man supplied, which consisted of tasty, dried morsels and then sometimes exotic, wet flesh. Once I grew accustomed to the change it was far better for me—I had been so hungry for so long it seemed a natural condition, but now I could eat my fill and lap up as much water as I could hold. I consumed more than my sibling kitties combined, and was now noticeably larger than any of them, though they all were unimpressed by my size and resolutely refused to play properly, continuing to mostly claw at my nose.

We mimicked Mother Cat and shied away from the hole when the human presence filled it, but otherwise dared to flirt with the very edge, drinking in the rich aromas from outside. Mother Cat sometimes went out at night, and I could sense that the kittens all wanted to join her. For me, it was more the daylight that lured, but I was mindful of Mother Cat and knew she would swiftly punish any attempt to stray beyond the boundary.

One day the man, whose fragrances were as familiar to me now as Mother Cat's, appeared just outside the hole, making sounds. I could sense other humans with him.

"They're usually way toward the back. The mother comes closer when I bring food, but she won't let me touch her."

"Is there another way out of the crawl space besides this window?" It was a different voice, accompanied by different smells—a woman. I unconsciously wagged my tail.

"I don't think so. How will this work?"

"We've got these big gloves to protect us, and if you'll stay here with the net, you can catch any cats that make it past us. How many are there?"

"I don't know, now. Until recently the female was obviously nursing, but if there are any kittens they don't come out in the day. A couple others, I don't know what sex. There used to be so many, but I guess the developer must have gotten them. He's going to tear down this whole row of houses and put up an apartment complex."

"He'll never get a demolition permit with feral cats living here."

"That's probably why he did it. Do you think he hurt the ones he caught?"

"Um, okay, so, there's no law against trapping and destroying cats living on your own property. I mean, he could have taken them to one of the other shelters, I guess."

"There were a lot of them. The whole property was crawling with cats."

"Thing is, I didn't hear anything about a big bunch of cats showing up anywhere. Animal rescue is a pretty tight community; we all talk to each other. If twenty cats hit the system, I would have heard about it. You okay? Hey, sorry, maybe I shouldn't have said anything."

"I'm fine. I just wish I had known it was going to happen."

"You did the right thing by calling us, though, Lucas. We'll find good homes for any cats we find. Ready?"

I had grown completely bored with the monotonous noises and was busily wrestling with the kittens when I felt Mother Cat stiffen, alarm jolting through her. Her unwinking eyes were on the hole, and her tail twitched. Her ears were flat back against her head. I regarded her curiously, ignoring the little male kitty who ran up, swatted my mouth, and darted away.

Then a light blazed and I understood her fear. Mother Cat fled toward the back wall, abandoning her young. I saw her slip soundlessly into the hidden crack just as two humans came in through the hole. The kittens milled in confusion, the male cats fled to the back of the den, and I shied away, afraid.

The light danced along the walls, then found me, blazing brightly in my face.

"Hey! There's a puppy in here!"